WE DON'T
TALK
ANYMORE

USA TODAY BESTSELLING AUTHOR

JULIE JOHNSON

You know who you are.

I love you as
certain dark things
are to be loved.

In secret,
between the
shadow and the soul.

Pablo Neruda

CHAPTER ONE

JOSEPHINE

I STARE up at the cabin ceiling, wishing I could evaporate. Through the floorboards, I can hear the telltale rhythm of Archer and Sienna screwing — those periodic moans, the tap-tap-tap of the headboard, the creaky springs in the mattress.

What a weird term for it. *Screwing*. Like their bodies are instruments plucked from some libidinous toolbox, jammed together out of necessity rather than affection. Makes the whole process sound mechanical. A chore. Like fixing an IKEA cabinet, not making love.

Making love.

Yuck. That's somehow even worse than *screwing*, in my humble opinion. Not that my humble opinion counts for all that much when it comes to sex, seeing as I'm a virgin with a capital V.

I'm also "Valentine" with a capital V. (That's my last name, not some fervid declaration of my favorite Hallmark holiday.) As nicknames go, it's not terrible — albeit not necessarily one I would've chosen for myself. But at a house party six months ago, one of the baseball jocks said, "Yo, Valentine! Pass me that beer, will you?" and I guess it stuck, seeing as it's all anyone at school calls me these days. Quite possibly because they couldn't be bothered to learn my actual name after six years of classes together.

Well... everyone except Archer. But that's only because we've been best friends since we were old enough to call each other anything requiring more than those goo-goo-ga-ga sylla-bles babies mouth at each other in daycare through drooling, toothless smiles. He calls me Josephine — a.k.a. Jo, a.k.a. JoJo, a.k.a Joe Shmoe — which is what my mother scrawled on my birth certificate after popping me out the same summer *The Wallflowers* released my namesake track, halfway through a mid-nineties heatwave. (My father initially wanted to name me Maude, after his dearly departed great-aunt. I send my deepest regards to gods of angsty alternative-rock for persuading him otherwise.)

So, that's me. Josephine Valentine. A girl named for a song no one my age has ever even heard. Which, honestly, is a pretty fitting interpretation of my entire high school experience thus far.

Since I was old enough to notice such things, I've always found myself on the fringes. Too artsy to blend naturally with the in-crowd, too obstinate to whittle myself into something they'd find more palatable at their cliquey lunch tables. Like a cheerleader. Or the student council president. Or a cokehead.

Anything, really, besides what I am — a deeply-unapolo-getic introvert, who'd rather spend her day out sailing or squir-reled away with a good fantasy novel than on display at Singing Beach, gossiping with girls who, it must be said, are more than a little intimidating. Only partly because of the way they fill out their bikini tops, while my own frame is flatter than a freaking hardcover. (I think the phrase "late bloomer" is embedded somewhere in my DNA.)

Much like the seagulls who roam boldly between sandy towels on the hunt for unattended snacks, the popular girls seem to travel in packs and strike the moment your back is turned. Predators with preening feathers, they smile prettily as they plot your demise.

Count me out.

Honestly, I wouldn't even be here at this stupid party if not for Archer. He dragged me along, insisting it would be more fun than sitting at home all alone on the final night of spring break, binge-watching yet another season of *The Great British Bake Off*, eating my body weight in mass-produced (likely carcinogenic) sour gummy worms while critiquing the contestants' shoddy use of fondant.

"It's senior year, Jo," he'd reminded me, grinning in that way that makes my knees go softer than buttercream frosting. "Last chance to tear it up before graduation."

"*Pass.*"

"Come on! Don't make me face the zombie hoard alone." He'd tugged a lock of my hair, then wrapped it absently around one finger, his eyes fixated on the strands as they caught the fading afternoon light. We were sitting in our spot, up in the rafters of the boathouse — our favorite hideout from the rest of the world — staring out at the ocean, our legs dangling in the wind. Below, waves gently lapped at the sides of the navy blue Hinckley picnic boat my father spent a fortune on (but is never around to use) and, beyond, the sun made its slow descent toward the horizon.

We've spent a million such nights up there — shoulders pressed together, sharing secrets in the dark. But this time, something felt different. Archer cleared his throat, uncharacteristically nervous.

"If you don't come to this party, who else will silently mock the masses with me? I need you, Jo. I'm not above begging..."

I folded faster than a freaking lawn chair.

What can I say? I'm powerless in the face of that persuasive smile. And that soft hair tug. And those bright, burnt-caramel eyes, fixed on mine with such playfulness in their depths.

Plus, I have to admit, Archer is probably right. This really is my last chance to quote-unquote '*tear it up*' before graduation. Between the upcoming senior prom and commencement ceremony, things are winding down in a very real way. The film is turning it's final reel. The curtains are about to close.

Fin.

The end.

Hasta la vista, baby.

It's almost tangible. Visceral. There's something in the air. Sure, it could just be the marijuana haze or the smoke from the fire pit drifting through the open windows... but I think it's more than that. We can all feel it. That bases-loaded, two-strikes, last inning sort of feeling has started to creep in. Responsibilities and college orientations and full-time jobs are hurling at us full force. In a few weeks, we'll be walking across a stage, shaking hands with Headmaster Lawrence, collecting our diplomas, and bidding high school goodbye.

Bidding childhood goodbye.

But for tonight... we are still seventeen, carefree and crazy, drinking cheap beer from tapped kegs, dancing in the moonlight, skinny dipping in the sea, wishing for a summer that will stretch on forever. (Or... if you're *me*... hiding out in a spare bedroom, listening to your best friend lose his virginity through the floorboards like the worst kind of voyeur.)

God, Jo.

You are seriously twisted.

Upstairs, Sienna lets out a moan loud enough to make a porn-star roll her eyes. I guess Archer is really living up to her expectations — and vice versa, since the mattress squeaks start coming faster and faster, a shrieking harmony to the pounding bass of my own frantic pulse.

Just finish, already, I want to scream at my best friend, feeling my heart contract in a surprising amount of pain. *Aren't virgins supposed to last, like, thirty seconds? Are you trying to set some sort of record up there?*

I pull a pillow over my head to muffle the sounds of them together, wishing for the hundredth time that I had some way out of this hellish scenario. If I'd known this was how my night would play out, I'd never have agreed to come. I certainly never would've allowed Archer to drive us, leaving me without a viable mode of escape.

"Oh, *Archer!*" Sienna screams, her voice breathy with desire. "Yes! Yes! *Yes!*"

I tell myself to get up. To walk out of this room, back to the party, where the crappy pop music they're blasting would over-power even Sienna's most bombastic fake moan. But I'm para-lyzed. Stunned immobile as a statue. Even more horrifically... there's an unexpected, unwelcome pressure gathering behind my eyes.

Why the hell am I crying?

If I'm honest with myself, maybe in the back of my mind... some delusional part of me thought Archer and I might lose our virginity together someday. Just as we've done basically every-thing else in our lives together, from swimming lessons at five to sailing races at ten to our first contraband beers at fourteen to getting our learners' permits at sixteen.

Given the three-point-five minutes of humpin-and-bumpin happening overhead, it seems my bestie would rather cash in his own V-card with the head cheerleader. It would be upset-ting if it weren't so utterly predictable.

Okay.

Fine.

It's pretty damn upsetting. But that doesn't mean it isn't also a cliché cut straight out of some eighties movie riddled with high school stereotypes.

Former wimp locates testosterone summer before junior year, makes varsity baseball roster, becomes chiseled heartthrob, wins affection of high school Queen B.

No, not bee.

B, as in *bitch*, which is what Sienna Sullivan has been since age nine, when she not-so-gently suggested I quit our youth-soccer team because my periodic asthma attacks were putting her chance at a plastic league trophy in jeopardy.

Gasp!

(Literally. Someone please pass my inhaler, would you? That last offensive play really knocked the wind out of me.)

I hear a groan through the floorboards. Deep-throated. Masculine. I'd know it was Archer even if I hadn't seen Sienna lead him into that bedroom. I know all his sounds. That little break in his laugh when he finds something really funny, *actually* funny, not when he's just trying to be polite in front of my parents. That half-sigh he does when I'm exasperating. The catch in his throat when he's worked up, battling back the slight stammer he had as a little kid.

Pressing the pillow harder over my face, I scream into it — a good, long one — until I run out of air. People are always doing that in movies and TV shows, as if it somehow releases the rage and pain pent-up inside. All it does is make me feel like I'm suffocating.

I can't quite explain why I'm in so much agony. It's not like I didn't know this would happen eventually. What did I expect? That he'd stay a virgin forever? Join a monastery? Become a priest? Abuse his right hand until he got tendonitis from excessive self-gratification?

Obviously, at some point, Archer was going to make that

much-lauded thrust from boydom to manhood. Most seven-teen-year-old boys on the baseball team are already well on their way to a half-dozen conquests — if not more. It's all they talk about. Which girls they've already *screwed*, the ones they still want to *nail*, how hard they'll *hammer* them when they get the chance.

Who knew so much carpentry was involved in copulation?

My point is, everyone (myself most definitely excluded) is doing it. It's only natural Archer would do it, too. I just didn't know it would be tonight. I wasn't prepared. I didn't have time to steel myself against this new reality. That's the only reason I'm so upset.

Right?

I should be glad Archer is getting some action. A best friend would be happy for him. Punch him lightly on the arm with a sly *atta boy* and roll my eyes as he relays the gory details. Listen with the attentiveness of a good pal.

His bestie.

His buddy.

His BFF.

But as I lay here blinking back tears, hands bunched into fists, heart pounding twice its normal speed... all I know is, if they carry on much longer, I think my ribs might crack under the strain.

"God! Yes! Oh, *Archer!*"

Squeak.

Squeak.

Squeak.

"*Yes!*"

A tear leaks out onto the pillow.

What the hell is the matter with me?

The sound of the door swinging open startles me upright. I yank the pillow off my face in time to see a couple stumble into the bedroom where I've taken refuge from the party still raging outside. They're a blur of roving hands and drugging kisses, their mouths fused as tight as their bodies as they stumble across the threshold. They've nearly made it to the bed by the time they realize they aren't alone.

I lock eyes with the girl, feeling heat rise to my cheeks. *She* doesn't look embarrassed, though — annoyed would be a more accurate description.

"Uh, excuse me?" I bleat. "This room is occupied."

She sighs, like I'm the biggest inconvenience of all time. I recognize her from the cheerleading squad. Candi Ciccirelli. When she signed my yearbook last summer, she dotted every lowercase *i* with a ridiculous little heart.

"Can't you, like, find somewhere else to..." She gestures vaguely at me, flipping her glossy fall of raven hair over one tanned shoulder. "...have whatever emotional breakdown you're currently experiencing?"

Only slightly mortified, I scrub the tears from my face with the sleeve of my sweater and slide off the bed. Escape isn't the worst idea. Staying here and listening to Archer and Sienna's final act sounds about as appealing as a root canal.

I grab my iPhone off the nightstand and head for the door, studiously avoiding eye contact with the couple as I walk out. Not that they even notice — they're already resumed their primal grope session.

Thirty seconds of overeager, over-intoxicated humping commences in five... four... three... two... one...

I sigh and step into the hall.

CHAPTER TWO

ARCHER

"OH, ARCHER!"

Acrylic fingernails rake across my chest. Bottle-blonde hair, stiff from too much product, falls over my bare thighs in a curtain. It's a scratchy distraction from the work her mouth is doing.

"You're so big," she moans around my shaft, like a line she lifted straight out of a porno. Her whole approach to sex is so overblown — puns intended — I wouldn't be surprised to look up and find a production team pointing cameras at us.

Take 2! This time with more fake moaning, okay? And... action!

It isn't how I imagined it. Sex, I mean. Maybe that's because I've always imagined it with a different girl. With...

No.

I shove that thought from my brain with brute force, a metal gate slamming down to keep it out permanently. I will not think of Jo. Not now, not here, not during... *this*. If I let myself remember that look in her eyes when she saw me walk upstairs with Sienna — that heartbroken awareness, that blind-sided shock — I'll never be able to stay hard.

Sienna is lapping at my cock like it's an ice cream cone on the hottest day of summer.

"You like that, don't you?"

Her fake nails scrape over sensitive skin, and I flinch in what I'm sure she thinks is pleasure.

"I'm gonna make you cum so hard you'll see heaven..."

Would it be impolite to put in my headphones, like I do at the dentist when I don't want to hear them drilling into my skull?

Jaw clenched, I stare up at the ceiling. My hands fist in the sheets as she picks up her pace. She pulls me all the way into her mouth, until I'm butting against the back of her throat.

Christ.

It does feels good, don't get me wrong. Not great, but... good. From the way the guys always talk about head in the locker room, you'd think I'd be levitating off the bed in sheer ecstasy by now. Hell, maybe I should be. Sienna is hot, and she definitely knows what she's doing. But whatever pleasure she's managing to stir up is at war with the guilt and pain and regret that's sitting like an anvil on my chest.

Focus, fuckhead, I scold myself. *Otherwise this is going to take forever.*

I grunt as her mouth moves faster. Its hard to describe the sensation. Warm, wet. A bit sloppier than I thought it would be. Like fucking a peach that won't stop moaning theatrically every time you dip in.

"Are you close?" she gasps, pulling back with a slurping sound. She's panting a little.

Am I close?

Not nearly.

"Yeah," I lie, barely recognizing my own voice. "I'm close."

I force myself to look down at her as she resumes. Her eyes are brown. They'd be pretty if they weren't rimmed with so much makeup. Every time she blinks those long false eyelashes, I think of caterpillars crawling across her face — which isn't helping my performance any.

Could I be any more of an asshole?

This girl is sucking me off with the enthusiasm of a Dyson, and all I can think about is how much longer it's going to take until I can get out of this room, away from her. Away from myself. Away from this whole fucking night.

By then, the damage will be done. I'll have accomplished my mission of pushing away the only person I've ever even come close to—

No.

I fortify the metal barricade around my brain with fresh bolts and iron shackles, so the thoughts can't creep in. So *she* can't creep in. I force my mind to blank, focusing only on sensation.

Sienna's mouth.

My cock.

But it's not working. Five more minutes tick by, and I still can't seem to finish. For all her faux enthusiasm, Sienna knows it too. Her lips smack together with a wet *pop!* as the suction releases. She sits up between my thighs. My still-hard dick points up at her, a soldier at attention, awaiting his orders.

"This isn't working," Sienna pouts, frustration plain in her voice. I can see why. She's probably never had to put in this much effort for something as simple as a BJ. She's so hot, most guys are ready to blow their load the first second her lips close over their tip.

Teenage virgins aren't exactly known for their stamina.

Brows furrowed, she contemplates me like I've got some

kind of anatomical issue. I can almost hear the thoughts turning over in her mind.

Whiskey dick?

Mommy issues?

Secretly gay?

Sienna prides herself on being the hottest piece of ass at Exeter Academy. I know that sounds derogatory, but it's a title she gave herself. She takes abundant pride in her so-called "body count" of boys whose v-cards she's collected, often bragging that she's got nearly a full deck.

Her fingernail talons dig into my skin as she crawls up my body, straddling me. With our faces inches apart, I notice her lips are swollen and red from her efforts. She leans in to brush them against my ear, a breathy whisper.

"Why don't you just fuck me instead?"

Her hair rubs against my cheek — straw-like, reeking of artificial strawberries — and I try not to grimace. At this point, I want to screw her about as much as I want to slam my own dick in the nearest doorway, but I don't protest as she wriggles into a better position.

She stares into my eyes as she slowly hikes her stretchy orange skirt up around her midsection. She isn't wearing underwear, which normally would be an exciting revelation, but I can't seem to feel anything anymore. Not turned on, not revved up, not anything at all except...

Wrong.

This is all wrong.

Wrong time, wrong place, wrong girl.

"Archer?" Sienna's head tilts. She's gazing down at me in a way I'm sure she thinks is sexy — duck-bill lips, hooded eyes — waiting for my answer. When I don't immediately give it, she takes my cock into her hands, pumping with the methodical expertise of a professional. "Don't be shy. I know you want to fuck me... "

Her voice holds no room for doubt. Why would it? She's fucked every guy on the baseball team. It's basically a rite of passage.

Chug a beer at home plate, then run the bases.

Toilet-paper Coach Hamm's house before the first game.

Prank the rival team from the neighboring town.

Hook up with Sienna Sullivan at a house party.

"Sure," I hear myself say in a dead voice, forcing my arms to lift from their place on the mattress. They're stiff — like I'm a robot being operated via remote control, my decisions in the hands of someone else — as I reach for the condom on the bedside table.

Tear off the foil.

Roll it on.

Reach for her.

Hate myself.

"Let's fuck."

CHAPTER THREE

JOSEPHINE

THE HOUSE LOOKS like the crime scene from a multiple homicide, bodies strewn everywhere. Jason Samborn is passed out in a heap on the pool table, a puddle of drool forming on the green felt. Several couples are hooking up right out in the open — writhing against walls, pressed together in semi-dark corners, too desperate to wait for their turn in one of the bedrooms or too intoxicated to care.

Following the pounding bass, I make my way toward the back of the cabin, where an open-concept kitchen and living room area looks out over the jagged Atlantic coastline. The water looms with dark presence, pressing against the rocks just beyond the edge of the terraced lawn.

For a summer house, this place is massive — bigger than most normal people's year-round homes. But Lee Park's family is anything but normal. His grandfather owns half of Singapore, along with a slew of other properties scattered across the globe. (Which makes him the third-richest kid in my graduating class, second only to Eva Ulrich, whose great-great-great-grandfather patented the tube sock, and Carl McDonald, heir to a multi-billion-dollar fast food empire.)

I step hesitantly into the sunken den area. Twin sisters Ophelia and Odette Wadell are snorting lines of Adderall off the glass coffee table, their identical platinum bobs swooshing around their faces as they chase with shots of chilled Grey Goose. Someone I don't recognize is face-down on the other half of the sectional, one hand still clutching a green Jell-O shot.

Classy.

In the kitchen, half the baseball team is huddled around the island playing beer pong with stacks of plastic red cups, a keg waiting at the ready. Every time a ball makes it in, a fresh round of cheering and chest-bumping erupts.

Amid the hubbub, one of them spots me. Ryan Snyder, varsity first-baseman. He's probably the nicest guy on the team — meaning he doesn't outright ignore my presence at their parties. He always waves to me when I hang out in the bleachers after school, waiting to catch a ride home with Archer when practice ends.

Ryan is attractive in that All-American, Abercrombie model sort of way — tall with sandy blond hair and six pack abs, which are currently on full display. His red bathing suit is still damp from the pool, riding low on his hips, and he's sporting a tan despite the fact summer has barely begun. It's hard to believe the New England sun is strong enough to produce such a deep bronze in May.

"Yo! Valentine!" he yells over the strains of the Drake song blasting from the speakers, halting me in my tracks. "Where have you been hiding? Get over here and do a celeb-shot for me. My partner disappeared."

My brows lift. "A what?"

"Celebrity shot." He proffers a white plastic ping-pong ball, grinning widely. "Come here, I'll show you."

I wander closer, hoping the low lighting hides any trace of my tears. "I don't want to do a shot, Ryan. I'm not drinking."

"I'm not talking about a shot of alcohol, dummy. I'm talking about subbing in for a throw on my team." He mimes tossing the ball into a cup, his wrist snapping expertly. "Haven't you ever played pong before?"

I shrug noncommittally.

"That's just sad, Valentine. Truly." Shaking his head, he herds me farther into the kitchen, his warmth pressing close at my back. He smells like chlorine and cigarette smoke, topped with a heavy dousing of canned AXE body spray. The teenage boy standard.

"Make some room, fellas. Valentine's my new teammate and she's about to own your asses," he says, steering me through the huddle of male bodies. They part in a Red Sea of baseball jerseys.

I look up at Ryan, mouth twisting wryly. "I wouldn't get your hopes up."

"Too late. I have extremely high expectations. Plus, you can't be worse than my last partner. I'm pretty sure he's puking in the upstairs bathroom at the moment." He winks playfully, blue eyes glittering in the low light. "Now, it's pretty simple. You see those cups?" His gaze moves toward the other end of the marble countertop, where ten cups are set up in a triangular formation.

I nod.

"You're going to sink this ball—" He presses the plastic ball against my palm. "—into one of them. Easy."

"Spoken like someone who has never watched me attempt any athletic activity. Ever."

He laughs and I feel something inside me brighten.

Maybe I'm not entirely socially stunted, after all.

"Don't stress, Valentine." Ryan's shoulder nudges mine. "I'll help you get the hang of it."

Stepping behind me, he slides his arms around my body and takes my hands lightly in his own. His chest brushes against my back as his head bows over my shoulder, the long flow of his hair tickling my neck.

Something nervous skitters down my spine, then pools in the pit of my stomach. I've never been this close to a guy before — besides Archer. And he doesn't count. We've been invading each other's personal space since long before we could even spell the phrase *just friends*.

"Now," Ryan says into my ear, his voice husky. "Aim for the center cup. Then toss gently. It's all in the wrist."

"All in the wrist," I echo dumbly, as if I have any concept of what that means. "Right. Got it."

He chuckles, the sound vibrating against my earlobe. I squirm a little. My skin suddenly feels too tight.

No wonder I'm a virgin. An attractive guy can't even permeate my safe little proximity bubble without sending me into a tailspin.

"Are you two playing pong or hide-the-sausage?" one of the jocks across the island calls, impatience plain in his voice. "Throw the damn ball or find a bedroom."

"Shut the fuck up, Chris," Ryan snaps, releasing my hands and stepping back a pace. "Ignore him. You've got this, Valentine."

I suck in a deep breath, square my shoulders, and eye the triangle of cups. They're about six feet away — not an impossible distance, but definitely not close enough to inspire confidence in my abilities.

Sending up a small prayer, I make my shot. The rest of the party fades out of focus as I watch the small white plastic orb sailing through the air. No one is more stunned than me to see it sink into the centermost cup with a decided thunk.

"Hell yeah!" Ryan yells, sweeping me into a breath-stealing bear hug. "That's what I'm talking about!"

"Beginner's luck." I shrug out of his hold, laughing breathlessly. His enthusiasm is infectious — I find myself smiling as he hands me a second ball.

"Toss again."

I do, this time missing by quite a wide margin. The ball bounces across the kitchen floor, then disappears beneath the Viking range. Biting my lip, I glance up at Ryan. "In my defense... I did warn you about my lack of hand-eye coordination."

"Hey, don't worry about it. You hit that first cup perfectly. You're a total natural, you'll see."

"What's the big deal?" a feminine voice cuts in, laced with annoyance. "She sank one stupid ball. Anyone can do that."

Sienna steps up next to Chris on the other side of the marble island. Her eyes are almost as sharp as her collarbones when they lock on mine. Her mouth — coated in bright pink lipgloss that matches her crop top — is twisted in a condescending smirk. I can't help noticing that her bleach-blonde hair is thoroughly mussed, as though someone's been running his hands through it.

Archer.

My smile falters.

Sienna grabs the white ball from Chris's hand and tosses it adeptly into one of our cups.

"Nice shot!" Chris cheers, his eyes never shifting from Sienna's cleavage. He's drooling so much, a Saint Bernard would be grossed out.

Without missing a beat, Sienna picks up another ball and — in a move I could never in a million years replicate — tosses it behind her back, like a contortionist. It sinks effortlessly into a cup.

"*That's* how it's done," she declares, planting a hand on her hip. Her bright coral skirt is so tight, it's practically fused to her skin. There's no way she's wearing underwear — and I'm not the only one who's noticed. Every guy in the room has his eyes fixed on her. They can't seem to look away. She's magnetic.

Maybe it's her perfectly bronzed skin, not a single tan line in sight. Maybe it's the crop top, stretched tight over a full set of breasts that make mine look like mosquito bites by comparison. Or maybe it's simply her confidence — that undiluted charisma that draws everyone's attention, whether she's on the top of a pyramid in her cheerleading uniform or standing in a kitchen surrounded by half-empty plastic cups.

Sienna smiles coyly. "Oh, I'm not done yet, boys... unless you've seen enough?"

They yell louder, egging her on.

She makes several more perfect throws in quick succession, until all but one of our cups contains a small white ball floating on the surface. Turning her back to the countertop with a hip-shimmy that makes the boys roar, she blindly tosses the last ball over her shoulder. It lands in the cup directly in front of me with a tidy little *plunk!* that signals the end of the game.

Much as it pains me to admit, it's pretty damn smooth.

Sienna knows it, too. She pivots around as the jocks explode into cheers, a self-satisfied smile on her face. A giggle escapes her glossy lips as Chris hoists her into the air. The other guys fall to their knees, adoring subjects chanting their queen's name — three syllables, over and over, drowning out the music.

"*Si-en-na! Si-en-na! Si-en-na!*"

"That's right, peasants!" She laughs down at her adoring

fans, arms waving over her head. "I am the Queen of Beer Pong!"

Something inside me deflates, but I manage to keep the smile on my face. Ever the good sport. Never one to make a scene. After all, plain little Jo Valentine — perpetual wallflower — wouldn't dare infringe upon the spotlight that's been fixed in Sienna's direction since the day she sprouted boobs, way back in third grade.

I know full-well I'll never possess whatever magic runs through Sienna's veins. It's not something you can acquire; it's something you're born with, like freckles or allergies or double-jointed fingers. My best imitation of her carefree allure would no doubt come across awkward and antiseptic. A little girl stumbling around in her mother's high heels.

When Chris finally sets Sienna back on her feet, she looks straight across the island at me. Her heavily-mascaraed eyes scan me up and down, seeming to pick apart every facet of my existence from my simple fishtail braid to my oversized white wool sweater to the lack of makeup on my face.

"Drink up," she says, jerking her head at the cups in front of me. "You lost."

I glance down at the cups. White balls bob like tiny ships atop the frothy yellow beer. It looks about as appetizing as urine.

I clear my throat. "I actually wasn't planning on drinking..."

"God, you are *such* a stick in the mud." Sienna rolls her eyes. "Why do you even bother coming to our parties? Stay home and knit something instead next time, for Christ's sake."

A few of the jocks muffle laughs into their beer cups.

Anger bubbles through me, undercut by a stream of embarrassment so thick, it's difficult to breathe around. Sienna Sullivan is the worst kind of popular — the type that revels in it. She finds joy in annihilating those below her on the social totem pole. Probably because she assumes we're plotting to steal her spot at the top. She'd never understand that some of us are quite happy on the bottom rungs; that we'd rather stay anonymous than step on everyone else in order to ascend the meaningless echelons of Exeter Academy.

"Come on, *Valentine*." My nickname is said in a mocking sneer through pouty pink lips. "Show us you're not the total Goody Two Shoes everyone thinks you are."

I bite my tongue to keep from snapping back at her. It would be a waste of breath. Nothing I say will make her magically morph into a better person.

"Well?" she taunts, eyebrows arching. "What's it gonna be?"

I shift back and forth on my leather flip-flops, wishing I could disappear. Sienna notices my uneasiness; her smile widens like a cat with a canary between its paws.

She's fully aware I hate being the center of attention. She's known since sixth grade, when I spelled the word EXTE-MORANEOUS as EXTEMPOR-*ANUS* in front of the entire school at our annual spelling bee, sending the audience into hysterics — and me, into a tearful rush off stage. (It took Archer two hours to coax me out from beneath the bleachers.)

The chance to humiliate me in front of the baseball team is too tempting for her to pass up.

"*Well?*"

I swallow hard. "I..."

"I'll drink them," Ryan offers, reaching for a cup. "I really don't mind—"

"No." Sienna's order stills his hand. She's looking at me, her eyes like blades. "You didn't even throw, Ryan. This isn't your game. It's hers."

There's a brief pause between songs. In the sudden quiet, I notice that the kitchen has gone strangely silent as Sienna and I face off. I can feel the weight of many eyes on me; the pressure of impending laughter swelling in the air like a summer stormfront. Everyone is watching. Waiting to see if I'll run away. Expecting me to bail.

Boring Jo Valentine never lets loose, never does anything unexpected.

On a normal night, that would likely be true. I wouldn't think twice; I'd just walk away. Shrug it off. Head home to watch *The Great British Bake Off* in my safe little bubble.

But this isn't a normal night. And beneath the annoyance I feel when I look at Sienna, there's something else, something deeper — a simmering resentment that has nothing to do with a game of beer pong.

"Screw it," I mutter, reaching for the closest cup.

CHAPTER FOUR

ARCHER

I SIT on the edge of the bed for a while after Sienna leaves, trying to clear my head before I go back downstairs. It's no use. No amount of deep breathing will be enough to wipe the memories of tonight away.

Or the guilt.

I'm not insulted Sienna didn't stick around. V-card in hand, she promptly kissed my cheek and vanished through the door. I seriously doubt I rocked her world, but she didn't seem to mind. For her, sex is more about power — about popularity — than physical pleasure. Just another tactic to make herself relevant.

Seeing how the guys on the team trail her around like love-struck puppies, it's a damn effective strategy. The way to a man's heart may be through his stomach, but the way to a teenage boy's sits directly behind his zipper. And Sienna is more than happy to trade a quick romp between the sheets for undivided male attention — however fleeting. Fake orgasms are just one more line item on her list of artificial qualities.

Fake tan.

Fake hair.

Fake nails.

Fake nice.

The girl adopts and discards new personality traits faster than most people change their socks. I honestly can't stand her. Terrible to admit, given I've just bonked her brains out and all, but it's the truth. It's also the only reason I let her lead me into this bedroom.

Better her than someone who might think it actually means something.

I drop my head into my hands and rub them over my face, hard enough to make stars burst behind my eyes. Slapping my own cheeks, I command myself to stop being such a mopey fucker.

I made a choice.

There's no taking it back.

No changing it.

Just living with it... and its fallout.

After all, that was the whole point of this charade, wasn't it? I didn't screw Sienna for my health; I sure as shit didn't do it for my heart. It wasn't a drunken mistake or a momentary lapse in judgment. It was a calculated move, designed to inflict maximum damage.

When I walked through this door, I knew exactly what I was doing — and who I'd be hurting. I knew I was drawing a line through my old life. Crossing out certain possibilities with permanent marker.

A face flashes in my head. One I'd memorized every facet of by age four; one I've spent every year since staring at with ever-increasing intensity.

Upturned nose, smattering of freckles.

Quick smile, dimpled cheeks.

Jo.

I slap myself again. *Hard.* Rattling every thought of her out of my skull. As if the physical pain I inflict on myself will somehow detract from the relentless ache inside my chest.

I'd cut my own heart out if I thought it would help. But there's no help for this.

For me.

For us.

I was fully aware it would be hard. But this — the pain I'm feeling, the unbearable *finality* of it all — is excruciating. I tell myself it will get easier with time, knowing it's a lie.

What's one more?

Add it to the list.

Hauling in a final deep breath, I force myself to leave the room. Hiding out up here like a coward, unable to own up to my own decisions... unable to face the hurt I know awaits me in a pair of wide blue eyes... is just putting off the inevitable.

Rip off the Band-aid, asshole.

Downstairs, the party has petered out a bit as the beer and the drugs weave their dark web. More than a few people are already passed out, sprawled on various surfaces. In the foyer, I head for the first keg I see and pump myself a beer. It tastes like foamed piss, but I chug it down anyway, then promptly refill my cup.

Chug it down.

Fill it again.

I have to drive home later, but that's the least of my worries right now. The promise of oblivion has a certain gravitational pull that cannot be denied. Anything that might blunt the agony headed my way like a freight train.

How the hell am I supposed to face Jo sober?

Taking a fortifying gulp, I search for her. Frustration

mounts as I walk through the house, moving from room to room, checking all her usual places and coming up short. Never a big fan of parties, she almost always winds up in some quiet corner or other, hiding out until we can leave.

Not tonight, it seems.

She's not on the front porch, watering strangers' plants. She's not outside on a pool lounger, staring up at the stars. She's not in the dark library, perusing the shelves. She's not propped in the bed of my pickup truck, waiting on me to drive us home.

Where the fuck is she?

A fissure of concern fires through my nerve endings, but I tamp it down with another gulp of beer. Eventually, I find my way to the back of the house, where most of the still-conscious partygoers are congregated. Sienna is snorting white lines off the coffee table, flanked on either side by the Wadell twins. She doesn't even look at me when I walk in.

In the adjacent kitchen area, half my teammates are playing pong. I wander their way, mouth opening to ask if anyone has seen Jo, but the words catch in my throat. She's right there, in the most unexpected of places — leaning against the refrigerator with Ryan Shithead Snyder's arm around her shoulders and a red cup in her hand.

I stop in my tracks.

The first thing that registers in my brain is how good she looks. No matter that I've seen her every day for as far back as I can remember, no matter that her face is more familiar than my own in the mirror. It slams into me, a fresh gut-punch each time.

In a kaleidoscope of skin-tight dresses and spray tans, she's a pure ray of light — that blonde hair half falling out of its thick braid, her skin a pale glow in the dimmed light, those ridiculous cut-off shorts she thinks make her look like a tomboy but actually just highlight how her legs stretch on for miles. Over the years, I've spent more time fantasizing about those legs than I care to admit.

Dangling from our spot up in the rafters.

Running toward me down the boat dock.

Kicking in the crashing waves.

Wrapped around my waist as I piggyback her across the lawn.

The second thing that registers is that she's drunk. Her eyes, those insane sky-blue eyes that always stare straight into my soul, are half-lidded. She's leaning against the stainless steel fridge doors, looking unsteady on her feet. I have to fight the urge to race to her side, to hold her up.

Someone's already there. Already doing it.

Already in my place.

Ryan, that fuckwit, says something that makes her giggle. She sways slightly off balance, and he uses the opportunity to pull her closer against his bare chest. My grip clenches so hard around my cup, I hear the plastic crackle in protest.

Son of a bitch.

Ryan's hands are all over her, roaming with a familiarity that sets my teeth on edge. I watch his dumb fucking fingers twist in the fabric of her sweater and feel a volt of something unpleasant snake through me. I want to close the distance and rip them off her. Violently. I want to grab her by the hand and drag her away from here, away from *him*, even though I know that's the absolute last thing I'm supposed to be doing tonight.

I can't help it. Reason, common sense, intelligent thought... they all evaporated the instant I saw her. My feet are moving before I can stop them, heading for her like a magnet. To hell with the consequences.

I'm halfway across the kitchen when a hand clamps down on my shoulder and stops me in my tracks.

"Yooooo, Reyes!" Chris Tomlinson pounds my back hard

enough to spill my beer, grinning like the Cheshire Cat. "The champ returns!"

Apparently, news of my conquest has spread through this party faster than mono. Annoying, if not entirely unexpected.

"So..." Tomlinson leans in, waggling his eyebrows. "How was she? Everything you imagined?"

"Lay off, Chris."

"You scored, right?"

I don't answer. I'm busy trying to see around him, to the other side of the kitchen where Jo is standing.

"Second? Third? Home run?" Chris pesters. "Don't tell me you choked at the plate?"

Annoyance flickers through me. "I'm not talking about this with you."

"Why so coy, Reyes?" He shoves me playfully. "I'm not getting any tonight, the least you can do is help a brother out with some details..."

Shouldering past him, I finally have a clear view of the refrigerator. Jo is no longer propped against it. She's nowhere to be seen. Ryan, either.

Panic burns through me, a hot rush in my veins. My head swivels, searching the blur of faces in the kitchen. I think I catch a glimpse of her heading out the patio doors, but they swing back closed before I can be certain.

Dammit.

"Where are you going, Reyes?" Chris calls as I walk away.

I don't even break stride. When it comes to my teammates, I'm far more interested in Ryan right now — specifically, what he's doing with my best friend.

I'm reaching for the handle when the patio doors fly open in my face. Andy Hilton — certified idiot, but hell of an outfielder with a throwing arm like a young Babe Ruth — stumbles inside, marijuana smoke billowing around him in a cloud. His eyes are bloodshot. He's grinning like a madman.

"Where's Tomlinson?" he barks.

I jerk my head toward the kitchen. My impatience spikes higher with each second that slips by. I can't stand not knowing where Jo is. Whether she's all right.

Is seventeen too young for a heart attack?

"Come on, Reyes," Andy says. Belatedly, I notice the net in his hand — the kind used for pond maintenance — and the flash of orange scales within. "You don't want to miss this, I promise. Got a special delivery here, just for Chris..."

Jesus Christ.

Andy plows into the kitchen, leaving a wet trail from the doors to the island. Against my better judgment, I follow.

"Catch of the day!" he screams, upending the net onto the counter. The fish plops out, its eyes round as marbles, its mouth opening and closing in useless pursuit of air. It thrashes around like a seizure victim. Everyone leans in, mesmerized by the sight.

My eyes jerk toward Andy. "Dude, what the fuck?"

"Tomlinson bet me you couldn't close the deal with Sienna," he says gleefully, his eyes on Chris — who's looking a little pale as he watches the fish squirm. "Since she already confirmed otherwise... it's time for him to honor his wager."

"It was a joke," Chris says weakly, eyes still on the fish.

Andy snorts. "You're only saying that because you lost."

"What was the bet?" I ask, though I'm not entirely certain I want to know the answer.

Andy is all to happy to inform me. "Loser swallows a fish from the Park family pond."

Chris shakes his head. "No. No way I'm doing this. I can't."

"Deal's a deal, bro. "

"Piss off, Andy!" His voice is slightly slurred. He's had so many beers, I'm surprised he's still cognizant enough to argue. "I'm not doing it."

"Don't be chickenshit."

"Lee will kill me, man. Those koi are his Mom's..."

"Lee's passed out on the sectional. He'll never know." Red-faced and panting in excitement, Andy reaches out and grasps the wriggling fish in one of his beefy hands. It escapes several times before he manages to maneuver it into an empty beer cup. He stares gleefully at Chris as he slides the cup slowly across the countertop.

"You want me to add some water, or do you prefer it sashimi-style?"

Chris makes no move to take the cup. No one else does, either. Most of the guys just stand there watching, waiting to see how it all unfolds. A few of them start laughing. Pounding Chris on the back in encouragement. Egging him on.

All the while, the fish is drowning on dry land.

My eyes are locked on the cup. I'm not sure why the sight of it bothers me so much, but I can't seem to look away. It rattles as the koi flops within, fighting for survival. His odds aren't looking good if no one intervenes.

Dammit.

The last thing I want to do at this moment is save a goddamned oversized goldfish, but it seems I have no choice. I can't leave the little guy in the hands of these clowns. Don't get me wrong, I'm not some PETA warrior. I've heard all the arguments for plant-based diets and vegan lifestyles — *"Fish are friends, not food!"* — but I still enjoy a nice piece of swordfish on the grill. I'm always in favor of a clam bake on the coals. Give me some melted butter and a claw-crusher, I will happily decimate a lobster in under five minutes.

The one thing I cannot stand is wastefulness. Entitlement. Some rich kid reaching down into your tiny-ass pond, where you were minding your own business, swimming around in happy circles, never knowing any better... and yanking you out, into the air, just for sport. Just because he can.

That's the shit I can't quite swallow.

In this room full of trust fund brats and fourth-generation millionaires, I probably have more in common with the fish flopping inside that cup. Not that they know that, of course. If they did, I'd never be standing here in the first place.

"Stop dawdling, Chris!" Andy hoots. "Drink up!"

Chris steels his shoulders and takes a deep breath, preparing himself. Annoyed — at myself, at my idiot teammates — I snatch the cup off the countertop before he has a chance to grab it.

"This is the most idiotic shit I've ever witnessed," I hiss through gritted teeth. "Where's the pond? I'm putting him back."

Andy groans. "Reyes, don't be a buzzkill! We're just having a little fun."

"Your definition of *fun* is not the same as mine, Hilton." I push past him on my way to the patio. Chris, I notice, looks more than a little relieved to see me go.

"Where's your sense of humor, man?" Andy yells at my back. "I used to think you were chill!"

"And I used to think you weren't an asshole. Things change." With that, I step through the doors, into the dark, and set off in search of the goddamned koi pond. Figures, it's on the farthest edge of the property — it's been that kind of night.

I glance down at the orange fish. He's still gasping for air, but he seems to be struggling less than before. Doubtful that's a good sign, I pick up my pace.

Hang in there, little guy.

I don't regret saving him from a brutal final swim in the

bowels of Chris Tomlinson's stomach; I do regret that this act of piscine altruism will undoubtedly delay my efforts to locate Jo.

An image of Ryan's arm sliding over her shoulders slams into my mind. His fingers, twisting in her sweater. Her eyes, glazed with the effects of alcohol.

Cursing under my breath, I break into a jog.

CHAPTER FIVE

JOSEPHINE

I'M DRUNK.

I'm not certain how I know this for sure, seeing as I've never even been tipsy before, but things are definitely... off-kilter. In a big way.

There's a slight haze wrapped around my brain. It's like staring at the world through fog. Everything is at once duller and brighter, louder and farther removed. Despite the disembodied sensation, I am acutely aware of myself in a way I've never before experienced.

The press of the steel refrigerator at my back. The scratch of the wool sweater against my skin. The warmth of Ryan's arm, wrapped around my shoulders. The slight tingle of nervous energy gathered at the base of my spine.

Chugging ten cups of beer will do that to a girl, I suppose. Not that I have much experience to go on. Besides the six-pack of IPAs Archer dared me to pilfer from my parents' spare fridge a few summers back, I've never had more than a few sips at any of these parties.

In retrospect, maybe I should have. I can't deny, the buzz is making it all much more tolerable. The music isn't nearly as jarring to my ears. The jocks' constant chest-bumping is almost endearing, now. Hard as it is to believe, even Sienna isn't bothering me — despite the fact that, when I drained my final cup, she merely faked a yawn, whispered '*boooooring*' under her breath, and wandered off toward the den to snort a few lines.

Whatever.

It's not like I was expecting her to do cartwheels in my honor, or anything. I don't need her praise. I'm proud of myself for proving I'm not a total Goody Two Shoes at least once before I put high school in my rearview. And Ryan, this giant golden-retriever-of-a-boy lingering by my side, seems proud of me, too. He's told me so twice already, his consonants running together like water.

"Hell yeah, Valentine! That's how it's done!" His broad shoulder nudges mine. "Thought you said you didn't drink?"

"I don't."

"Could've fooled me."

I look up at him. His face is a bit out of focus, like a photograph snapped at the wrong shutter speed. In fact, it's not just his face. The entire room is looking more like a double-exposure with every passing moment. I regret skipping dinner as the beer swirls inside my empty stomach.

"You want to play again?"

"Definitely not." I shake my head vigorously. The move makes the room spin even more than before. I grab the edge of the countertop to steady myself.

"Hey, you okay? You look a little..." Ryan's hand, warm and solid, lands on my shoulder. He squeezes gently through the fabric of my sweater, which suddenly feels too hot against my skin. I'm flushed and woozy, as though all the blood in my veins has rushed straight to my head.

"I'm fine," I say. *Slur.* "I think I just need a little fresh air."

"I'll come with you."

"No, that's okay..."

But my weak protest is quickly brushed aside. Ryan's arm is already around my shoulders, steering me toward the patio doors, over the threshold, into the night.

Outside, it's quiet. Music drifts from the open windows, but otherwise there's only the low hum of voices from the jacuzzi tub, where a handful of people are bubbling like lobsters in a pot. The surface of the pool gleams, a black mirror, as we pass by, stepping over discarded beer cans, cigarette butts, and plastic cups.

What a mess. I would not want to be Lee Park tomorrow morning. (Or, more accurately, the Park family maid. No one in this socioeconomic bracket does their own menial labor.)

It's dark at the edge of the property, where the manicured lawn meets the unforgiving Atlantic. An outcropping of boulders rebuffs the ocean's persistent advances. Ryan steers me toward one with a flat top.

"Here," he says softly. "Sit with me for a bit."

Sitting feels good. Stable. With solid rock beneath me and solid muscle at my side, the earth rights on its axis just enough for things stop spinning. Behind us, the party rages on, but we are far-removed from it out here in the darkness, where there are no bright lights or pounding bass beats — just a starry sky and the faint crashing of waves against the rocky beach. Breathing deeply, I time my inhales to each sea swell: in through my nose, out through my mouth. Steadying myself against the alcohol undulating in my system.

"Feel better?" Ryan asks after a few moments of silence.

"Yeah. Thanks." I swallow hard. "You don't have to stay with me. If you'd rather go back..."

"Nah." His shoulder brushes mine. "Could use a little air

myself, to be honest. If Chris beats me at pong again I'll never hear the end of it."

"I definitely didn't help you on that front."

"You did just fine."

"Right. Tell that to Sienna, *Queen of Beer Pong*," I blurt in a mocking tone I'd never normally use around anyone except Archer. Apparently, my verbal filter has been rendered null-and-void by beer.

Ryan laughs. "Don't let Sienna make you feel bad. She's just..." When he trails off, I glance over at him. He's rubbing the back of his neck, staring out at the water. "She's gotten used to being the center of attention around here. She can be a little territorial — especially when it comes to girls she's threatened by."

"*Me*? A threat? In what world?"

"You don't see yourself very clearly, do you Valentine?"

I blink slowly at him. His face is still a bit blurry. "To be entirely forthright... at the moment, I'm not seeing *anything* all that clearly, Ryan."

A quick grin spreads across his face. "Hey. You're funny! I never knew you were funny. You're always so shy."

"I am not shy!"

"Not tonight." He laughs again. "But usually you keep to yourself, if you even bother coming to our parties — which isn't often."

"It's not like I really fit in here."

"What do you mean?"

"I mean..." I chew my lip, regretting that I ever opened my mouth. This conversation is heading somewhere I'm not certain I want to go. "I'm not like the rest of you."

"You half-alien or something?"

"I don't usually drink. I don't really party. I'm not..." *Popular,* I add silently.

"Valentine, I'm going to let you in on a little secret."

"Oh yeah? What's that?"

"Not one person here feels like they truly belong. Why do you think everyone gets so wasted at these parties?"

My nose scrunches in thought. "To hook up?"

"Well, yeah. But also because beer is like... social lube. It makes everyone less of a tight ass."

I laugh so hard, it comes out a snort. Not my most attractive attribute, but I'm too tipsy to contain it.

"Laugh all you want," Ryan says somewhat defensively, fidgeting with his fingers. "It's true! When you're buzzed, you don't worry about saying the wrong thing or screwing everything up."

His shoulders have gone stiff. It's possible I shouldn't have snorted at him. I remember my mother telling me a million times — *men like making jokes, but they can't stand feeling like one.*

"I'm not laughing at you," I assure him, attempting to get a hold on the mirth bubbling inside me. "It's just... what a poignant metaphor, Ryan. I don't know what your plans are for after graduation, but might I suggest a career in poetry?"

A chuckle vibrates through his shoulder, into mine. "There's that sense of humor creeping out again. Careful, Valentine — I might not let you pretend to be shy around me anymore."

"Oh, I think my secrets are pretty safe. Or have you forgotten our high school days are numbered? After a few more weeks, we probably won't cross paths ever again."

"Ouch! Dagger to the heart." He scowls playfully at me. "You can't shake me that easily. There's still a handful of baseball games, then playoffs, prom, and, like, a million graduation parties to get through."

I have no response to offer. Not one he'd appreciate,

anyway. Frankly, I'm not certain I'll be attending the majority of the events he's just rattled off. The senior prom — four hours trapped on a party cruise around the Massachusetts coast with a hundred of my fellow graduates dressed in their best formalwear — sounds like a chapter pulled from a tome of my worst nightmares. And then there's the small fact that, as of this moment, I don't even have a date.

In another lifetime, I thought maybe Archer would ask me. After tonight, that seems about as improbable as me receiving an invitation to Sienna Sullivan's post-grad sunset soiree.

"It's a small town, Valentine," Ryan, bless his naive heart, reminds me. As if a town's size makes any difference when it comes to being an outcast. Even this small Massachusetts microcosm we call home is full of people who don't fit in. Myself included.

Manchester-by-the-Sea.

Population: 5,000

Number of parties I attended to prior to Archer making the the varsity baseball roster and dragging me along as his weirdo sidekick: 0

"There's a whole summer to waste before college orientation!" Ryan bumps my shoulder with his again. "Bonfires, beach days, you name it. Just because we aren't passing each other in the halls every day, doesn't mean we can't hang out."

My eyes widen. "You and me?"

"Yeah. Why not?" It's dark, so I can't be sure, but I think his cheeks are a little red. Gesturing back toward the house, he tacks on, "But also, I'm sure the guys on the team will throw a bunch more parties like this one. It'll be chill. You should come."

"Maybe."

"Sounds like a no."

"Parties aren't really my scene."

"What is your *scene*, then?"

I shrug noncommittally.

"Come on. That's all I get? A shrug?" Sighing, he shakes his head. "Josephine Valentine. Always so mysterious."

A scoff pops out. "I'm not even slightly mysterious."

"Then tell me something about yourself. What do you like to do? You know, when you aren't boycotting fun parties and kicking ass at beer pong."

"Um..."

"Don't overthink it. Just spit it out."

"Sailing," I blurt abruptly. "I like sailing."

"That's cool. You have your own boat?"

"Yeah, a 20-foot Alerion. She's fast, but also small enough for me to take her out single-handed." I smile at the thought of my most prized possession, bobbing at her slip back home. "It was a sixteenth birthday present from my parents."

"Most girls probably would've preferred a convertible."

"I guess." I shift against the stone, uncomfortable. "But I usually get a ride everywhere with Archer, since he lives right next door. I wouldn't have much use for a car of my own."

"Right, I forgot. You and Reyes." He sighs. "You've been his little shadow for as long as I can remember. Before he joined the team, I don't think I'd ever seen him without you by his side."

I'm not sure what to say to that, so I don't say anything at all. We lapse into silence. It's not an uncomfortable one, though. Just the sound of the waves and the thudding of my pulse, beating a bit too fast inside my veins.

"So what's the deal with you two, anyway?" Ryan asks suddenly.

"Me and Archer?" I squeak. "There's no *deal*. We're just friends."

"Uh huh."

"You don't sound very convinced."

He shrugs. "Just not sure I buy it."

"Buy what?"

"That a guy and a girl can ever really be *just* friends."

Feeling brave, I nudge his shoulder with mine. "What about you and me — we're friends now, aren't we?"

He's silent for such a long beat, I begin to regret my words. *Damn.* Maybe I overshot. Maybe I misread this entire situation. Maybe he's just a nice guy taking pity on the weird loner girl at the party and—

"What if I said I didn't want to just be your friend, Valentine?"

My mouth gapes in shock at his question. I blunder with fragments of disbelief and incomprehension, trying to cobble them into a single coherent thought... trying to figure out what I'm supposed to do next.

Ryan doesn't seem confused. Not at all. He's following a script no one bothered to share with me — looking into my eyes, leaning closer. So close, I can smell the beer on his breath, can see the freckles dotted across the bridge of his nose.

I feel dazed — from the alcohol in my veins, from his unexpected words, from this entire night. I can't move. I can't do anything except watch him narrow that gap between us, his mouth heading straight for mine.

He's going to kiss me, I think stupidly. *My first kiss. It's finally happening.*

At seventeen, it is a milestone long overdue. But now that it's finally arrived, I'm oddly unsettled — which makes no sense at all. How can something I've been waiting for forever somehow feel so incredibly rushed?

Probably because it's happening with the wrong person.

I push away the unwelcome thought and try to focus on the boy in front of me. The one who finds me *funny* and *mysterious.* The one who wants to kiss me in the starlight, with the waves crashing a stone's throw away. The one who is actually interested in being more than just my friend.

I'm not sure what's more pathetic — the fact that, in this moment, with Ryan's mouth a hairsbreadth from my own, I can't stop wishing I was about to kiss someone entirely different... or that I'm still wasting wishes on that someone, when he's probably inside at this exact moment with his tongue in some other girl's mouth.

Stop.

Thinking.

About.

Archer.

Closing my eyes, I square my shoulders and brace myself for the brush of Ryan's lips. Only... it never comes. Instead, I hear the sudden rush of footsteps, followed shortly by the dull thud of a fist making impact with a cheek. I hear a male roar — one I recognize all too well.

"Get the fuck off her!"

My heart stops.

I know that voice.

Ryan's warmth is ripped abruptly from my side. By the time I manage to open my eyes and register what's going on, he's sprawled in the grass ten feet away. Standing above him with clenched fists, his chest pumping harder than the pistons of a steamer engine, is the last person in the world I expect to see at this moment.

"*Archer!*" I spring to my feet, stumbling a bit in the process. "Are you out of your mind?!"

My best friend doesn't look at me. He's too busy glaring down at Ryan, who's still sprawled in the grass moaning lightly, clutching his cheek. A bruise is already blooming.

"Oh god, Ryan..." I wince, starting in his direction. "Are you okay?"

"He's fine."

Archer's voice is cold as ice. I actually shiver at the sound of it, my steps faltering to a sudden stop halfway between the two boys — one on the ground, looking as bewildered as I feel, the other looming like a thunderstorm, electrically charged with inexplicable anger.

"You hit me, man!" Ryan clambers to his feet. "What the hell?"

Archer offers no explanation. His jaw is locked so tight, I'm not sure he's able to breathe, let alone speak. For the life of me, I cannot fathom what's set him off. He's never acted like this before, in all the years I've known him. Not once.

Of the two of us, I'm the one with the temper. I'm the one who flips out and storms off, sulking until he talks me down with that calm voice, those deep eyes. We balance one another — me a boiling froth, him a steady undercurrent. Where I'm dramatic, he's unperturbed. While I overreact, he takes everthing in stride.

At least... usually.

This black rage of his, this swelling anger, dark enough to blot out the stars... it's a side I've never seen before.

A side I'm not certain I like.

"Archer..." His name comes out almost as a plea. "What is going on?"

Ryan glances at me. "Come on, Valentine. I think we should go."

"She's not going anywhere with you, Snyder." Archer steps forward, his eyes locked on Ryan with lethal precision. "You should walk away. Before I make you walk away."

"That a threat, Reyes?"

"A promise."

"*Archer!*" I cry out, half-angry, half-astonished by his behavior.

His eyes cut to me for the briefest of seconds. When I sway on my feet, still not one hundred percent in control of my balance, he looks swiftly away again, his jaw even tighter than before.

"Look, man..." Ryan's nostrils flare. "I don't know what your problem is, but—"

Archer cuts him off. "Right now? *You.* I told you to piss off once already. You won't like the way I tell you again."

Rage gathers inside my chest, overriding all the confusion and embarrassment fighting for purchase. Before I know it, I'm barreling in my best friend's direction, so angry, I can barely see straight. (The buzz isn't helping on that front, either.)

My palms slam against his shoulders, full force. "Have you gone *insane?*"

He barely even rocks backward — which pisses me off so much, I do it again. Harder. He grunts this time, but doesn't move more than an inch.

Is the boy made of stone?

"What is the matter with you?" I ask, my words punctuated by a third shove to his shoulders. "You can't just go around—" Another shove. "—punching people—" And another. "—for no good reason!"

Before I can land one more hit, Archer grabs my wrists, manacling them in a steely grip. Disarming me seems to cost him almost no effort — like controlling an overtired toddler or swatting a meddlesome fly. I don't even have time to summon indignation; in the space between two heartbeats, I find myself hauled up against his chest, our joined hands crushed between our bodies.

Normally, he's a half-foot taller than me. Like this, dragged up onto my tiptoes, we're nearly nose to nose.

"*Stop*," he grunts.

I jerk in halfhearted protest at his order, knowing all the while it's futile. He's a million times stronger than me. I couldn't get away if I tried. And if I'm being candid, I'm not trying. Not really. Something about Archer's anger up close is disarming. It tempers my rage with undeniable curiosity.

What's gotten so under your skin, Archer Reyes?

"Let me go," I whisper thickly. "You're acting like a total psychopath right now!"

"The girl who just shoved me six times is angry I hit someone?" His eyes narrow on mine. "Certain sort of irony in that."

"At least I had a good reason!"

"So did I."

"And what might that be?"

A muscle jumps in his jaw. "He was touching you."

"*And?*"

The muscle jumps again, but he remains silent.

"So what if he was touching me?" I ask, not even caring that Ryan is within earshot of this mortifying exchange. "Maybe I *wanted* him to touch me, did you ever think of that? Did you?"

Fury is still rolling off Archer in waves — it's there in the rapid rise and fall of his chest, in the stiffness of his posture, in the furrowed brow — but when he speaks again, it's in a flat voice that lets me know his emotions are now on a tight leash.

"He was taking advantage of you."

I roll my eyes. "Don't be ridiculous."

"He was."

"*How?*"

"You're drunk, Jo."

"I am not!" I yell, indignant enough to lie.

"You can't even walk straight!" he yells right back. "And if you think I'm going to stand by and watch as some asshole gets you wasted just so he can put his hands all over you—"

Ryan attempts to interject. "Bro, chill! I wasn't—"

"We'll settle this later, Snyder." Archer's eyes cut to his teammate with a look so full of promise, it makes my heart skip a beat. "Now... *evaporate.*"

Ryan shoots me an apologetic look before he bolts back toward the party, where it's safe. I can't blame him. Archer is in full-on, overbearing asshole mode. I wouldn't stick around either.

"Thanks a lot!" I glare into Archer's face, mere inches from my own. "You humiliated me! Are you happy?"

"Happy he's not touching you when you're too wasted to consent? Yeah. I am happy."

"So you can get drunk and have—" I can't bring myself to say *sex.* "—and hook up with whoever you want, but I can't even let a boy kiss me without you beating him into the ground?"

"It's not the same thing," he growls. "He was taking—"

"Advantage of me?" I shake my head. "And what exactly were you and Sienna doing tonight? Playing Scrabble? Because she wasn't sober. In fact, she was snorting lines off the coffee table with the commitment of a housewife in the candle aisle at HomeGoods." I pause for a loaded beat of silence. "Or did you think I didn't know that you slept with her?"

Archer actually flinches.

Good.

I'm glad I still have the power to wound him. God knows he's hurt me enough, tonight. Glaring into his face, I try to read the emotions in his eyes but he shields them from me, staring fixedly over my shoulder. He offers me nothing — no answers, no apologies, no explanations.

I'd hit him again, if he weren't still holding my hands.

"Right, I forgot! Silly me!" I try to laugh, but my voice

cracks pathetically. "The rules don't apply when *you're* the one getting some."

He expels a frustrated sigh. "I'm not fighting with you about this, Jo."

"Well you sure as hell had a lot of opinions a few minutes ago!" I shake my head. "You know what? I don't even care what you have to say. Spare me your sexist, double-standard bullshit."

His furious gaze snaps to mine. "Then spare me the doe-eyed innocent act. You know as well as I do that these guys are just looking for a warm body. Forgive me if I don't want my best friend winding up one more meaningless notch in their belts."

"Ryan isn't like that!"

"Ryan Snyder is exactly like that. These guys... they're my teammates, and they're decent enough to spend an afternoon at the batting cages with. Beyond that, they're not winning any prizes for chivalry. They'll fuck anything with a pulse. For all I know, they made a bet out of it — first to nail Valentine gets bragging rights."

Ouch.

My stomach drops to my feet. I reel back, desperate for some space, only to realize I'm still a captive. His hold on me is stronger than iron — and I'm not just talking about his hands on my wrists.

"So that's all this was?" I ask flatly.

"All *what* was?"

"One friend looking out for another." I stare at him, too worked up to hold back.

His gaze flickers back and forth across my face, reading me like a book. "What else would it be, Jo?"

"You tell me."

"I don't know what you're talking about."

"And I don't know why you can't just admit it!"

"Admit what?"

"That it bothered you!" I snap. "Seeing me with Ryan."

His eyes flare. "Don't be ridiculous."

"You were *jealous*." I poke him in the chest with the tip of my finger. "Admit it! You couldn't stand seeing me with someone else. Because deep down, in some twisted way... you think I belong to you."

There's a long beat of utter silence. So long, I start to count the waves as they crash, a relentless metronome. I reach a dozen before I begin to feel the tingling of regret creeping up my spine. A dozen more before Archer takes a deep, shuddering breath.

"You're drunk, Jo. You don't know what you're saying, and you're going to regret it in the morning."

My heart fails inside my chest when he says that. Suddenly, I want to be anywhere but here. Anywhere but with *him*. I want to crawl into bed, cry my eyes out, and forget this entire night ever happened. Or, at the very least, escape my own mind for a few blissful hours of unconscious sleep.

Defeat and despair intertwine inside me in a tight knot, filling up my lungs, blocking off my airway, pressing at the back of my eyes. I don't want to cry. If I start, I may never stop.

Forcing my mouth open, I speak very carefully — each word like a bullet in the air. "Let me go, Archer."

"Jo—"

"*Now*. I mean it."

He does.

In the sudden absence of his steadying hold, the sky spins precipitously around me. I lurch sideways and nearly fall over, only managing to catch myself at the very last moment. So much for my insistence re: *sobriety*.

When stability returns, Archer is watching me from a careful distance with his arms crossed over his chest. I can't stand to see the *I-told-you-so* look on his face, so I stare down at my feet instead.

"I really hate you right now," I tell him, voice hollow.

"I really don't give a shit." He pauses. Extends his hand out to me. "Come on. I'll drive you home."

I ignore his hand — and his eyes — as I beeline for the driveway.

CHAPTER SIX

ARCHER

I DRIVE us home in strained silence.

It's nearly three. The streets are empty of traffic, but I stick to the back roads in case a cop is cruising to meet his monthly ticket quota. The last thing I can afford is to be pulled over — not with Jo in the car, not with potential scholarships on the line. Not in general.

Since I got my license last year, I have braked fully at every stop sign. I don't run reds. Hell, I don't run yellows. The guys on the team give me shit for it — *"Reyes, my grandma drives faster than you!"* — but they wouldn't understand. If a cop pulls them over, they get off with a verbal warning. A free pass. A sedate "Say hi to the folks for me, son."

Me?

I get the quizzical "How did you afford this nice truck?" look. I get my plates run. And, as soon they see the name REYES pop up in their system, I get the book thrown at me.

Big thanks to my brother Jax for making our family notorious in this town.

The windows are cranked down, letting in a stream of

warm, early-summer air. Jo's got her head hanging out like a dog. I can't decide if it's because she's drunk or because she can't stand to look at me. Maybe a little of both.

My grip tightens on the wheel and I grimace as pain shoots through the knuckles of my right hand. Using my pitching arm to smash in Snyder's face wasn't the smartest choice. But honestly, the way things have been going lately, losing my shot at a scholarship due to an idiotic, self-inflicted injury would just be icing on the fucking cake that is my life.

I resist the urge to press more firmly on the gas pedal. Some days, when I'm out for a drive alone, I'd like nothing more than to steer this truck right off the road, onto the sand, into the ocean. Let sea water fill up the cab slowly, let my limbs start to float. Wait until only an inch of air remains at the ceiling. Gasp at it like a goldfish yanked from his pond. Wonder whether the water is dragging me under or offering me deliverance I'm too blind to accept.

Jo would freak if she ever heard me say something like that out loud. Hell, she'd probably have me signed up for bi-weekly therapy sessions within the hour, so I could sit in a beige-on-beige "safe space" and discuss my feelings with a neutral third party observer. I might even attend, just to appease her. But it wouldn't change anything. No therapist in the world can fix all the shit that's gone wrong in my life these past few weeks.

Neither can Jo. That's why I haven't told her about any of it. If I did, it would only put her square in the middle of a situation highly prone to going sideways. Because she'd do exactly what she always does — make *my* problems *her* problems. Attempt to fix it. And get herself hurt in the process.

I can't let that happen. I'd rather have her hate me than see her damaged by the fallout from my family implosion. After all she's done for me, after all we've been through... she deserves a life untouched by emotional shrapnel. Even if that life doesn't include me anymore.

At the next intersection, I glance over at her. She's still ignoring me, hiding behind the curtain of her hair. Loosed from its braid, it blows around her face, rippling like sand dunes on a windy day.

God, she's beautiful.

God, she must hate me.

I should be happy my plans to push her away are working so effectively. But I'm not happy. Just the opposite. The prospect of losing the best thing in my life has opened up a bottomless pit inside my gut. Each moment we're at odds gnaws a little more into my stomach lining. And there's nothing I can do to make it better.

Creating some distance between us is the smartest option. The only option. But now that the ball is rolling, I can't help second-guessing myself. I can't help wishing that any moment now, she'll look over at me and murmur, "It's okay, Arch, I forgive you."

I sigh.

Josephine Valentine is not, by nature, a forgiving person. She's known to hold grudges. She gets angry at authors for killing her favorite characters, then refuses to read another word they write. (George R.R. Martin has undoubtedly received hate-mail from her.)

She still talks trash about the guy who cut her off in line for the gondola when we went snowboarding last season. Same for the girl in the Bentley who stole our parking spot on the first day of school.

She boycotts a certain coffee shop downtown because a barista there once made a racist crack about the soy milk request for my latte.

Yo soy Archer. Haha!

Jo almost threw the aforementioned latte right in the hipster's face. I had to drag her out the door, kicking and screaming like a feral cat the whole way. To this day, whenever we walk by that place, she blatantly glares through the display window, making it clear all is not forgiven.

But...

She's always forgiven *me*.

We've had fights before, of course. I've pissed her off plenty over the years. You can't be best friends since birth without a few epic blowouts.

Age eight: broke the arm off her favorite American Girl Doll in an ill-advised round of tug-of-war. Cue all of my allowance, up in smoke.

Age ten: went fishing with my older brother and failed to invite her. Cue meltdown of unmatched proportions.

Age twelve: refused to partner with her in the local talent show for a mediocre rendition of "Defying Gravity" from the musical Wicked. Cue first — but not last — "I hate you, Archer Reyes!"

She's pissed me off plenty, too, don't get me wrong. There was the time, at thirteen, when she hijacked her father's boat and crashed it into a sandbar, nearly getting us both killed — not to mention grounded for an entire summer. At fifteen, when she barged into my bedroom without knocking and caught me red-handed — literally — watching porn. At sixteen, when she showed me one of her baffling sewing patterns and proceeded to call me a "low-brow jock with no appreciation for design." And just a few months ago, when she insisted I only entertain baseball scholarship offers from schools within a two hour drive of Brown — which just so happens to be where she was accepted early-decision, and plans to attend this fall.

But this fight feels different.

It *is* different.

Deep down, even if I want her to forgive me, I know she shouldn't. It's safer for her to be out of my life — at least, for the foreseeable future. Safer if she hates me so much, she can't stand to be in the same place at the same time.

Despite all previous efforts to push her away — dodging her in the halls, sitting at the jock table at lunch, jamming my schedule full of baseball practices and hours at the batting cages and yes, even my teammates' lame parties on the weekends — she hasn't gotten the hint. Hasn't backed off in the slightest. The busier I get, the more determined she becomes to make time together: arranging Sunday afternoon sails, showing up at my door, ambushing me as soon as she hears my truck rolling down the driveway.

Turns out, cutting Jo out of my life is harder than cutting off a limb. She won't let go. Not without extreme measures.

For instance, blatantly screwing another girl.

If I could physically avoid her, I wouldn't have to take things so far. Given that we live on the same property, that's basically impossible. Jo has a way of making a even a three-acre estate feel intimate. She spends more time in my tiny bedroom than she does her own waterfront suite.

We pull up to the wrought iron gates that mark the start of the private drive. I punch in a code on the small electronic keypad and they swing inward with a metallic clang. Pulling the truck off asphalt and onto imported pea-stone, I creep up the driveway slowly, so as not to wake anyone.

After a moment, Cormorant House comes into view. It's impressive, even after all this time — a sprawling, twelve-bedroom stone mansion perched on a cliff overlooking the Atlantic, complete with a full guest cottage, in-ground swimming pool, boathouse, private dock, and separate staff quarters. Built in an opulent châteauesque style, it's been a Valentine property since Jo's ancestors struck industrial gold in the

Gilded Age, building the country's first ever railroad— though, her father only inherited it twenty or so years ago.

For almost as long as her parents have occupied it, mine have maintained it. Though everyone has always been careful not to use the word "servant," instead throwing around euphemisms — "housekeeper" for my mother, "handyman" for my father — I've known since I was no more than three that the Reyes clan could never afford to live in this house, this zip code, this very town on our own.

We exist here at the behest of Jo's father. Were he to simply snap his fingers... we'd be out on our asses, exiled from the the only home I've ever known before the ink on my parents' severance check was dry.

Rounding the circular driveway, I slow to a stop at the front walk and turn off the engine. Jo makes no move to get out. For a moment, we sit in total silence. I have to curl my hands around the steering wheel to keep from reaching for her, from crushing her against my chest in a hug — the kind we used to give each other without a second thought, back when things were so much simpler.

"I don't know what to say to you," she whispers finally. Her voice is soft; I strain to catch all her words. "That's never happened before."

My jaw tightens, holding in the desire to apologize. If she forgives me, this whole night — everything I did with Sienna — was for nothing.

I can feel her looking at me. Waiting for me to say something. To make this better between us, like I always do when we disagree. But I keep my eyes fixed straight ahead, my lips pressed firmly shut.

"I don't know what your problem is, Archer, but I hope you get over it. Soon. I didn't even recognize you, tonight. You were so angry. So out of control. It was like..." She pauses. "Like staring at your brother."

Jesus.

I suck in a sharp breath. I can't help it. Her words are a calculated blow, directly to my soul. And she knows it. She knows better than anyone how hard I've tried to distance myself from the reputation Jaxon created for our family. She knows how much I've struggled to detangle my identity from his.

Jo isn't done speaking. "You need to get over this knight-in-shining-armor act. We aren't kids anymore, Archer. I don't need you to protect me from the bullies. I don't need you to watch my back."

Bullshit, I think but don't say. She may not want to hear it, but she does need a shield to keep her safe; a sword to slay her demons.

The kids who go to our academy are assholes. Always have been, always will be. I've spent my life putting myself in the path between her and them. She's not even aware I'm doing it, most of the time.

Case in point, tonight. Ryan Snyder. I shouldn't have hit him. I realize that. I realized it the moment my fist flew out, the moment he went sailing through the air like a sock puppet. The moment Jo's eyes sprung open and she started looking at me like a stranger.

And yet, if I could go back, I'd probably do it again.

Snyder may look like a Ken doll, but he's no dickless innocent. Beneath that floppy hair and sensitive facade lies a true player. He's hooked up with half the girls at Exeter Academy — plus just about every other private school in New England. The guy has so many notches in his bedpost, it starting to look like an authentic Native American woodcarving. Over my dead body will he add Jo to that piece of work.

Her voice gets even smaller. Still tipsy, she's struggling to articulate her thoughts. The ones that manage to escape are laced with undeniable pain. "You know, hard as it might be for you to believe, I'm not totally *repulsive*. I—I—"

I'm horrified by the devastating crack in her voice; even more so when I look over and see tears welling in her big blue eyes.

Christ.

I clutch the steering wheel tighter, a useless lifeline against the avalanche occurring beneath my ribcage. My chest feels like it's caving in on itself. I wish the ground would swallow me up, suck me down to Hell. It would be a reprieve from this torture.

Still...

I say nothing.

I offer no comfort.

I hate myself.

"I just can't... You need to realize..." She shakes her head vigorously, as if to clear it. "Not every human male on this planet sees me as a platonic little sister!" she says finally, fumbling for the door handle as the first wave of tears spills down her cheeks. "You're just going to have to get used to it!"

With that, she slams the door and sprints up to the house, her strides weaving like a rum-soaked pirate. I wait to start the engine until she's securely inside, door locked behind her, porch light extinguished. Leaving me alone in the dark night.

"Fuck!" I yell, slamming my fist against the steering wheel so hard, I'm surprised it doesn't crack. "God *fucking* dammit!"

It takes all my strength not to peel out down the driveway. To keep my tires at a gradual crawl. Messing up the pea-stone won't make me feel better. It will, however, make more work for my father in the morning.

Dramatic exits aren't as satisfying when you think about the groundskeeper responsible for cleanup duty.

Leaving the circular driveway behind, I branch off onto the smaller route that leads past the swimming pool and tennis court, around the guest house, all the way to the wooded edge of the property. It is here, far inland, away from the coveted water views and prime real estate, hidden by a thick grove of maple trees like a blemish behind an artfully placed hat, that we make our home.

Gull Cottage — so named by the fading, hand-carved sign hanging above the front door — is a small, single-story dwelling with a simple farmer's porch. Three bedrooms, one bathroom, no frills. Built in the mid-1960s, it lacks the historical flare of the main house, as well as the creature comforts.

But it's home.

I park my truck next to my father's in the small clearing on the side of the cottage. My shiny, souped-up, black Ford F-150 — a blatant bribe from the scouts at Vanderbilt last spring, after they came to see me pitch — looks even more ridiculous sitting beside the beat-up pickup Pa's been using to get around the grounds for as long as I can remember. I eye it pitifully as I walk past — chipped paint, nonexistent suspension, evidence of a hard-day's labor still sitting in the leaf-strewn bed.

Jo's dad drives a brand new Tesla. Just brought it home last month.

Inside, the lights are off, my parents long-since asleep in their room. But Ma's left the dim bulb above the stove burning for me, along with a plate of something that smells too good to pass up.

She knows I'm always starving when I get home late.

Peeling back the foil, I find homemade empanadillas. They're cold but I shove one in my mouth anyway, far too impatient for the microwave. Still chewing, I put the plate of leftovers in the fridge, flip off the stove light, and walk down the short hallway, passing Jaxon's darkened room on the way to mine.

I don't know where he is. And I don't care.

At least, that's what I tell myself.

Jax is the reason my life is so screwed up right now. I have every right to hate him. But there's a part of me that can't turn away from my brother, even after everything he's done to tear our family apart. To threaten all my parents have worked so hard for. To jeopardize not just his own future, but mine as well.

I beeline straight for the bathroom. I need to shower Sienna off my skin; to wash away my sins with scalding water. Even on the hottest setting, it's not enough to make me feel any better. I stand beneath the spray until it runs cold, leaning back against the tile wall and trying to forget.

All of it.

The scrape of acrylic nails against my skin. The cloying smell of artificial strawberries. The look in Jo's eyes. The break in her voice before she climbed out of my truck and slammed the door.

Not every human male on this planet sees me as a platonic little sister!

Christ, if she only knew how I see her... how she makes me feel... the things I'd like to do with her... to her... she'd never use the word *platonic* around me ever again.

The clock on the desk in my messy bedroom declares 3:36AM in its scornful red glow. I have to be at the field in five hours, ready to pitch. Coach is already going to be in a foul mood, seeing as half the team will be showing up hungover and his star pitcher has a set of swollen knuckles. That means *sprints.*

Lots of them.

My muscles tense in anticipation as I collapse face-first onto my bed, not even bothering to yank on boxers or crawl under my covers. Much as I wish I could close my eyes and escape my life for a while, I'm too worked up to sleep. I scroll my phone instead, pulling up a bookmarked playlist of videos.

Not porn. Not the latest episode of whatever dumb sitcom the networks are circulating this spring. Not the viral prank videos my teammates are always forwarding.

The greats.

Crisp white uniforms with blocky red lettering, iconic fixtures against the bright green grass. The same clips I've watched over and over, a million times, since I was old enough to access YouTube by myself; since I realized there was a way to foster my Red Sox obsession even without being able to afford season tickets.

I study the players — their technique, their focus, their presence on the field. I watch the plays unfold, smooth as a choreographed dance, each throw made with instinctual precision. The Green Monster looms large, a fixed backdrop against the Boston skyline, dwarfed only by the talent on the diamond below it.

Pedro Martínez.

Nomar Garciaparra.

David Ortiz.

Manny Ramirez.

When I finally drift off, images of my idols still playing across my iPhone screen, I dream of the day I'll be standing on that pitcher's mound at Fenway Park, throwing a perfect game. And I dream of the blonde girl with blue eyes, sitting front-row behind home plate, the name on her fan jersey a match for the one on our marriage certificate, cheering me on.

CHAPTER SEVEN

JOSEPHINE

THE SUN IS AN ASSHOLE.

I blink awake to a shaft of light beaming directly into my bleary eyes. Given the pounding in my temples, either an elephant sat on my head while I was sleeping, or I'm experiencing my first-ever hangover.

"Ugh," I grunt, forcing my body upright. Almost immediately, I realize being vertical is a terrible mistake. I fall back against my pillows as my stomach lurches queasily. I'm not sure if I need to throw up everthing in my body or shovel down the biggest breakfast known to modern man. Make that lunch, seeing as it's already past noon.

What happened last night?

Beer pong — that's what. I have only myself to blame for being in this state. I wince as memories flood back to me in fragments.

Lifting a red cup to my lips.

Stumbling in a monochrome kitchen.

Sienna Sullivan's pouty pink lips.

Ryan Snyder's face, alarmingly close to my own.

Archer's fist, slamming into that same face.

My eyes snap wide open.

Archer.

I'd nearly forgotten our fight — not to mention the reason I decided to get so wasted in the first place. It's not typical of me to reach for alcohol to numb my pain. Then again, nothing that happened last night was typical. Certainly not overhearing my best friend being deflowered by the head cheerleader.

Mortification swiftly overtakes me as I realize what Archer must be thinking. I reacted to his hookup like a jealous girlfriend, not a platonic friend. I'm actually quite grateful I can't recall the full details of our fight on the drive home. The memory of me slamming his truck door with enough dramatic flair to land me a spot at Julliard will haunt me until the end of my days.

Granted, I'm still angry at him for being such an asshole... but my anger has temporarily been subdued beneath the weight of utter embarrassment. I'm not sure I'll ever be brave enough to show my face in front of him again — or Ryan, for that matter.

Poor guy tries to kiss me and gets his lights punched out instead.

When I'm certain I'm not going to throw up, I drag my carcass from my bedroom to the kitchen. I have to break twice on the stairs, grabbing the thick mahogany bannister like an invalid, leaning over to catch my breath. My fuzzy bunny slippers mock me, a remnant of simpler times, before boy-crushes and beer-fueled outbursts.

I'm never drinking again.

In the kitchen, I'm greeted by the sound of cheerful humming drifting through the open windows. Flora, Archer's mom, is outside wiping down the glass with a bottle of vinegar, as she does at least twice a week. The constant spray off the ocean coats Cormorant House in a thin layer of salt; by the day after tomorrow, every one of its many windows will be in need of cleaning again. It's a task that would drive Sisyphus himself mad.

But Flora has the patience of a saint. She's one of the kindest people I've ever met. Since I was small, she's been as much as mother to me as she is to her sons — always making sure I'm well fed and in bed at reasonable hour, never letting me out of her sight without a kind word or a pat on the cheek.

I flinch whenever my parents refer to her as our house-keeper or her husband, Miguel, as our handyman. To me, they're family. Far more than the distant cousins who live clear across the country and only show up for occasional, obligatory holiday visits.

Sometimes, I feel closer to Flora and Miguel than I do my own parents. Not that I'd ever say that out loud. Mom and Dad are good people. They do love me; that's never been in question. But they love their careers, too. I respect them for how hard they work — even more so when I consider the fact that they could've lived more than comfortably on the mere interest earned by my father's inheritance.

Most trust fund kids want to party their way across the world; very few use their money for something as noble as a nonprofit that aims to save it. But that's Vincent and Blair Valentine for you — solving global hunger one day, one dollar, at a time.

I don't mean to sound flippant. I'm quite aware that the work they do is important. How many kinds can say their parents spend their days ending food insecurity in at-risk populations across the globe?

The company they co-run, VALENT, is more than a profession; it's a calling. It's their second child. (Perhaps their favorite child.) Still, when they're home, I never want for affection or attention. They're invested in my life. They want to know how I'm keeping busy, to see my recent report cards, to take the boat out for a spin around the Misery Islands. It's just...

They're not actually home all that often.

Between speaking engagements and business trips and funding meetings and site visits to each of their many aid distribution centers... they're never here more than a handful of days out of every month. Rarely on the same schedule twice.

There is only one day out of the entire year I can count on their presence with any sort of certainty. One day I know they are guaranteed to be here when my eyes open in the morning.

June 5.

My birthday.

The Valentine family doesn't ascribe to many traditions or even celebrate every holiday together — *"Starvation doesn't take a vacation, Josephine,"* Mom told me over a grainy video-chat last Thanksgiving, her satellite connection spotty in the Sudanese desert — but we do have June 5.

At eight on the dot on the anniversary of my birth, the opening strains of the song "Josephine" begin blasting through the house. Every speaker. Top volume. I race out of bed, fly down the stairs, and find my parents waiting predictably in the kitchen with a stack of blueberry pancakes almost as high as the stack of presents on the table.

I don't even care that most of the gifts were picked out by executive assistants I've never met. I *live* for that day. I spend all year waiting for it. Mom and Dad. Home. Together. In the same, actual room. At the same, actual time.

I don't doubt, if they could, they'd be with me more frequently. They'd want to see every new design in my sketch-book. They'd cook me dinner twice a week and we'd eat together, at a table, like a real family. They'd ask typical parental questions — about my homework, about my crushes, about my favorite teachers at school. They'd wonder why I prefer the vintage sewing machine Archer bought me from a consignment shop over the shiny new one they had delivered via courier last Christmas.

But... those things... they seem so insignificant compared to their work at VALENT. And even if I miss my parents, even if I'm lonely sometimes... I'm not alone.

Not really.

Though it certainly isn't in their job description, the Reyeses took me firmly under their wing. They've never made me feel like an obligation. Or even like what I am — a ward they're paid to watch over. I've been their surrogate daughter since the very start.

It was Miguel who held my handlebars and taught me how to ride a bike — Archer pedaling like a Tour de France racer by my side, his own training wheels removed weeks prior; Jaxon already halfway to the front gates, determined to leave the "babies" in his dust.

It was Flora who stayed late on windy nights when I was scared of the dark, watching cheesy movies with me on the Hallmark Channel even after she'd worked a full day, putting her feet up on a coffee table she'd polished only hours before.

I don't think I would've survived my childhood without them. I can't count the number of times I ran through the maple thicket to Gull Cottage in need of assistance with something, be it algebra homework or a disastrous experiment with pink hair dye or a terrifying hissing sound in the basement that turned out to be an outdated water heater, not a monster at all. Warm hands and kind words were only a five minute walk; three if you cut around the pool and dodge across the tennis courts.

When my parents first hired the Reyeses, they were a young, childless couple seeking steady employment in a new country. I'm certain they never expected to still be working here two decades — two children — later. I'm equally certain they never anticipated their youngest son would befriend the daughter of their employers. But Archer and I... we were inevitable. Born one day apart, inseparable every day since.

For a long, long time, sheltered behind the gates of Cormorant House, running wild along the beaches with the wind in our hair, carefree in a way only children can be, we didn't realize there was anything strange about our friendship. We didn't see the differences between our families. Our socioeconomic situations. Our inherent opportunities.

We were just...

Best friends.

The truth is, I have far more in common with Archer than I ever have the pretentious kids who fill the halls of our private academy. Always have. Of course, none of them know Archer doesn't come from money. They definitely don't know my parents pay his tuition — a concession they made after I declared, with surprising conviction for a twelve year old, that I would not step a single foot into Exeter Academy of Excellence without him by my side. I was simply not willing to spend grades six through twelve in his absense, while he made a new best friend at the public school across town.

Selfish of me?

Surely.

Yet, for some reason, Archer agreed to attend and, in the end, despite enduring six long years surrounded by the spoiled offspring of privilege, Exeter actually gave him a boon in the form of our varsity baseball team.

It was there, last spring, under the stadium lights on a meticulously-groomed pitcher's mound, that he threw his first perfect game against the rival academy. Propped on the cold metal bleachers, a cup of weak hot chocolate clutched in my hands, I watched his star begin to rise that night.

Every game after, it ascended a little higher. It wasn't long before the scouts caught wind of him. They came from universities and colleges all across the country, touching down at Boston Logan Airport and trekking forty minutes north just to see Archer Reyes pitch in person.

Now, midway through a stellar senior season, he has his pick of any program he wants. Full financial ride, plus perks — like the truck from Vanderbilt, the hand-stitched glove from UCLA, the sleek set of bats from Florida State. No matter where he signs his official Letter of Intent, if he plays well enough over the next few years, there's no question of him going pro in the MLB someday.

Would he have ended up here — world at his feet, more verbal offers than he knows what to do with — if I hadn't dragged him to Exeter along with me? Or would his talent have gone unnoticed on a crappy public high school team without the resources to foster his skills?

It doesn't really matter, I guess.

He's here now.

He's made it.

In my humble opinion, he was always destined for greatness, one way or another. It drives me crazy that the kids from school would look down on him if they knew his real background; if they realized he wasn't actually my neighbor — one who magnanimously gives me a ride every day in his very shiny, very expensive truck — but the son of our staff.

"So, she lives," Flora says, breezing into the kitchen, interrupting my reverie. "I thought you were going to sleep the whole day away."

I lift my head from the tabletop, where I've been slumped

for the past twenty minutes, summoning the energy to raid the fridge. "If only."

"Mmm, I heard Archer come in late. What were you two up to last night? Not any mischief, I hope?"

"Just a stupid party."

She peers closer at my face, tipping my chin back with her fingertips so she can examine me thoroughly. My bloodshot eyes and wan complexion are a dead hangover giveaway.

"Well." She *tsks*. "If you feel as bad as you look, I guess that's punishment enough."

I laugh.

Flora technically has the authority to ground me in my parents' absence, but we both know she rarely finds occasion to wield it. In my defense, it's hard to get into trouble when your typical Friday night involves a kindle, a Netflix account, and a new sewing pattern. If I'm feeling particularly extroverted, I might drag Archer out for a night sail or sit up in the boathouse rafters, counting shooting stars.

I know, I know — I'm a wild child.

This social dearth not entirely my fault. These days, Archer is so busy, it's hard to catch him in a free moment. The closest we've come to quality time lately was him inviting me to the party last night — which, given how it all played out, is not exactly my idea of *bonding*.

Flora rummages around the cabinets for a bowl, then ladles in a large helping from the pot simmering on the stove. It's steaming hot when she sets it in front of me. She presses a spoon into my limp hand.

"Eat. You'll feel better."

"What is it?" I ask, already dipping my spoon into the thick broth, lifting it toward my mouth.

"*Asopao de pollo*. Chicken stew. My grandmother's recipe, from back in San Juan. It will help you."

Flora is an amazing cook. If she told me her soup cured cancer, I'd believe it. I finish my serving in an embarrassingly short span of time. She silently refills my bowl, then settles into the seat across from mine to watch me eat.

"You can talk to me, you know."

The spoon halts halfway to my mouth. "I know that, Flora."

"I mean..." She hesitates for a moment. "Even if it's about Archer. He is my son and I love him, but I know he isn't perfect. If you two had a fight—"

"What makes you think we had a fight?" I wince at the defensiveness in my own voice.

"I can't help noticing you two aren't spending as much time together, lately. I wondered if something happened." She looks at me so kindly, I want to cry. "It's normal for friends to fight, *mija*."

"We don't fight. Not really. He's just so busy, lately." I shrug to cover my own sadness. "I don't think he has time for me anymore. Or maybe he likes hanging out with the guys on his team better than me."

"That can't be. You two are thick as thieves."

"Everything's changing, though." I set down my spoon and sit back in my chair. Like magic, my hangover is already ebbing away. "Maybe it's better this happens now. In a few months, we'll be at different colleges anyway. We were bound to grow apart eventually, right?"

Flora's eyes hold many truths, but she does not put words to them. I think she knows I'm saying this to convince myself as much as I am her. Thankfully, she doesn't push me on it. She merely clears my bowl, humming lightly as she carries it to the sink.

"Thank you," I tell her, meaning it. "I do feel better."

"What are your plans for the day?"

I glance out the freshly-cleaned windows. Across the

expanse of grass, where Miguel is riding the lawnmower back and forth in regimented lines, I spot the American flag whipping around on its pole down by the boathouse.

"Looks like a steady southwestern breeze. I think I'll head out for a quick sail around the islands."

"Don't go too far." Flora clucks. "You know I don't like when you're out there by yourself."

I roll my eyes. "You worry too much. It's not even that rough, today."

"Take your radio, anyway."

"Always."

"And your lifejacket!"

"*Flora*." The way she's acting, you'd think I was a rookie.

"Okay, okay. I'll stop smothering." She pauses a beat, then says lightly. "You could always wait for Archer. He should be home from practice in about thirty mi—"

"Bye!" I call over my shoulder, already racing for the stairs.

No freaking way do I want to sit around here, waiting for Archer to come home like a pining wartime widow.

Frankly, I don't want to see him at all.

———

I YANK the jib sheet tighter, grinning as I feel the Alerion pick up speed. Her sails are perfectly trimmed, catching the wind as we fly away from the dock, out toward open water.

The secluded cove in front of Cormorant House is calm as a lake, shielded from the swells by a natural breakwater of rock and sand. With the exception of a brutal Nor'Easter that hit when I was nine, sweeping away our private dock and ripping all the shingles off the boathouse, we've luckily been spared the worst of the Atlantic's hair-trigger temper.

Clear of the cove, the water's chop intensifies — as does the wind. My sailboat, *Cupid*, starts to heel, cutting through the side of each swell like a blade. She's agile. Aerodynamic. Built for speed, no matter what conditions are thrown at her.

I always laugh when people describe the ocean as peaceful; when they set a picture of it as the background on their computer screen, like some aspirational point of reference for serenity and calm. Anyone who spends time on the ocean knows there's nothing peaceful about it. It is a chaotic monster, clutching with greedy hands. Do not ever mistake its still surface for serenity; it could swallow you up without so much as a ripple.

Rounding the tip of Crow Island, I set my course for the spit of land that marks mouth of Manchester Harbor in the distance. There's no need to consult a chart; I've been exploring these waters since I was old enough to hold a tiller. I know what areas to avoid, where lethal rocks lie in wait, ready to scupper an unsuspecting vessel.

Leaving a wide berth around the shoals, I meander southward, keeping the white sands of the infamous Singing Beach to my starboard side. It's still too cold for the sunbathers who crowd there in the summer months, clutching beach chairs and coolers, laughing as the dunes squeak musically under their steps. By late June, tourists will arrive in droves, forking over $40 to park for a single afternoon at the shore. ,

Lobster bouys of every shade and pattern imaginable bob in the shallows, each marking the location of a trap on the sandy bottom below. They grow fewer and farther between as I head into deeper waters. So do the other boats — not that there are many out today, anyway. Besides a handful of commercial fishing rigs on the horizon, I have the whole stretch of coast to myself.

I shiver as the wind picks up, spraying the cockpit with icy foam. I'm glad I layered a long-sleeved shirt beneath my sweater; by nightfall, it'll be freezing out here. May can be cruel in New England — a tease of summer tempered by sheer unpredictability. One day, it's eighty degrees and sunny; the next, you're hunkered down in monsoon rains, hoping your lines hold.

I clutch the tiller more firmly as the water wrestles with my rudder, trying to drag me off course. This far out, the swells are capped with white, cresting at the tops as they slam relentlessly into *Cupid*'s red sides. The wind has risen to a steady howl, whipping the hair around my face, stinging at my eyes.

I should probably turn back.

Head home.

Retreat to calmer waters.

Instead, I yank my sails in tighter, chasing the salty tang of exhilaration across the expanse of blue. The most myself I ever feel is out here, away from the world — reduced to no more than a distant red speck a stranger squints to see clearly from the safety of the shore.

Sometimes, I wonder what would happen if I kept sailing, straight on through the night, across the Atlantic, not stopping until I either hit England or sank to the depths of Davy Jones' Locker.

How long would it take someone to notice I was gone?

Would anyone care if I never came back?

Sudden loneliness surges through my veins, panging deep in the chambers of my heart. I find myself wishing Archer was with me after all; that I wasn't so alone amidst the vastness.

For so long, he has been my most vital tether to the shore. He has kept me grounded, reeled me in whenever my sails began to overpower me. With that assured grin, those steady eyes, those strong hands... his hold on me was a lifeline I never knew I needed.

Until I thought I might lose it.

Even Flora can sense it. He's pulling away from me. I've felt it for weeks now — long before he got tangled up with Sienna at that stupid party. Something is simply... off. I know it in my bones. But every time I try to bring it up, he dodges. He changes the subject. He shuts down completely.

It's infuriating.

And painful.

And a million other feelings I can't properly put into words — not without unbearable thoughts creeping in.

He's grown tired of me. Tired of the way I rely on him. Tired of being the extroverted half in an imbalanced equation.

He finally sees what everyone else always has: Josephine Valentine is not worth sticking around for.

Leaning into the breeze, for just a moment, I close my eyes, drop the tiller, and surrender, allowing the elements to take full control. Growling gusts thrash my sails with wild fury. Merciless waves pitch *Cupid* up and down, spilling over the sides and into the cockpit, saturating my tan Sperry Topsiders. We churn sideways, veering off course like a spinning top on the surface of the sea, caught in a dangerous current.

Over the cacophony of clanging of lines and flapping sails, at the mercy of howling winds and frothing swells, I wonder.

How long will I survive without my tether to the shore?

A rogue wave splashes freezing water into my face, snapping me back to my senses. I quickly pull in the lines. With the tiller firmly in hand once more, I point the bow back toward the distant outline of Crow Island, and the cove beyond. If I squint, I imagine I can see the glowing light of the boathouse, nested there against the dock, waiting for me in the lengthening shadows. And, hidden in the trees beyond, a dark-haired boy walking up the steps of a small cottage — dirty cleats on his feet, worn glove in his hand, secrets hidden behind his once-clear eyes.

CHAPTER EIGHT

ARCHER

ON THE MOUND, the world narrows.

Leather in my left.

Ball in my right.

Tension coils in my spine. My lungs yield, breathing now a secondary concern. I trace the ball's seams with my fingertips, adjusting my grip. Weighing the familiar curve against my calluses.

When you're first learning to pitch, back in Little League, coaches tell you to focus on the catcher's mitt if you want your ball to break in the strike zone.

That never felt specific enough for me.

I look harder. *Closer.* Using every bit of my concentration, until the brand name on the glove's lower heel becomes legible. Until the mitt breaks into discernible parts — webbing, pocket, pads. I find the seams. The individual laces that weave their way up the finger stalls.

I find one, single stitch.

And when I have it in my sights, when I've locked onto that tiny, far-off detail with the precision of a laser...

I let the ball fly.

In this game, there are as many types of players as there are pitches. Sluggers, runners, fielders, closers. Splitters, sliders, curveballs, changeups.

I'm an ace.

A power pitcher.

A flamethrower.

My four-seam fastball is already breaking triple digits on the radar-gun — unheard of in most pre-collegiate divisions. It's not uncommon for me to pitch a no-hitter, striking out every batter who swings against me. They tremble when they step up to my plate.

And it is *my* plate.

My stadium.

My team.

That might sound conceited but it's the truth. One I earned, one I refuse to be ashamed of. I worked my ass off to get here. I practice twice as hard as any other guy at Exeter. I had to — my parents couldn't afford private coaching sessions, couldn't rent out the cages for hours at a time, couldn't pay for the best equipment, couldn't send me away to training camp.

To make the varsity team junior year, I dragged my ass out of bed at every morning at the crack of dawn and jogged six miles to the field before the sun was up. By the time the rest of the team showed up for practice at nine, still yawning into their gloves and wiping crust from the corners of their eyes, I'd been at it for hours. And when they called it quits the day, heading off to play video games or make-out with their girl-friends, I'd still be there. Throwing until my arm gave out — or, until Jo arrived to drag me home for dinner.

"That's it, Reyes! Looking good out there," Coach Hamm calls from the dugout, giving an approving nod when my fast-ball slams into Chris Tomlinson's catching glove at bone-bending speed. Behind the cage of his face mask, I think I see him wince.

"Hilton, you're up!" Coach jerks his chin at Andy. "Snyder, in the hole."

Three quick sinkers, and Andy's out. At his best, he's no great hitter; with a hangover, striking him out is child's play. He tosses his helmet to the dirt and storms off the field, looking like someone pissed in his Cheerios. I'm surprised he made it to practice at all. He was so drunk last night, if he blew a breathalyzer right now he'd probably still be over the legal limit.

Ryan Snyder steps up, aluminum bat glinting in the sunshine. Judging by the glare he's directing my way — and the mottled purple shiner surrounding his right eye socket — he's yet to forgive me for punching him last night.

Oh well.

No big loss, there. We were never friends. Just teammates — brought together by necessity rather than actual cama-raderie. If he wasn't such a solid first baseman, I wouldn't put up with his chameleonic bullshit at all.

Snyder is a poser. When he's trying to get into a cute girl's pants, he becomes whatever, *whoever*, she wants him to be. The jock, the poet, the comedian, the tortured soul. Sensitive, quiet, funny, outrageous.

He does it so skillfully, most girls never know they're being played. But the moment they sashay away, titillated by his attention, that oozing charm goes up in smoke, replaced by cocky bravado. And once they let him under their bra straps, into their beds? Snyder uses the locker room bench as his personal stage, bragging to a captive audience about his latest lay. I've lost count of the times he's chronicled his weekend conquests after practice on Monday.

Gentlemen don't kiss and tell; privileged white boys use

more details than J.R.R. Tolkien describing the trees of Middle Earth.

Smallest tits of all time, but she let me cum on her face!

I've seen dogs with better teeth, thought she was going to chomp my dick off...

Look at the scratches on my back! The girl was a total animal.

I hit all four bases, then slid around to the dugout, if you know what I mean...

When I think of Snyder talking about Jo like that, something inside me — something dark — stirs to life. My grip on the ball tightens, the red seams digging painfully into the pads of my fingers.

"Let's go, Reyes! We ain't got all day," Coach Hamm yells. He's holding the speed gun behind the safety of the backstop, ready to record my next pitch. Every week, the scouts call to check in, wanting a full report. And every week, they ask the same question.

Has he made his decision, yet?

The metallic gleam of Snyder's bat catches my eye as he swings it up into position. When our eyes meet, a smug smile spreads across his bruised face.

"Better get going, Reyes. Don't you know, if you move too slow, you'll miss your opportunity? Things you thought were yours, things you took for granted... they'll slip right out of your hands." He pauses, smile widening to a full-fledged grin. "Say *hey* to Valentine for me, will you? I'm really looking forward to getting to know her better."

I start for him, nearly stepping off the mound before I catch myself. He's baiting me — and, *dammit*, it's working. I react without thinking, filled with the sudden desire to balance out his face with a second shiner on the left side. To pummel him until he realizes my best friend is off limits.

I tell myself Jo is too smart to fall for him, that she'll see through his facade in seconds... but then I remember how pissed she got when I hit him last night... how she moved to comfort him when he went sprawling in the grass...

Great.

I've made this jackass a martyr.

"What's the hold-up, Reyes?" Coach calls, sounding confused. "We got a problem here?"

"Yeah, Reyes," Snyder mocks, leaning into his stance. "You have a problem with something?"

Hauling in a deep breath, I try to regain focus, but all I can think about are Snyder's hands beneath Jo's sweater, his fake charm working on her like a drug.

My fists itch for violence.

Get ahold of yourself, the voice of reason inside my head orders flatly. *You did not work this hard to get tossed off the team for violating the Exeter code of conduct.*

Crouched behind the plate, Tomlinson is signaling for a curveball — two fingers, pointing down at the packed dirt between his feet.

I shake my head.

He signals again — one finger. Fastball.

I nod.

Taking my position, I let the world narrow until it all fades into background noise — Snyder's sneering confidence, Coach's concerned frown, the scouts' pressure to choose. The nightmare that is my brother Jaxon. Even the mess I've made with Jo. All of it goes out of focus until there's only one thing remaining.

Leather in my left.

Ball in my right.

I crank back my right arm, hike up my knee, and throw with all my might — with every bit of my rage channeled into tensing muscles and blinding speed. The ball is a blur as it sails past Ryan's swinging bat, straight into Tomlinson's glove.

Strike.

Ryan blinks, looking dumbfounded. The smug smile is gone from his face.

Behind the backstop fence, Coach is yelling. Holding the speed-gun in the air. Grinning ear to ear as he yells out the numbers on the screen.

102 mph.

It's the fastest pitch I've ever thrown.

I LINGER at the field after practice ends, running mindless laps around the track. I'm in no great rush to get home. Things with Jo are a tangled catastrophe; it's easier to avoid her entirely than attempt to work out the knots with both hands tied behind my back.

My teammates are long gone by the time I finally call it quits. I head for the dugout, rubbing the sore muscles of my pitching arm as I grab my equipment bag. After a night of no sleep and a full day on the field, I'm dead tired. A walking zombie. With any luck, that means I'll fall into bed tonight too exhausted to dream, let alone think.

The last place I want to spend time is inside my own head, second guessing all my decisions.

My truck is the only one left in the parking lot. It's already getting dark, shadows of each light pole stretching across the asphalt like skeletal fingers. My cleats echo with every footstep, a solitary patter. My mind is far away — already back at Cormorant House, wondering what Ma made for dinner, how Jo spent her day, whether Pa ever got the lawnmower running. It was giving him trouble this morning.

I don't notice the men leaning against the cab until it's too late. When they push off and step toward me, I go still, my arm freezing halfway to the tailgate, my stomach vaulting into my throat.

"Reyes, right?"

The leaner of the two men grunts the question at me. His eyes are shifty, darting back and forth across the parking lot for some unknown threat. Behind him, the beefier man stands in silent silhouette. One look at them — the tattoos, the low-slung jeans, the piercings, the vaguely menacing demeanors — makes it clear they're not Manchester-by-the-Sea locals. The criminal element in this town is typically limited to speeding tickets and illegal parking fines.

Still, I've seen them before. I'd bet my pitching hand they're the same guys who've been following me around — an almost-indiscernible presence, shadowing my movements from a careful distance in a black Ford Bronco.

I'm not sure when, exactly, they started trailing me. I noticed them for the first time about a month ago. We were on the way to school — Jo in my passenger seat prattling on about her parents' latest, greatest save-the-world initiative — when I glanced in my rearview mirror and did a double-take.

Wasn't that same Bronco behind me yesterday?

After that, I started paying better attention to my surroundings. Suddenly, they were everywhere I looked: parked in the woods by the front gate, driving in the lane behind mine on my way home from practice, idling across the street as Jo and I bought paper cups of sugary lemonade from a little kid's neighborhood stand.

I guess I should've known it was only a matter of time before they made actual contact. It's not like Jaxon didn't warn me.

"Uh..." I clear my throat, trying not to sound intimidated. "Who's asking?"

"You don't need to know."

I arch a brow. "Then I guess I don't need to talk to you."

At my flippant tone, the big guy takes a step forward, bringing his shoulder parallel with his partner's — and his full bulk into view.

My heartbeat kicks up a notch. At six-foot-three, I'm not a shrimp by any measure; I don't often feel intimidated. But this guy could turn me into mincemeat with one squeeze.

"Look," the skinny, shifty-eyed one says. "All you need to know is, we're... associates of your brother. We need to talk to him about some business."

"What sort of business?"

Not the legitimate kind, I'm guessing.

He ignores my question to ask one of his own. "Have you seen him lately?"

"Can't say I have."

"He's lying," the giant grunts, cracking his knuckles with a sickening *pop*. His hands are big as holiday hams.

My grip is so tight around the strap of my equipment bag, I'm sure my own knuckles have gone white. I try to relax, but with my fight-or-flight instincts screaming to head for the hills, zen is somewhat out of reach.

Shifty-Eyes steps forward. "You lying to us, kid?"

"No."

"Then just tell us where you think your brother is. Or..." He pauses to glance at the living mountain beside him. "My partner here is real good at making people talk about things they don't want to. Maybe you'd rather deal with him?"

I swallow hard. "Look, the truth is, Jaxon comes and goes as he pleases. Always has. Since he got out of Cedar-Junction two months ago, he's only been home a handful of times — either to grab spare clothes from his room or because he knows his P.O. is coming by."

"Any idea when that'll happen again?"

"No. We don't exactly keep in touch."

"He's your brother," Shifty-Eyes says doubtfully. "You must know something."

I shrug. "Last time Jax came home, he swiped all my parents' emergency cash in the middle of the night and left without so much as a note. He might be my brother, but he isn't exactly my favorite person in the world. So the way I see it? The less he comes around, the better."

It's not a lie — not really. At least, not the part about Jax getting out of jail two months ago. Or cleaning out the cookie jar of cash off the counter. Or only showing up for the benefit of his parole officer.

He's broken my parents' hearts so many times, I'm running out of glue to fix them. Being the best second-born in the world can't make up for the damage inflicted by the son who came first.

"If he comes around again, we need to know about it," Shifty-Eyes says. "Immediately."

"Mhm. What is it you want from my brother?"

"Don't worry about that. Be more worried about what'll happen to you if we don't track him down."

My teeth grind together. "If you have problems with Jax, that's fine. But leave me and my family out of it. We have nothing to do with this—"

Before I can finish, I find the equipment bag ripped from my hands and myself in a chokehold — courtesy of the giant. For such a big guy, he moves fast. I didn't even see him coming in time to dodge.

So much for all those agility drills Coach is always forcing on us.

My muscles strain against his hold, but it might as well be titanium. His arm tightens around my neck, compressing my windpipe until I can't breathe. I have no choice but to submit — a limp puppet in the arms of a sadistic master.

He peels my right arm away from my side as his partner lowers the tailgate with gleeful snigger. I don't fully understand what's happening until they lay my hand flat against the metal edge of the truck bed, in the space where the tailgate snaps shut.

Horror dawns all too quickly.

"Maybe you need a reminder of what you have to lose here," the giant growls in my ear. "One slam, your baseball career is over. Is that what you want?"

I stare at my hand — my pitching hand — poised on the edge of ruin. If they snap the tailgate closed, every bone will be crushed in an instant. Pulverized beyond repair.

Goodbye baseball.

Goodbye scouts.

Goodbye scholarship.

Goodbye future.

"Please," I croak through a half-closed throat, desperation plain in my voice. "Please, don't—"

"We don't want to, kid. But we need you to understand how important this is." Shifty-Eyes comes closer, my equipment bag clutched in his hands. Held immobile, I can only watch as he reaches into the side pocket, pulls out my phone, and dials a number. A second later, his own pocket begins to ring.

"Now you have my number. Name's Rico. You'll get in touch if Jax comes by again. Right?"

I attempt to nod, but it's damn-near impossible in a chokehold. His grip is unrelenting. My breaths are so shallow, I'm barely getting any air at all.

Setting my bag and phone on the truck-bed, Rico turns back to me. My mind is still reeling, but I try to focus long enough to catalogue some of his features. The compact build, a few inches shy of six feet. The pockmark scar just below his left eye. The dark hair, buzzed short against his skull. The tattoo on his neck — a king's crown, its blue-black ink a startling contrast to his tan skin.

I flinch as he pats my cheek. He smirks, clearly enjoying himself. "There's a good boy." His eyes flicker to his partner. "Let him go, Barboza."

The giant drops me without hesitation. Gasping for much-needed air, I collapse forward like a rag doll. My uncooperative limbs refuse to catch me in time. My bare knees and palms jolt against the rough pavement, leaving a considerable chunk of skin behind. Pain sears through me as blood wells to the surface. I'm so grateful all my bones are intact, I barely register it.

By the time I manage to catch my breath and clamber back to my feet, the men are gone. Except for a brood of hungry ducklings quacking for dinner in the pond beside the parking lot, I'm totally alone in the quiet. I blink rapidly, trying to get ahold of myself. Trying to slow my thudding pulse. Trying to forget the paralyzing terror that's defined the past few minutes.

Moving very slowly, I shut the tailgate, climb into the cab, and start the engine. I drive home in total silence, stopping at every red light, never pushing the gas above the speed limit. All the while pretending not to notice how my bleeding hands tremble against the leather steering wheel.

"YOU MISSED DINNER."

I stop halfway down the hall, then backtrack toward the

living room. "Ma, I didn't even see you. What are you doing sitting in the dark?"

"*Qué tonto eres.* Waiting for you. What else? Now, sit and spend a little time with your mother. I won't be here forever, you know."

Rolling my eyes, I ease into the rickety armchair across from hers. "That's a bit dramatic."

"Dramatic would be me yelling about you getting blood on the living room furniture." She pauses carefully. "What happened to your knees?"

I sigh. My mother's brown eyes may be soft in appearance but they are sharp in focus. They miss no small detail. "I tripped in the parking lot after practice."

"That doesn't sound like you." She crosses her arms over her chest — the classic maternal interrogation pose. "You've never been clumsy."

"First time for everything, I guess. I wasn't paying attention. My bag strap tangled around my legs. Before I knew it, I was on my ass in front of the entire team. Everyone laughed." I rub the back of my neck sheepishly. "I'm just happy the scouts weren't there to see it."

My mother watches me for a long moment, weighing my words in silence. Finally, she tilts her head to the side and says, quite softly, "*Mijo,* don't lie to me."

I push to my feet. "It's no big deal, Ma, honestly. I didn't even realize I was bleeding until you pointed it out. Let me go clean up." I drop a quick kiss on her cheek, pretending not to see the skeptical purse of her lips. I swear, the woman is a human lie detector.

"When you're done cleaning up from your *fall*..." She lets the word dangle for a beat. "There's dinner on the stove. I made *asopao.*"

My stomach rumbles, suddenly ravenous. I haven't eaten all day. "You know that's my favorite. Thanks, Ma."

"If you must know, I made it for Josephine. She was in quite a state this morning. No thanks to you."

I stop in my tracks.

What, exactly, did Jo say to my mother?

Glancing back, I find Ma watching me with an unreadable expression. For a moment, I wonder if Jo told her about last night — Ryan, Sienna, the whole enchilada. If so, I'm about to get a proper ass-whooping.

"What do you mean?" I ask carefully.

"What do I mean?" Ma scoffs. "She was so hungover she could barely drag herself out of bed!"

A wave of relief sweeps through me. I'd happily take a grounding for underage drinking to avoid discussing the many complexities of my relationship with Jo. "And that's somehow my fault?"

"Of course it is! Josephine is a good girl. She wouldn't be out all night at a party if you hadn't dragged her there."

"You always take her side. You realize that, don't you?"

"*Always* is an overstatement. I only take her side when I know she found herself in trouble because of you. Which, I must say, has been happening for as long as you two have been friends."

"So I'm a bad kid. A bad *influence*. Is that what you're saying?"

"I'm saying that girl would do just about anything to make you happy. You know that. You've known it since you were small." She pauses. "You could ask her for the moon, she'd do her best to pull it down from the heavens for you. Don't take that kind of devotion for granted. That's all."

"I don't take it — her — for granted. But I never asked for her devotion. I never asked for anything from her."

She shakes her head. "*Mijo*. For such a smart boy you can be incredibly short-sighted."

I hold up my hands in surrender. "I'm going to shower."

Gritting my teeth, I force myself to walk out of the living room before I say something I can't take back. Or worse — before the real reason for my bloody knees and battered heart spills out in a torrent.

CHAPTER NINE

JOSEPHINE

I CAN'T SLEEP.

My thoughts roar too loudly to ignore, clanging around inside my head like the pendulum of a grandfather clock. For hours, I toss and turn in my bed, agonizing over my fight with Archer. Wondering if he's staring up at his own ceiling right now, going over it a million times inside his head.

Wondering if he even cares at all.

It's late — past midnight — when I'm forced to concede that no matter how long I lie here, I'll never be able to quiet my mind enough to sleep. Shoving back the thick duvet, I slip out of bed. I don't bother turning on any lights as I slide my feet into flip flops. Moving into the hallway, I make sure to grab my favorite hoodie off its hook by the door.

My lips twist in amusement at the words printed across the front in all-caps. *GREEN MONSTAH* — an homage to Fenway Park's most notorious feature. I pilfered the ridiculous garment from the box of old clothes Flora sorted together for donation last summer. A reject from Archer's closet. I figured nobody would notice if it suddenly appeared in mine.

When I tug the sweatshirt on over my pajama set, it falls past the hem of my shorts, midway down my bare thighs. It doesn't smell like Archer anymore, but the feeling of my arms inside his sleeves somehow makes me feel closer to him.

This time of night, Cormorant House is dark and totally silent. With my parents in Zambia and the Reyeses sleeping soundly a whole acre away, I am completely alone in the drafty mansion. The floorboards creak beneath my feet as I move along the hallway, down the grand staircase, across the vaulted atrium.

When I slip silently out the side door onto the stone terrace, I shiver as the crisp night air wraps me in its dark embrace. I'm glad I grabbed the sweatshirt. It may be almost June, but Massachusetts has not yet yielded fully to summer heat.

The manicured lawn is lit by moonlight as I make my way down the sloping gravel path. The sound of lapping waves grows louder with each step. I round a bend and the stone boathouse comes into view, silhouetted against a backdrop of ocean. Beside it, the dock juts out into the inky waters of the cove. Cupid is a mere shadow at the far end, bobbing against her lines, her mast swaying slightly with each swell.

The boathouse is my favorite spot on the property. An architectural feat, half its foundation is embedded in the rocky shore while the other half hangs out over the water. The arched entryway is just high enough to drive a small boat beneath. My father's 29-foot Hinkley fits perfectly at the interior slip, sheltered from the elements in his absence.

The boathouse was built back in the 1800s, along with the rest of the estate. Not much about it has changed in all the years since. Except for a few necessary modern upgrades — lights to illuminate the dock, some electrical outlets — it looks like a relic straight out of some Newport high society period piece. No furniture, no running water. No heat or air conditioning. Just stone walls and exposed wood beams.

And the rafters, of course.

Archer and I discovered the lofted space by accident, ages ago. Accessible via a rickety ladder bolted to the back wall, it's used mainly for storage — a set of Cupid's extra sails, seat cushions for the Hinckley, spare engine parts, a few cans of paint. Between the boxes of tools and various equipment, there's just enough space for two people to sit, legs dangling over the edge, and watch the sun set slowly over the cove, turning blue shallows to an orange-pink masterpiece.

It's become our secret spot. A hidden clubhouse of sorts. As we got older, on the rare occasions my parents were home or visiting relatives required my full attention, we'd leave messages for each other there, staying in touch even when we couldn't hang out in person. As the years passed by, small items found their way up into the rafters, an eclectic accumulation of items stolen from the main house.

An old camping lantern to light the dark. A wool blanket for cold nights. A stack of books. A set of perfectly good pillows my parents put out to the curb approximately six minutes after purchase, convinced they didn't match their new sofa.

I step into the stone boathouse, moving almost on autopilot. It's pitch black inside, but my feet know the way. Past the Hinkley, floating in its slip. Along the interior wall. Grope until I find the ladder rungs.

Up.

Up.

Up.

One foot after another.

At the top, I heave myself through the gap and scamper into the loft on all fours. I don't bother getting to my feet — the sloped roof is quite low in this section. Hands extended in front of me, I crawl my way toward the front of the rafters, where I know the lantern waits.

All around me, boxes of boat supplies are shadowy outlines in the darkness. If you stare at them long enough, your eyes start to trick you into thinking they look a bit like someone standing there, watching you. They don't freak me out anymore. I've spent so many nights up here, I know every square inch of the place. The precise location of each human-like coatrack and imposter mop handle. Which is probably why it's such a goddamned shock when I move forward and my palm lands not on wood flooring, but something soft.

Squishy.

Alive.

The monster grunts as my hand slams into it. I scream and reel backward, but there's nowhere to go. My back bumps into a crate, sending loose tools rattling in all directions. My heart, suddenly pounding twice its normal speed, is lodged so firmly inside my throat, I can't even scream.

Panicked, I try to stand. To run. To get away from this horrid creature, at any cost. Instead, as I find my feet, my head bonks against something harder than a rock. I think it might be a skull.

The monster lets out another painful grunt as we collide. I'm not sure how it happens — I can't see a freaking thing — but one of us trips over something and we both go down, our limbs tangled together like wisteria vines. I end up on top, the full brunt of my body landing hard enough to knock the wind out of my own lungs. Probably his as well, given the way he wheezes.

When I try to wriggle away, two arms wrap around my body like bands of iron, pinning me in place. Instantly, I'm rendered immobile. Pressed so close against him, I can feel every angry exhale of his chest, every furious pant against my lips. His features are still in shadow, impossible to make out clearly.

"What the hell!" the monster growls beneath me, sounding pissed as hell... and, it must be said, remarkably familiar.

"*Archer?*" I gasp.

"No, it's the fucking boogeyman," he snaps sarcastically. "Who the hell did you think it was?"

"Not *you*, obviously! What are you doing up here, lurking in the dark like an axe murderer?"

"I wasn't lurking, I was sleeping! Or I was, until a crazy person barreled into me like a bull in a china shop."

"Oh."

"Yeah."

Relieved I'm not about to be chopped into itty-bitty pieces, I relax against him. My pulse drops back to normal speeds. My breathing slows. But as my panic fades, something else arises in its place: acute awareness — of Archer's hard body beneath mine, of the scant inches separating our faces in the dark, of how good it feels to be in his arms.

I should pull away. Create some space between us. But I don't. And Archer doesn't push me off, either. For a long moment, we simply lay there in the darkness, legs intertwined, breaths mingling.

Perhaps it's because we're here, in our spot... perhaps it's because we can't see one another properly... perhaps it's simply because it's the middle of the night, and the rest of the world is asleep... but for whatever reason, in this moment, it's as though we've pressed pause on our fight. Set our anger aside in a momentary truce.

A temporary ceasefire.

"I'm sorry," I murmur. "I didn't mean to wake you."

"Well I didn't mean to scare you," he murmurs back.

"Couldn't sleep either, huh?"

His head shakes. "Nah. Too much on my mind."

"The scouts?"

"Among other things."

I recognize the strain in his voice. It's more than just our fight. Pressure is mounting for him to make a decision regarding college baseball. Most athletes have long-since signed their letters of intent, locking in their offers as soon as they received them. But Archer is leveraging his senior season in his favor, letting the best universities in the country woo him until the final hour with incentives — both financial and educational.

Last I checked, he'd narrowed his many options down to Florida State, Vanderbilt, Ole Miss, and (my personal pick) Bryant University. As his sole New England choice — and, coincidentally, a mere thirty minute drive from my dorm at Brown — I've been not so subtly rooting for him to join the Bulldogs in Rhode Island since the day they made their first overtures.

"Have you narrowed your list down further?"

"Not yet."

"Deadline is coming up," I tell him needlessly.

"Mhm."

Everyone expects him to announce his decision at the end of the season — preferably, after he's led Exeter to a State Championship title. I can practically see it now: him holding a gold trophy aloft in front of a swarm of press, grinning as he shakes his new coach's hand. With just two regular games left before playoffs, that gives him mere weeks to make the biggest commitment of his life.

"It's a big decision. It's normal to be nervous. But you'll make the right one," I assure him. "I know you will."

His voice grows achingly soft. "Sometimes... it feels like I've been handed this amazing stroke of luck and at any minute, it's all just going to evaporate from my grip."

"It's not luck, though. It's training. It's years of hard work."
I sigh. "How many times did I drive to the field and drag your
ass home after a full day of practice? How many mornings did
you go for a six-mile run, even in the rain and snow and sleet?
How many nights did you make me watch YouTube clips with
you, studying footage and learning technique?" My lips twist.
"You aren't lucky, Archer. You're talented."

He's quiet for a long moment. My body rises and falls each
time he takes a breath, a boat upon a sea of rolling swells.
When he speaks again, his voice is low. Full of gravel.

"Right now, I feel pretty lucky."

I suck in a sharp breath. If I didn't know better, I'd swear
he's talking about something besides baseball. My heart, only
moments ago in danger of combusting from terror, is now in
danger of combusting from another emotion entirely.

Not a platonic one.

Tension mounts in the air around us, almost tangible. I
wonder if he feels it, too. If he feels anything at all besides innocent friendship. I'm not sure what possibility scares me more —
that he's totally oblivious to this state of emotional suspense... or
that he does feel it, but would rather pretend otherwise.

"Lucky?" I say lightly, forcing a laugh. "Even though I
nearly flattened you?"

His arms tighten around my back as he snorts. "For such a
small person, you land with a surprising amount of force."

"Hey! Are you calling me fat?"

"No. Just... *dense.*"

"I am not dense!" I scowl. "You're dense — in the head!"

His chuckles vibrate my entire body. "Good comeback, Jo."

"Oh, shut up," I hiss, even though I'm fighting off chuckles
of my own. "I guess in the future, we need to sort out custody of
the rafters. Write out a contractual agreement for who gets to
use them whenever we have a stupid fight. How 'bout I get to

sulk up here on weeknights, you get weekends? We can rotate major holidays. Do you want Easter or Christmas?"

I'm joking, but he doesn't laugh. Beneath me, his body goes stiff — as though he's just remembered to be angry. A second later, his arms unlock from the cage they'd created around me and drop to his sides.

Ceasefire, over.

I instantly want to snatch back my stupid words. To rewind ten seconds to the quiet sanctuary of his embrace, when things actually felt normal between us for the first time in far too long.

From the unyielding set of his muscles, I know there's no point in even trying. Biting my tongue, I force myself to roll off him. To sit up. To reach into the darkness, seeking out the familiar metal edges of the camping lantern.

I turn the knob and dull light suffuses the loft. I blink at the sudden change in brightness, my eyes struggling to acclimate. When they do, I see Archer is already sitting at the edge of the rafters with his back to me — spine ramrod straight, staring fixedly out the windows to the ebony ocean beyond. Dressed in gray sweatpants and an Exeter t-shirt, his bare feet swing in the air. His dark hair is tousled with sleep.

"You can have it," he says haltingly. "Full custody. I won't come here anymore."

Tears spring to my eyes. I blink them away before they can fall. Taking a deep breath, I try to steady my voice before I respond. "What does that mean?"

He doesn't say anything.

"What does that mean, Archer?" I repeat, scooting closer to him. I'm careful not to brush my shoulder against his as I swing my legs over the edge.

I stare at his face in profile. He looks tired. Deep shadows are etched beneath his eyes, evidence of more than one sleepless night. As I take in the uncompromising set of his jawline, the rigidity of his posture, I wonder how his mood could shift so quickly from laughing with me to loathing me.

The truth is, as hurt as I was on Friday, as angry as I was afterward... there was never a doubt in my mind that we'd work through this fight. That, eventually, we'd smooth things over and they'd return, if not totally to normal, than at least to a semblance of it. But as I look at him now, in this moment, I feel the first tendrils of uncertainty begin to swirl inside me.

Maybe he doesn't want to fix it.

"It means exactly what it sounds like," he says in a hollow voice. "I don't need this place anymore."

I flinch, as though he's dealt a physical blow. He might as well have. He said, *I don't need this place anymore.* Didn't he mean...

I don't need you anymore.

"W-why?" My voice quivers. "Why are you being like this?"

"Like what?"

"So— so cold to me. I don't understand what's happening. I don't understand why you're acting like such a jerk lately!"

He doesn't look at me as he takes a breath. His voice is empty of all emotions, stripped down to its most essential elements — vowels, consonants, meaningless letters. "I'm just being realistic. We aren't kids anymore. No matter what school I end up at, I'm not going to be able to run to the rafters and hide whenever things go wrong in my life. And neither will you." He pauses. "It's time to grow up. It's time to move on."

"Fine," I retort thickly. "If that's how you really feel."

"It is."

"Great!" I'm trying very hard not to cry. "Then leave. Get out of here. Go ahead and *grow up* and *move on*—" My words crack off. My hands fist in the thick material of my sweatshirt, just so I can stop their shaking. When I remember it once belonged to him, I'm overwhelmed by the desire to peel it off my skin, to toss it dramatically into the sea.

In the static silence, Archer climbs slowly to his feet. He's so tall, he has to hunch slightly to avoid the low ceiling. He takes two steps, then stops. He's still not making eye contact. His shoulders are as rigid as his words.

"Don't stay out here too long by yourself. It's late."

I swallow down an incredulous scoff. "As if you care?"

His hands clench at his sides. He doesn't say another word. He just walks to the ladder, crouches down, and slides his legs through the gap in the floor. I don't say anything as he grips the upper rungs and begins to descend. But as I watch the top of his head about to cross the threshold, I can't hold my tongue anymore.

"I always knew you were destined for better things. Fame. Fans. Fenway Park. I always knew you'd leave this little town behind. *Always.* I just... I never thought you'd leave me behind, too." A tear slips down my cheek. I scrub at it angrily with my sleeve. "I thought we meant more to each other than that."

Apparently, Archer doesn't agree. Because a second later, he vanishes from view. Down the ladder. Out of my sight.

Out of my life.

I sit in the boathouse until the sun comes up, crying long past the point of tears. When the sky finally breaks open, unfurling into pale blue-pink petals, the new day dawns alongside an entirely new reality.

One in which Archer Reyes is no longer my best friend.

BEFORE FULL LIGHT, I head back to the house, climb into bed, and don't move — not when my alarm begins to blare, not when Flora comes to check why I'm not downstairs in my uniform, ready to leave.

"I'm sick," I tell her, my voice muffled beneath the heavy duvet. "I'm not going to school today."

I must sound as terrible as I feel, because she doesn't push me. She doesn't even take my temperature. A gentle "Okay, mija" drifts to my ears before the door clicks closed. I'm grateful for the privacy. The last thing I want to do is explain why my eyes are so red and puffy.

I strain my ears, listening for the telltale rumble of a truck engine, for the distant click of the front gates that assures me Archer is gone for the day. All I can hear are birds chirping outside my window, building summer nests in the weeping willow trees.

Exhaustion clutches at me, a relentless suitor. I let it pull me under, thinking I might escape my misery with sleep. But I only dream of things that make my heart ache — narrowed caramel eyes, full lips spitting cruel words.

It's time to move on.

I jolt awake, eyes watering.

Flora comes up with lunch on a tray for me. I send it away untouched. I have no appetite. I feel half alive. Hollow. Like someone's taken a commercial fishing hook and gutted me, right through the stomach.

I tell myself I'm not waiting for Archer to text me. To call me. To show up at my door and apologize. To beg forgiveness for being such a jerk, plead temporary insanity, and assure me he's back to his normal self.

He does none of those things.

Crazy as it sounds, even after everything, a small part of me was hopeful he'd try to mend things between us. Every hour that ticks by without hearing from him, I feel a little more of that hope wither inside my chest.

Eventually, I summon enough energy to pull my laptop beneath my sheets. I click on *The Great British Bake Off*, losing myself in the comforting monotony of strangers competing to create the best blueberry custard tart. The light outside fades, shadows lengthening as the day wanes from afternoon to evening and finally to full night.

Flora brings more food for dinner. It grows cold on my bedside table before she takes it away.

My laptop runs out of battery halfway through episode eleven. I don't bother locating the power cord. I curl more deeply beneath my cocoon of blankets, close my eyes, and, for the first time, allow myself to consider what the following day will bring.

Today, I got away with avoiding everything; tomorrow, that free-pass officially expires. I'll have to go to school. To face my life.

To face him.

And if I want to get through the day without dissolving into pathetic tears in front of the wolves that roam the halls of Exeter Academy of Excellence...

I'm going to need a contingency plan.

CHAPTER TEN

ARCHER

FUCK.
My.
Life.

CHAPTER ELEVEN

JOSEPHINE

TUESDAY MORNING DAWNS clear and bright.

I blink awake six minutes before my alarm. Kicking off my duvet, I practically vault out of bed and race for the bathroom. I speed through my shower, leaving my damp hair to dry naturally. No time for blow dryers, today.

I throw on my uniform — pleated green and black plaid skirt, coordinating blazer, crisp white shirt. My stockings have a tear, which delays me a bit rummaging around for fresh ones, but a glance at the slim silver watch on my wrist shows I'm still on track.

With a heavy stack of textbooks pressed to my chest, I creep down the grand staircase, grimacing at every creaky step.

Historic houses make sneaking around a varsity sport.

At the bottom, I pause, straining to hear any sign of Flora in the kitchen — faint humming, the clatter of pans, a refrigerator clicking shut. But there's nothing.

All clear.

I step off the landing, round the atrium corner, and slink down the hall to my father's study. Inside, it smells of old leather-bound books and fresh furniture polish. I find it odd that there's no dust; that the imposing mahogany desk shines brightly even in its neglected state. I suppose Flora still cleans in here, even if my father isn't around to appreciate it.

The top desk drawer isn't even locked. And the key fobs are exactly where I thought they'd be — in plain view, nestled in a small box. Mine for the taking.

I grab one at random, caring less about my mode of escape than the act of it. My thumb traces the design engraved on the fob's surface: a pair of wings inset with the letter B. As I pocket it, a fissure of exhilaration quakes my rule-oriented foundations.

I've never stolen a thing in my life. Not a pack of chewing gum, not a hotel bathrobe, not an apple from the produce aisle. Certainly not a car.

How many years in the slammer do you get for grand theft auto?

Today, I'm willing to risk it.

Backtracking my steps, I find my way to the side door off the atrium that leads to the garage. The fleet sits there, tucked beneath satin dust covers like thoroughbreds left to wither in their stalls. A shameful waste of horsepower.

I sort them by their distinct shapes — the low-slung Porsche, the stately Rolls Royce, the angular Aston Martin, the sharp-edged Tesla. And, at the far end, my destination: the boxy Bentley.

My father has more automobiles than any one man requires — especially a man that's rarely even on this continent enough to get behind the wheel. I suppose that works in my favor, though. It would be much harder to steal one of his cars if he were actually home to notice.

I yank the dust-cover off the Bentley and pile it in a corner. Clicking the fob, I grin as the headlights flash in response and reach for the door handle.

"I wouldn't take it if I were you," a voice says casually.

I jump about a mile into the air. The fob clatters to my feet, then skitters beneath the chassis. Whirling around, I come face to face with Miguel. I didn't even notice him crouched down by the front of the Porsche, a tire-pressure gauge in his hand.

"I—I'm not—I wasn't—"

"Stealing your father's Bentley? Sure you were." Miguel chuckles. When he does, his caramel eyes crinkle up at the corners — just like his son's. Looking at him is like staring into the future. He's Archer in thirty years. Salt and pepper hair, a few wrinkles gathered around his temples. Still handsome in that roguish way that makes women on the street turn their heads.

"You'd make a pretty lousy criminal, JoJo," Miguel tells me cheerfully.

"I'm sorry. I just..." I trail off. I have no reasonable explanation to offer him. I chew my lip as I wait for the axe to fall. Miguel never gets angry — not that I've seen, at least. But his quiet disappointment is infinitely worse than any raised voices or raging words.

"What was the plan? Sneak in here and steal a car to avoid riding with Archer?"

I blink, stunned. "How did you—"

"My wife talks. *A lot*. She indicated you and my son have been... at odds lately."

Of course Flora told him. I'm surprised she hasn't taken out a billboard in the center of town.

JOSEPHINE AND ARCHER HAD A FIGHT!

I sigh deeply. "I just thought... maybe... a little space might not be the worst thing. I'm sorry. It was a stupid idea, and I definitely didn't think it through."

"That's true." Miguel nods slowly. "I mean, for starters..."

He jerks his head at the car beside me. "The Bentley's basically out of gas. You'd make it about three blocks before you ran out."

"Oh." Color floods my cheeks. "I didn't know that."

"Figured as much. That's why I stopped you."

"*That's* why you stopped me?"

"Well, sure. I've got a busy day ahead of me. I can't be playing your knight-with-shining-gas-can, rescuing you from the roadside." He reaches into his back pocket, pulls out a key, and tosses it my direction. Baffled beyond belief, I manage to catch it with my fingertips before it clatters to the cement floor.

"Uhh..."

"Take the Cabriolet," Miguel says, pulling off the cover, revealing a hunter green convertible with a tan ragtop roof. "She's got a full tank and fresh oil."

I walk toward the Porsche. Even if you know nothing about cars, it's spectacular — a vintage 1965 model, with a front trunk compartment and round, buggy headlights. It reminds me of something Audrey Hepburn or Elizabeth Taylor would drive around in, cruising down Hollywood Boulevard between movie sets.

Nothing else in this garage can hold a candle to it. Not the Rolls Royce with its regal glamour or the Bentley with its astronomical price point or even the brand new Tesla with it's self-driving pizzazz.

"Miguel, I can't take the Porsche."

"Sure you can. It's warm today — perfect for riding with the top down. Just do me a favor? Don't crash it. This car costs more than most people make in a year." He pauses. "More like two years, now that I think about it."

I swallow hard. "No pressure."

"JoJo."

I look up and meet his eyes. His steady gaze reminds me so much of Archer, it makes the breath snag in my throat. "Yeah?"

"Cars are made to be driven. Not to sit idle, waiting around for someone to finally appreciate them."

Miguel strokes his hand gently across the tan ragtop. Unlatching it with care, he folds the cloth back into place, exposing the convertible's creamy, camel interior. The wooden steering wheel. The gear shifter, sticking out of the floor.

I whistle appreciatively, excitement sparking to life. I've only driven the Porsche twice before, and never beyond the gates of Cormorant House. The circular driveway provided a perfect makeshift learning course for lessons last year — first in Miguel's beat-up truck, then with my father's fleet.

Archer was infinitely annoyed that I mastered manual transmissions so much faster than he did. Ever since we got our licenses, he's wanted to sneak the Porsche out for a clandestine drive up the coast. If he knew I was about to do it without him, he'd be apoplectic.

Not that I care.

"For what it's worth," Miguel says suddenly, drawing my attention back to him. "That same advice applies to human beings, JoJo."

"What?"

"You can't spend your days waiting for life to happen to you, safe in a weatherproof hangar. You have to get out on the open road. Crank the windows down. Let the wind mess up your hair. Maybe end up on a route you never saw coming." He winks playfully. "Then again, I'm just a handyman. What do I know?"

"Miguel—"

But my words fall short; he's already walking away. "Get going now, kiddo. You don't want to be late for school."

MIGUEL WAS RIGHT — it is a beautiful day. Warm and sun-drenched, the air rife with the promise of summer. I take the winding route to Exeter Academy, following the Essex Coastal Scenic Byway through salt marshes and small inlets, past pebble beaches and crystalline coves. I shift gears, letting the Porsche fly when I reach a secluded straightaway. Above all, I try not to think about Archer.

At this, I fail miserably.

I can't help it. This is the first time in a decade we haven't carpooled to school. In our younger years, Flora would drop us off together. Even after I got my license last summer, I never considered asking my parents for a car of my own. Why would I, when I had Archer to take us everywhere in his truck?

How naive of me to think there'd never come a day when his passenger seat is the last place on earth I want to be.

The Exeter parking lot is already filling up when I arrive. I pass row after row of shiny new cars — one black-on-black Ford F-150 conspicuously missing from their ranks — and finally locate a free spot in the very back, by the track that loops around the baseball field. In the distance, the first bell rings, a ten minute warning till the start of class.

I've barely shut my door when a massive yellow Jeep Wrangler screeches to a stop in the space beside mine. Ryan Snyder ambles out of the driver's seat, the grin on his face somewhat undermined by the nasty shiner around his eye.

"Sup, Valentine."

"Ryan!" I gasp. "Your eye!"

"Eh. Looks worse than it is." He grins wider. "You still think I'm handsome, don't you?"

A blush spreads across my cheeks. "Um. We should probably head inside. The bell's about to ring... "

He chuckles as he walks to my side. Before I can protest, he promptly removes the stack of textbooks from my arms.

"Oh! You don't have to—"

"I want to." His blue eyes are practically sparkling in the morning light. He glances down at the books. "What do we have here? AP Biology, AP Chemistry, AP Physics... Someone's an overachiever."

"More like the daughter of overachievers."

"Parents have high expectations of excellence, huh? I can relate. I'm a triple-legacy at Yale. Never had much of a choice about my college plans. I think my first onesie had Handsome Dan on the front."

I steal a peek at him as we cross the parking lot. Ryan Snyder may look like a J. Crew model in that dark green blazer, but he's clearly got brains lurking beneath his chiseled beauty. You don't get into Yale on familial connections alone — even if you are a third-generation shoe-in.

"I'm sure your parents are proud of you."

"I guess." He shrugs. "I wanted to go to Dartmouth but I'm not the one paying, so..." He trails off. "Anyway. I don't think I had a chance to ask you the other night... where are you headed in the fall?"

"Brown."

"Ah. A fellow Ivy Leaguer. Hence the impressive books. You planning to study science?"

"If my parents have their way? Yes. They've got it all planned out. Undergraduate degree in Biology with a focus on Nutritional Science. Masters in Public Health, followed by an internship at their nonprofit. Eventually, taking over the reins and running the company."

"And you? What's your grand plan?"

I try to focus on his question, rather than the other students making their way to the front door. Several of them are blatantly staring at us. By first period, the news will have swept through every classroom.

Ryan Snyder was carrying Josephine Valentine's books this morning! And he had a black eye, to boot!

"Earth to Valentine. Am I boring you?"

"No! Sorry," I murmur guiltily. "I want to study fashion."

"Let me guess — you're hoping for a stint on *Project Runway*? Future designer to the stars? Kardashian fashion consultant?"

"Not exactly." I roll my eyes. "The design side is interesting, but I want to learn about the whole industry. From sketching new styles to manufacturing lines to stocking the shelves."

"That's cool."

"It's not *cool*, actually." My brows pull together. "Do you know how many harmful dyes and chemicals are pumped into our rivers every year, just to make the uniforms we're wearing right now? Do you know how many people live below the poverty line, working in sweatshops to sew them together?"

"I'm guessing a lot."

"Yes. A lot. And no one is doing anything about it." I shake my head in exasperation. "I want to start a fashion brand that does things differently. One that actually pays the people who make my clothes a livable wage. One that creates clothing without destroying the earth in the process."

"I'd say '*that's cool*' again, but I'm afraid you'll yell at me."

I snort-laugh, somewhat mortified by my tirade. He probably thinks I'm a total freak. "Sorry. I'm a bit on-edge today. And I tend to get revved up when I talk about this stuff."

"Never apologize for being passionate about something, Valentine." He glances at me again. "I just can't believe I ever thought you were shy."

I duck my head, hair falling around my face in a curtain. I hope it hides my blush. (Judging by the way a group of sophomore girls giggle behind their notebooks as we pass by, I'm guessing that hope is futile.)

We've reached the front door. Juggling my books, Ryan reaches out and holds it open for me.

"How gentlemanly," I tease, walking inside.

"I'm trying to impress you, if it wasn't obvious." He's smiling as he passes my books back to me. "How am I doing so far?"

"What fun would it be if I told you?"

With that, I turn and walk away, heading for my locker. It's at the tail end of the senior hallway with the rest of the alphabetical rejects, crammed in between Kenny Underwood and the Wadell twins.

"You're killing me, Valentine!" Ryan calls after me, loud enough to make everyone in earshot turn around to stare.

Unfortunately, three minutes before the final bell, the senior hallway is packed with lingering students — all eager witnesses to my embarrassment. They whisper under their breath as I walk the gauntlet. The weight of many watchful eyes rests heavily on my shoulders, an unfamiliar burden for a girl who is usually borderline invisible. I pray my cheeks aren't as flushed as they feel.

I'm spinning open my combination lock — 3-34-14 — when the Wadell twins flank me on either side, their matching pink backpacks the same shade as the gum they're snapping in tandem. There's not a hair out of place in their glossy platinum bobs; a far cry from my windswept mane. Driving with the top down creates more volume than the best blow-dryer on the market.

"Hey," Ophelia says.

"Hey," Odette says.

"Can I help you?" I grunt, distracted. They've made me mess up my combo. I start over.

Twice to the right...

3...

"So are you, like, dating Ryan now?" Ophelia asks.

I ignore the question.

Once to the left...

34...

"How'd he get that black eye?" Odette wonders.

Back to the right...

14...

"Everyone's saying Archer gave it to him," Ophelia informs me.

"And that they're, like, fighting over you now," Odette adds.

I press my lips firmly together. Yanking open my locker door, I shove my textbooks inside haphazardly. I don't care if they fall out later; I'm desperate to escape this conversation.

Interrogation.

Grabbing a blank notebook, my lab goggles, and the first pencil I see, I shut my locker with a metallic slam and walk away without a word.

"Rude," Ophelia declares.

"Totally," Odette agrees.

Overhead, the tardy bell rings. I'm officially late for biology.

I sigh.

It's going to be a long day.

ARCHER and I don't share any classes together — something that normally annoys me. Today, it's a blessing in disguise. I slug through biology lab, only half paying attention to the frog I'm supposed to be dissecting. Unfortunately — for my GPA as well as the amphibian — I end up extracting its liver instead of a kidney.

My teacher, Dr. Gilmore, seems more upset than I am. She's accustomed to me being her star student, not phoning it in like one of the stoners.

"Are you feeling well, Miss Valentine?" She's staring down at the liver-less frog in my tray, an indent between her auburn eyebrows. "I know you were out sick, yesterday..."

"I'm fine."

"Well. I suppose even valedictorians have off days," she clucks. "I'll get you a fresh specimen so you can start over..."

I pull myself together long enough to survive the rest of the anatomy workshop, along with Chemistry and Physics. But in the back of my mind, lunchtime looms like an ever-darkening shadow. The whole senior class eats at the same time; no matter where I sit, I'm certain to cross Archer's path.

As the clock marches onward toward noon, I fidget in my uniform, crossing and uncrossing my legs so many times, I'm sure the kid sitting next to me thinks I have a urinary tract infection. When the bell rings, I bolt from my seat like a sprinter off the blocks.

The Exeter cafeteria offers a meal service that makes most five-star hotel spreads look shabby. (Our exorbitant tuition fees, hard at work.) I typically load up my tray at the salad bar, then eat with Archer beneath our favorite tree in the courtyard — a spot we staked out at the start of senior year.

Right now, that's definitely not an option.

I head for the parking lot instead. Sitting in the Porsche, I munch on stale trail mix, sip a grapefruit seltzer, and tell myself I'm perfectly fine.

So what if I have no other friends to sit with? At least I'm not a total loser, eating alone in a bathroom stall — which seems to happen in every high school movie I've ever seen.

So what if the boy I've loved forever doesn't want anything

to do with me, even in a platonic way? At least I never embarrassed myself by telling him how I really feel.

So what if the future I thought was certain is now nothing but a question mark? At least, in a few months, I'll be away at college, starting fresh somewhere new.

I'm fine.

I'm fine.

I'm fine.

Except I'm not fine at all.

CHAPTER TWELVE

ARCHER

JOSEPHINE VALENTINE IS AVOIDING ME.

Josephine Valentine is driving me insane.

Yesterday, there was the fake-sick routine. And I get it, I really do. I was a dick that night at the boathouse; she was understandably upset.

But when this morning rolled around, I went to pick her up at her front door only to have my father inform me — quite merrily, I may add — that she'd already left. In the Porsche, no less.

She knows how I feel about the Porsche.

I pulled into the parking lot just in time to see her walking into school with Snyder, practically swooning as the fuckhead held the door open for her. I almost crashed my truck, craning my neck to keep them in my sights.

Since then, she's turned into a goddamn ghost — never in any of the places I look for her. Not the courtyard at lunch, not her locker between classes, not the Creative Arts wing where they keep the industrial sewing machine she uses for her fashion designs. I hit dead end after dead end, never catching more than a glimpse of her across a crowded hallway.

The flash of a fishtail braid.

A fragment of her laughter.

You can't be anywhere near her, I remind myself over and over, stalking the halls like a penned-in tiger at the zoo. *Not until things with Jaxon are under control. Not until it's safe.*

But taking care of Jo is an impulse ingrained so deeply inside my psyche, it's not easy to shake. I can't stand the thought of her being isolated at school; left alone at the popular kids' mercy without me there to intervene. It's driving me to utter distraction.

And distraction is one thing I really can't afford. Not tonight. It's the second to last game of the season, an away match in the neighboring town. I'm certain several scouts will be there to watch me pitch. Vanderbilt. Bryant. Maybe even an MLB recruiter. But with my thoughts so tangled up in Jo, there's no way I'll deliver the performance they're expecting. I need to get my head on straight before I'm standing under the stadium lights in five hours, making an ass of myself.

In an attempt to clear my mind, I cut my last class, climb into my truck, and go for a long drive down the coast, keeping mostly to the back roads. It's a perfect time of year. Flowers in full bloom, tree boughs hanging heavy with green. Landscapers mowing lawns, nannies pushing little kids on swings at the park.

I cruise through several coastal towns, almost on autopilot. Beverly, Peabody, Salem. The streets flow by outside my windows in a blur, barely making an impression. I don't have any real destination in mind. I just drive.

After nearly an hour, I wind up at the lighthouse on the tip of Marblehead Neck. Shutting my engine, I sit and watch the waves crashing against the shore, spraying sea-foam into the sky. Gulls circle overhead, occasionally dropping shells to crack them open on the parking lot asphalt. Swooping down, they devour the spoils with throaty cries of victory. On nearby rocks, cormorants sun themselves, their black wings spread wide.

There's plenty of harbor traffic on a warm day like this. Sailboats of all shapes and sizes crisscross the blue expanse, growing smaller and smaller as they head out to sea. When my eyes catch on a small red one, my heart lurches inside my chest.

Rationally, I know it can't be Cupid — Jo's Alerion is docked miles and miles away, at its slip in Manchester. Still, I strain to keep the small craft in my sights. As if somehow, by holding onto it, I might also hold onto the girl whose face it conjures in my mind. The girl who slips away from me a little more each day, bound for far-flung horizons where I cannot follow.

My eyes sting in the wind. I brush an escaped tear off my cheek. Breathing deeply, I wait until the sailboat fades into an indiscernible speck before I climb back into my truck and head for home.

GULL COTTAGE SITS QUIETLY in the clearing, giving no indication of the danger awaiting me within its walls. I whistle lightly under my breath as I jog up the steps, fiddling with my keys.

My parents will be working up at the main estate for several more hours. I doubt I'll see them until late this evening, when I get home from my game.

I lift the key toward the lock. My hand goes still before I can insert it. My pulse begins to pound faster inside my veins. Every hair on the back of my neck raises in high alert.

The door is already ajar.

I was in a rush this morning. Maybe I didn't pull it closed properly...

Except, I'm always careful to close the door. Always. If I don't, I get a long-winded lecture from Ma on the surprising prevalence of burglaries in wealthy towns with tiny police departments.

As if we own anything worth stealing.

Using the tip of my key, I push the door open wider and peer through the crack. There's no indication anyone is inside — no strange noises, no furniture upended.

Just in case, I slide my iPhone out of my back pocket. My palm is sweaty against the glass screen as I toggle it open. I have no one to call for help, but I feel better with it in my hand when I widen the gap between door and frame.

My pulse thuds between my ears, a steady drum beat. Stepping across the threshold, I creep into the cottage as quietly as possible. My eyes scan the room, taking inventory of every item. Searching for the smallest details out of place.

Everything looks exactly as I left it.

"Hello?" I call tentatively, taking a few more steps into the living room. "Ma? You here?"

Silence booms back at me.

My shoulders slump as the tension leaves me in a whoosh. Shaking my head at my own paranoia, I walk toward the kitchen in search of a snack.

Must've left the door open after all. Let's hope Ma doesn't find out, or I'm in for—

The thought explodes into fragments as something hard slams into the back of my skull. Pain sears through me, blinding. I fall to the hardwood. A second before I hit the floor, the world flickers into darkness.

I BLINK AWAKE, groaning in pain.

Whatever they hit me with must've been heavy, because it knocked me out cold. My head is pounding like an anvil's been dropped on it.

I attempt to feel the lump forming beneath my hair, but my hands aren't cooperating. They aren't moving at all, in fact. Dazed, I open my eyes and discover both my wrists bound to the arms of a dining chair with several layers duct tape. No matter how hard I tug, they don't loosen.

Fuck.

"So, Sleeping Beauty is finally awake," a man says, crouching down to meet my eyes. I recognize him from the parking lot; Rico, the shifty-eyed gangster who threatened me after practice. "I was worried Barboza caused permanent brain damage."

A low grunt reverberates from my left. My eyes follow the sound to his partner, the hulking giant. He looks ridiculously oversized amidst my parents' aging dining room set.

"Disappointed we haven't heard from you, kid." Shaking his head, Rico makes a *tsk* sound. "Thought, after our last little talk, you understood we weren't overflowing with patience."

"I haven't seen my brother."

"Well, that's a damn shame." He pauses. "For you."

Barboza steps forward, cracking his knuckles menacingly.

"What do you want from me? I can't force Jax to appear," I say, trying hard to keep my voice steady. I don't take my eyes of those massive fists, coming ever-closer. The feeling of them around my neck, cutting off my air supply, is burned forever into my memory.

"We know that. We aren't unreasonable." Rico laughs lightly. "That's why we thought Jaxon might need a little... incentive... to pop his head out of whatever hole he's hiding in."

I gulp in a breath. "Incentive?"

"Mmm. Say... his little brother ends up in the hospital with a terrible injury." His head tilts in thought. "Or... maybe his mother steps out into traffic. Women can be so clumsy, can't they? I'm sure he'd attend the funeral."

My hands curl around the arms of the chair. "If you even think about going near my mother I'll—"

"What? Kill me?" Rico laughs. "I like your spirit, kid. We should've recruited you instead of your shithead brother."

"I'll pass, thanks."

Rico smirks. "The thing is, what I think doesn't matter. It's not going to make a damn bit of difference to our boss. He's been real patient so far... but his patience is about to expire. If Jaxon doesn't start clearing his debts soon, we'll have to collect from his family. Which is your family, *ese.*"

"Is that what all this is about?" I scoff. "Money?"

"Your brother owes us a debt."

"How is that possible? He's been behind bars for two years. I seriously doubt he's been racking up a balance at whatever establishment you work at." My lips twist. "Let me guess — underground cockfight ring? You two look like you enjoy a good cock."

Barboza takes a step closer. His voice rumbles like a freight train. "You got a smart mouth, kid. Happy to shut it for you — permanently."

"Barboza, chill." Rico spins one of the dining room chairs around and sits on it backwards, facing me. "Life on the inside isn't like out here — all rainbows and glitter and sunshine. Jaxon took protection from the Kings to avoid becoming some-one's bitch. He knew that protection came at a price."

The Kings.

The Latin Kings.

Jesus Christ.

My eyes drop to the tattoo on Rico's neck. The five-pronged

crown — an irrefutable symbol of one of the most notorious gangs in the Boston area. I should've put two and two together before. I should've realized that these were no mere ex-cons seeking payback for jailhouse beef with my idiot brother, or enemies he pissed off before he went away.

They're members of the Latin Kings.

The world of crime is about as far-removed from the quietude of Manchester-by-the-Sea as I can fathom, but word of their violence is widespread enough to reach even here. The gang dominates the local news channels these days — nervous reporters detailing the recent uptick of deaths in the city, police speculating a change in gang leadership. Someone new in charge, with a penchant for killing.

Ma watches while she cooks dinner, clutching at the cross around her neck as images of gore play out on the television screen.

Drug busts.

Carjackings.

Kidnappings.

Murder.

No matter how many sting operations the Boston Police Department conducts... no matter how many gang members they arrest... none of it has much effect. Every time they cut off the head of the monster, another seems to spring instantly back in its place.

Needless to say, these are not the kind of people you want to mess around with. Not if you value your life.

If I could get my hands around Jaxon's throat right now, he'd be a dead man. I knew he was in trouble — enough to scare him off the grid, enough to make him warn me of the fallout heading for us a few weeks back, pale-faced and shaking as he packed a bag in the middle of the night. I had no idea he'd gotten himself entangled with something like this, though.

If I thought it would help, I'd call his parole officer myself. But sending my own brother back to jail won't protect my family from this. Not the heartbreak of losing him all over again; not the repercussions from men like Barboza and Rico.

If they're brazen enough to break in during broad daylight, knock me unconscious, and duct tape me to a chair... they're not going to back off just because I get the cops involved. If anything, that'll just piss them off further... and put my family in even more danger.

I clear my throat, trying to keep the panic buried. "I don't know how much Jax owes you, but you're not going to find anything of value here. Look around — look at where we live. It's not exactly the Taj Mahal. We don't have anything to offer you."

Rico scratches absently at the pockmark scar on his cheek. "Bet that big house up on the point has plenty."

My heart skips a beat. I take a deep breath, swallowing down my fear and fury. I make sure my voice is very level when I speak. "The people that live there have nothing to do with my family. We just work for them. I'm sure you know that already."

"Mhm." Rico stares me down. "You seem pretty tight with that girl."

My heart stops entirely. "Who?"

"The blonde with the legs."

"*Her?*" I snort incredulously. My heart pounds a mad tattoo. "She's nothing but an obligation. A stuck up brat, like the rest of the kids at my school. My parents used to make me drive her around. That's it. If I never see her again, it'll be too soon."

My words hang in the air between us, heavy with deceit. I can't tell if he believes me. He doesn't say anything. He merely runs a hand over his buzzed head, his eyes narrowed in thought.

"Speaking of driving... that's a pretty shiny truck you're cruising around town in. You know, for a kid without any money."

"You want my truck? Fine. Take the damn truck," I offer, feeling desperate. "But that makes us square. You leave me and my parents out of this from now on. No more threats. No more unexpected drop bys. Stay away from us."

Rico grins at his partner. "He thinks he can negotiate. Isn't that cute, Barboza?"

Barboza does not look particularly tickled by my gall. As far as I can tell, the man has exactly one facial expression — an uncompromising, unflinching stare, delivered through soulless eyes. Violence emanates from his skin like perfume.

"The thing is, kid..." Rico blows out a breath. "Our boss wants more than just money from Jaxon. Your brother has some connections in this neck of the woods. Connections we'd like to absorb into our network. You feel me?"

I stare over his shoulder at the cabinets on the other side of the kitchen. My jaw is locked so tight, I can barely breathe.

Drugs.

Of course this is all about drugs. It always is, with Jax. Before he was sent to Cedar-Junction Correctional Institution, he was a part-time dealer, full-time junkie. Life with him in this house was erratic at best. I never knew which version of him I was going to get — the loving brother I grew up with or the drugged-out monster who'd hijacked his body.

Growing up, Jaxon was constantly in trouble — first with my parents, then with his teachers, later with the local cops. His crimes escalated with age, from smoking pot in his bedroom to getting busted with a stockpile of pills in his sock drawer to full-fledged dealing at every high school party.

You want Oxy? Adderall? The best pot on the East Coast? Talk to Jaxon Reyes.

Truth be told, I was relieved when he finally got arrested two years ago. Locked up, at least he'd be sober. At least my parents wouldn't have to watch their child slowly killing himself anymore. At least I wouldn't live in the constant fear of walking into his bedroom, finding him overdosed on the carpet.

After looking the other way on petty misdemeanors for years, when the police pulled him over with a trunk full of narcotics, they'd finally had enough. They threw the book at him.

Drug possession with intent to distribute.

A felony.

At nineteen, he was tried as an adult, slapped with a $20,000 fine (paid by Jo's parents, since mine couldn't afford it), and sent to state prison on a three year sentence. With good behavior, Jax shaved it down to two before getting released on parole.

I never visited him while he was in there. I couldn't bring myself to. I was too angry at him for throwing his life away, for fragmenting our family beyond repair. For making Ma cry into her pillow every night; for making Pa grow still and silent under the weight of his own grief.

Not that they'd ever hold it against him. They still loved their son. Every Sunday, they made the long drive to Cedar-Junction, two hours round-trip just for a few shared moments behind plexiglass. They'd come home with red-rimmed eyes and tell me how well he was doing, how healthy he looked — proud of him in the way only parents can manage, even after their kid fucks up immeasurably.

Jax *was* different, when he came home two months ago. Older. Colder. And clean. His eyes were clear. His temperament was even. For the first time since I was ten years old... I thought I might get my big brother back.

I should've known it would never last.

"Jaxon has a lot of product to move," Rico tells me bluntly, snapping my focus back to the present. "So far, he's not holding up his end of that bargain."

"My brother isn't dealing anymore. He's sober. He served his time. He's trying to start over."

"Is that what he told you?" Rico shakes his head. "Then he's a liar. Someone with his ties to this world can't just step away from it. Not ever."

"You make Jax sound like some one-man drug cartel, not a small-time dealer."

"Give credit where it's due. Before he got busted, your brother built his own little empire up here. At nineteen, he was moving so many pills, we heard about him out in Springfield." Rico's pupils are pinpricks. For the first time, it occurs to me that he might be high. "The Kings have been trying to expand north for years. But this area is a hard nut to crack from the outside. We need someone with a foot in the door."

Enter: Jaxon.

I shake my head in disbelief. "A handful of pot-smoking, pill-popping rich kids can't possibly be worth all this effort. I'd think it's hardly worth your time."

"See, that's where you'd be wrong. These rich kids you speak of, the ones with bottomless wallets and access to Daddy's credit card... they're the biggest untapped resource this side of Boston. But if someone like me or Barboza tries to sell to them, they're more likely to call ICE on our asses than actually buy what we have to offer."

"So you think Jax is going to be... what? Your liaison to the trust fund set?"

"They know your brother. They trust your brother. He's not some homeboy off the street. If he tells them to try the latest, greatest designer party drug, they'll fork over any amount of cash to snort it up their noses." Rico pauses, staring at me. "If your brother won't step up... maybe you will. We can give you a tryout, kid. Find out if dealing runs in the family."

"I won't," I say flatly.

Before I can blink, Rico whips a gun out of the waistband of his jeans and presses it to my face. "You will if we say you will. Understand?"

I flinch against my bindings, but they hold fast. My lungs seize as fear overrides every one of my senses. I can't think, can't breathe, can't speak. I can't do anything at all except stare at the sneering face inches away from mine.

The cold metal barrel presses harder into my cheek, indenting the flesh. "I asked you a question, kid. *Do you understand?*"

"I understand," I rasp, my words garbled.

"Excellent."

The gun disappears as quickly as it appeared. Tucking it back into his waistband, Rico pushes to his feet, crosses to the countertop, and grabs my keys. He tosses them playfully into the air. They jangle as they land in his hand.

"Much as I'd like to take you up on your offer of new wheels, I'm in a generous mood. You can keep your truck — for now. Just don't think about using it to leave town." He pauses. "We'll be watching."

Barboza grunts his agreement.

"And kid — I hope you're smart enough not to call the cops. If you do... your brother's as good as dead. Wouldn't bode too well for the rest of your family, either." Rico grins. "Wonder if there's a bulk discount on caskets?"

Jesus.

"I won't call the cops," I promise in a voice hollowed out by fear. "I won't call anyone."

"Good. And when you do see your brother... make sure you

tell him about our little visit to his childhood home. Make sure he knows, if we have to visit again, we won't be so nice."

Flicking open a stiletto, Barboza slices off my duct tape bindings. I wince as the blade nicks the sensitive skin inside my wrists, leaving thin trails of blood behind.

I'm free, but I don't move.

Not an inch.

Not a muscle.

"We'll see you soon, kid," Rico calls as they head for the door. Their heavy boots thud across the porch. "Count on it."

CHAPTER THIRTEEN

JOSEPHINE

FOR THE REST of the week, I achieve the impossible.

I mange to avoid Archer.

At school, I make myself scarce — switching out my books at strategic times when I know the hallways will be empty, spending free periods in the Creative Arts wing working on my sketches, eating lunch in my car. At home, I stick to my side of the estate — lounging at the pool, sailing around the islands, hitting tennis balls on the empty court, studying for the upcoming AP exams in my bedroom.

I do not go back to the boathouse.

For all I know, Archer is avoiding me as well. He's in no rush to make amends, that much seems clear from my lack of texts, phone calls, and drop-ins. He's undoubtedly busy after school, his schedule packed with baseball games and extra practices. With the regular season winding down, I'm sure his coach is already prepping for the start of playoffs next week.

Friday night marks the final game against Exeter's biggest rival — St. John's Preparatory School, the all-boys academy a few towns over. Our team is bound for the State Championships regardless of the final score, but the Exeter vs. St. John matchup is always a big event. Half the town turns out to tailgate, their faces painted green, bodies plastered with Exeter paraphernalia. Everyone even loosely associated with the academy attends — alumni, students, staff.

Everyone except me, that is.

No way am I going to sit in the bleachers and cheer Archer on to victory. Not when we're so at odds.

By Thursday afternoon, the impending game is all anyone can talk about. I weave through clumps of students in the hallways, listening to the chatter with a detached sort of acceptance.

You're going tomorrow, right?

Reyes is going to crush it!

St. John's is going down this year.

Do you have your tickets yet?

I spin my locker combination, wishing I hadn't forgotten my headphones at home.

"How's it hanging, Valentine?" Ryan asks, planting his shoulder against Kenny Underwood's locker as I'm exchanging my textbooks after lunch.

"No complaints, Snyder."

"Ouch! Did you just last-name me?"

"You last-named me first!"

"But everyone calls you Valentine."

Not everyone.

I shrug and shut my locker. "Do you need something?"

"Why yes, now that you ask." He grins widely. "I desperately need to know where you'll be sitting tomorrow night. Want to make sure I can find you in the crowd. I didn't see you on Tuesday at our away game." He waggles his eyebrows as he leans in, whispering conspiratorially. "And, trust me... I looked."

My cheeks heat. "I actually didn't go to Tuesday's game."

"Seriously? I thought you came to all our games. I don't think I've ever seen you miss one."

I laugh in surprise. "I had no idea you took such careful notice of my presence these days."

"Oh, I've been noticing you for quite a while, Valentine. That, I can assure you."

"Well, I'm sorry to disappoint."

"You could never disappoint me." He pauses. "That said... I'll see you tomorrow, right?"

"Uh... actually..."

"Don't tell me you aren't coming! I was counting on you to cheer me on. And Tomlinson's having a party afterward to celebrate the end of the season. One last rager before we head to playoffs. You can't miss it." His expression becomes almost bashful. "I thought... when the game ends... we could drive over together. And then I'll bring you home afterward. At a reasonable hour, even — Scout's honor."

I blink, startled. I may be socially stunted, but even I know that in teenage-boy-speak, attending a party together is a big deal. A prelude to an actual date. Foreplay to the foreplay.

"You're killing me with these long silences, Valentine," Ryan says, his blue eyes dropping to his feet. "Don't tell me that means you're preparing to say no..."

"I'm sorry, Ryan, but I —"

"She'll be there," a cheerful female voice interjects from behind me.

"We'll make sure of it," an eerily similar voice adds.

Jumping in surprise, I whirl around. The Wadell twins are leaning against their lockers, blatantly listening to our entire exchange. Before I can ream them out for eavesdropping, Ryan extends one balled hand toward them.

They both fist-bump him, giggling.

"Sweet." Ryan gives my shoulder a quick squeeze, winks playfully, and walks away. "See you tomorrow, Valentine!"

When he's gone, I glance at Ophelia and Odette. They're both sucking on lollypops — the big, pink kind with bubblegum in the center. They offer no explanation for their interference.

"Why did you do that?" I ask suspiciously.

"Because clearly you were about to say no to Ryan." Odette shrugs.

"Total self-sabotage." Ophelia nods.

"I still don't see how it's any of your business."

"Sweetie, we all know at a private school, nothing is ever private." Ophelia moves her lollypop into the side of her mouth, rounding out her cheek. "Ryan's hot. And he likes you."

Odette's eyes narrow. "Don't you want to go out with him?"

"I barely know him!"

"Is that even relevant?" Ophelia asks.

"Isn't getting to know someone better the whole point of going out with them?" Odette adds.

She does have a point. "I... I'm not really looking to date anyone right now..."

"*Date?* Who said anything about *date?*" Ophelia's nose wrinkles. "It's just a party."

"Just a party," Odette echoes, nodding.

"Right..." I find myself murmuring. I feel like I'm being conversationally bludgeoned into compliance. Resistance is futile.

"Great." Ophelia grins. "So you'll go to the game!"

"I didn't buy tickets," I lie. "So even if I wanted to—"

"We have an extra! You can sit with us." Odette smirks. "We were supposed to take our second-cousin Molly, but she's a total drag. Our Mom will let us ditch her if we explain the direness of your situation."

"But I really—"

"We'll pick you up!" Ophelia announces, pushing off her locker. "You live over by Crow Island, right? The big house on the point?"

"Um, yes, but—"

"Cool. See you at seven!" Odette calls over her shoulder as she walks away, after her sister.

"Bring beverages!" Ophelia tacks on, just before they step around the corner, out of sight.

For a second, I just stand there, totally frozen, wondering what the hell just happened.

Why do I feel like I've been bamboozled into something I never wanted in the first place?

THE FOLLOWING EVENING, I pace back and forth on the front steps of Cormorant House. It's hot outside, a muggy late-May evening. Sweat dots my brow. I'm wearing bright white sneakers with my favorite jean cut-off shorts — the ones with ripped hems I bought forever ago. They're a little tighter than they were last summer, riding high on my thighs, but I didn't have time to upend my closet in search of a looser pair. At least the dark green t-shirt is breathable, hanging loosely around my sides. The front bears an image of a howling wolf — Exeter's official mascot.

I glance at my watch.

7:07PM.

They're late.

A fissure of nerves spikes through me. Maybe they aren't coming. Maybe they were *never* coming. Maybe this was all just some elaborate prank to make me feel like an idiot and—

The outer gate buzzes.

I race to the intercom box embedded by the front door and

punch in the access code. A few moments later, a custom-painted bubblegum-pink Range Rover rolls up the circular driveway, braking to a halt at the bottom of the steps. The passenger window rolls down. Odette sticks her head out.

"Will you be my *Valentine?*" she sing-songs, grinning.

I roll my eyes, laughing as I jog down the steps. The plastic grocery bag swings with each step. I wince as its weight clangs against my kneecap.

"You brought beverages?" Ophelia asks, turning to face me once I'm settled in the back seat.

I hold up the bag. "Grapefruit seltzer."

The twins look at each other and burst into raucous laughter.

"She brought *seltzer!*" Odette wheezes.

"Cutest thing I've *ever* heard!" Ophelia snorts.

My brows lift. "Did I do something wrong? I can get regular water if you guys don't like bubbles..."

For whatever reason, this makes the twins laugh even harder.

"Don't worry, Josie." Odette's finally calmed down enough to speak. "You don't mind if we call you Josie, right?"

I sort of *do* mind, but I don't say anything. In my experience, when the popular kids pick a nickname for you, there's very little point in protesting.

"*Anyways...*" She fixes her lipgloss in her handheld mirror. "Like I was saying, don't worry about it — we brought extra."

"Check the YETI," Ophelia suggests, jerking her chin at the seat beside mine, where a large cooler rests. When I open it, my eyes widen. It's fully stocked with a dozen or so spiked lemonades.

Of course they meant alcoholic *beverages.*

"Oh," I murmur, feeling like an utter idiot. "I didn't realize—"

"Don't sweat it, honey." Odette glances over her shoulder at me. "Pass up a lemonade, will you?"

I pull out a bottle. It's cold with condensation as I hand it to her.

"Now crack one for yourself!" she orders, twisting off the cap. "We have to toast to the Wolves winning tonight! It's good luck."

I don't let myself think about the brutal hangover I experienced last time I put alcohol into my body. I don't let myself think about anything. Frankly, I'm tired of thinking. Tired of doing what everyone expects of me all the time. Tonight I just want to be a normal teenager for once.

Tonight, I just want to forget.

Clinking my bottle against Odette's, I twist off the cap, put it to my lips, and let a large gulp pour into my mouth. Flavors explode across my tongue — tart lemonade, sickly sweet sugar. The sharp after-burn of alcohol.

"'Atta girl!" Odette cheers, pumping her fist in the air.

I cough slightly, taking another large sip.

We roll through the exterior gates of Cormorant House, onto the main road. Ophelia meets my eyes in her rearview mirror as she accelerates. "Gorgeous house, by the way."

"Thanks." A thought occurs to me. "How did you guys even know I lived here?"

They look at each other briefly.

"Our Dad subscribes to Architectural Digest," Odette says finally. "There was that article a few years ago—"

Oh.

The photo spread.

How could I forget?

For a week straight, Cormorant House was a circus of florists and photographers and lighting consultants. Interior designers and historical society members and journalists. They catalogued the entire property, pouring over the most minute details. While they interviewed my parents at length, for the most part they ignored my presence — like I was a particularly well-mannered family pet, trained to sit nicely but never to speak.

The profile was eventually published alongside a picture of me and my parents on the front steps. It took about a zillion takes to get one with all of us smiling at the same time, my braces glinting in the sun. But when the magazine hit shelves six months later, the article's title was far more mortifying than my untimely orthodontia.

NEW ENGLAND'S OLD MONEY: BEHIND CLOSED DOORS AT CORMORANT HOUSE WITH THE INDOMINABLE VALENTINE CLAN

I found the whole thing so pretentious, I like to pretend it never happened.

"Right," I say slowly, taking another big sip of my lemonade. "The article."

"It's a stunning house." Ophelia's eyes flicker to mine again. At the next stop sign, she pulls a JUUL vaporizer from her center console and puffs on it twice. "You could have, like, a Gatsby-level party there."

Odette squeals. "Oh my god, *yes*! Fill the pool with champagne and swing from the chandeliers!"

"Not sure how my parents would feel about that..." I mutter.

Despite my protests, there's a certain allure in the idea. The thought of Vincent and Blair's faces if they walked in after their latest business trip to find fifty drunken teenagers rampaging through their picturesque estate...

"At least think about it," Ophelia encourages. "We still need a location for the prom after-party. Lee Park was supposed to host it, but his parents flipped after his last rager. Apparently someone fucked with his mom's koi pond."

"Did you say *after-party?*" My brows lift. "I thought prom was the party."

Odette giggles. "Oh, you innocent little flower. Everyone knows the after-party is more fun than some corny, school-sanctioned dance. The only reason to even attend is for an excuse to rent a limo and get all dressed up."

"Don't forget the corsages!" Ophelia's lips part to release a thin stream of vapor from one corner of her mouth. "And the competition for Prom Queen, of course."

"As if it's even a competition." Her twin rolls her eyes. "We all know Sienna is going to get all the votes. Who needs to stuff the ballot box when you've banged half the boys in our grade?"

Ophelia snorts. "True. But I don't care about a stupid crown anyway. My dress is Alexander McQueen. That's as close to royalty as I need to be on prom night."

Odette glances at me. "Did you pick out a dress yet?"

"Dress?" I grimace. "I don't even have a date."

Brakes screech. The Range Rover slams to a stop in the middle of the road as both twins turn fully around in their seats to face me. Their mouths are agape in identical expressions of horrified disbelief.

"Prom is two weeks away, Valentine," Ophelia says gravely.

"I know."

"Most girls locked in their dates ages ago," Odette informs me, equally grave. "We're going with a set of twins from St. John's."

I laugh. "Seriously? Twins with twins?"

"Cute, right?" Ophelia winks. "But honestly... we assumed Archer asked you."

"Totally assumed," Odette agrees.

The laughter withers on my tongue. "At one point, I

thought he might... but lately things have been so weird between us..."

Odette's nose scrunches up in thought. "Weird *how*, exactly?"

I shrug.

"Come on. Spill it." Ophelia puffs her vape again. Before I can answer, a car pulls up behind us, beeping angrily at the roadblock we've created. Unruffled, she merely rolls down her window and waves them onward. The dark sedan zips around the Range Rover with an angry squeal of rubber.

"Get out of the damn road!" the driver yells as he passes.

The twins appear unfazed.

"*Anyway*," Ophelia says, lips twisting. "You two hooked up, is that it? Ruined the sanctity of your friendship by finally screwing?"

"No! Absolutely not."

"It's fine. You can tell us. Everyone at school already thinks you two have been doing it for ages."

Great.

My teeth grit. "We didn't hook up."

"Never?"

"Never."

"Not even once?"

"Not even once." I sigh. "We're just friends!"

"Maybe you *were*. But at some point, one of you must have started wanting to be more." Ophelia shrugs. "That's the only explanation for the new awkwardness between you."

"It is not the *only* explanation!" I insist. "There are plenty of other reasons—"

"Oh my god!" Odette cuts me off in a gleeful tone. "You, like, totally love him! *Oh my god.* Look at her cheeks burning, O! Do you see it?"

Her twin nods. "Totally see it."

My cheeks flood with even more color. "*I don't love him.*"

"Look, it's okay. You don't have to lie. We won't tell anyone." Ophelia pauses, growing contemplative. "I am sorry, though. Falling for a friend is the worst kind of painful if they don't feel the same."

Odette nods. "Unrequited love... *ugh.* The angst. The torturous, torturous angst."

"For the last time," I practically growl. "I don't love Archer. He definitely does not love me. We're just—"

"Friends?" Ophelia finishes doubtfully. "*Right.*"

Odette's eyes are brimming with sympathy. "Have you told him how you feel?"

I glance sharply out the window. I suppose there's no use lying. They don't believe me anyway. "No," I murmur softly. "He doesn't know."

"And you think... he doesn't return your feelings?"

I shake my head. "Definitely not."

"But you'll never know for sure unless you tell him," Ophelia points out. "Maybe he's hiding his feelings too, because he's just as afraid to cross the line between friendship and... something more. Maybe he's scared you'll reject him and it'll ruin everything."

Her words tumble inside my head, stirring up feelings I'm not sure I'm equipped to process. Giving me foolish hope for something that's never going to happen.

"He slept with Sienna," I say bluntly, grounding myself back in cold reality. "At the party last weekend. I think that makes it pretty clear he doesn't want to be with me."

"Oh..." The twins cluck their sympathy. "We didn't know."

For a moment, the car is completely silent. I stare out the window, trying to keep a tight leash on my tears. I will not waste any more on a boy who doesn't deserve them.

"You know, this is *exactly* why we don't have any male

friends," Odette announces, shattering the quiet. "Lines get crossed. Feelings get hurt. Sexual tension gets in the way... Such a mess."

Her twin glances at her and snorts. "O, we don't have any male friends because we always sleep with them."

"That's true, too." Odette pouts against the glass rim of her lemonade bottle. It's almost empty. "Did Archer ask someone else to prom?"

I shake my head. "I don't think so."

"Is he planning to?"

"No idea."

"Hmmm." She tilts her head to the side. "Well, if he doesn't get his act together, we can definitely scrounge you up a date."

"You guys don't need to do that..."

The twins make eye contact. I listen in amazement as they fly through a roster of male names, their mouths moving rapid-fire.

"Chris Tomlinson?"

"Taking Sienna."

"Andy Hilton?"

"Taking June Woods."

"Steve Abbott?"

"Going with George Massey."

"Wait. What about Ryan Snyder?"

"Bringing that slut from St. Mary's."

"Damnit."

They persevere, running through practically every boy in our class. All of them already have dates or are deemed too weird to take me.

"It's okay, guys, really," I assure them, flinching as another car zips past us with an angry beep. "Forget about this. We should just go to the game—"

Odette's expression has grown dark. "Don't worry, Valentine. It's short notice, but between our connections at St. John's and Deerfield...."

"And Pingree!" Ophelia interjects.

"Mmm. Pingree, too." Odette smiles reassuringly. "We'll find you someone hot and hunky, who fills out a suit like Brad Pitt at The Oscars. Don't worry. You can even ride in our limo! There's plenty of room. We rented a stretch."

Ophelia leans forward. "A pink one, obviously."

They both giggle.

I swallow another sip of my lemonade to quell the nervous butterflies swarming in my stomach. "Look... it's super sweet of you guys to offer, but I'm not even sure I want to go to prom."

The silence is deafening.

"You have to go to prom." Odette sounds more serious than I've ever heard. "It's, like, the pinnacle of your senior year experience. A night you'll always remember. You can't just skip it."

"Non-negotiable," Ophelia agrees.

Looking at them, I realize this is a fight I'm not going to win. More surprisingly, it's a fight I don't desire to win.

I've never had female friends before. Ever. And the thought of doing stereotypical girly things — getting ready together, styling our hair, sharing makeup, gossiping over our dates — actually sounds rather...

Lovely.

I've spent all six years at Exeter terrified to be myself around my peers. Especially the female ones. I always felt somehow insignificant next to them. An ugly duckling, masquerading amidst a flock of perfect swans. But as I stare at the Wadell twins, who've now gone out of their way to include me in their plans on more than one occasion... I begin to wonder if most of that insignificance was a figment of my imagination.

Maybe the popular kids didn't exile me to the bottom of the

social totem pole; maybe I exiled myself, rather than risk letting anyone besides Archer get to know the real me.

"Well?" Odette prompts.

"What's it gonna be?" Ophelia nudges.

I hold up my hands in surrender. "Okay, okay. I'll go to the stupid prom."

They both scream so loud, it makes my eardrums ache. Turning back to face the steering wheel, Ophelia resumes driving toward Exeter. Odette and I finish our lemonades, exchanging our empty bottles for full ones. We dance in our seats to the beat of a new Ellie Goulding song blasting from the speakers.

"Tonight is going to be so much fun!" Odette yells over the music, rolling down her window and howling like a wolf. "*Ahh-wooooo! Ah-wooooooo!* Go Wolfpack!"

"Stop it, O!" her sister chides. "You're gonna get me pulled over!"

But Odette is on a roll. "*Ah-wooo! Ah-wooooo!* Come on, guys! Howl with me!"

I shake my head, laughing at her ridiculousness.

The stadium lights come into view in the distance; we're nearly there. When we pull into the parking lot, every square foot is jammed full of excited Exeter fans in green and black attire, tailgating in their truck beds with coolers, lawn chairs, and portable grills. We roll slowly down the rows, looking for a free spot.

Odette howls out her window at a cluster of freshman boys. "*Ah-wooo!*"

They howl right back at her, even louder. The group beside them soon joins in. And then the group beside *them* adds their voices to the braying chorus. Howls spread across the entire parking lot in a domino effect, until the sky is a vibration of lupine enthusiasm.

"*Ah-woooo!*"

"*Ah-wooooo!*"

"*Go Wolfpack!*"

Ophelia and I roll down our windows.

"*AH-WOOOO!*"

I scream as loud as I can, my howls harmonizing with hundreds of excited Exeter fans. By the time we locate an empty spot, I'm having so much fun, I've almost forgotten why I was dreading coming to this game in the first place.

Almost.

CHAPTER FOURTEEN

ARCHER

"GET your head out of the clouds, Reyes!" Coach yells from the dugout as we run back onto the field to finish the final inning. "Let's show these boys that fastball you've been working on all season long! No more free passes!"

He sounds frustrated.

Hell, *I'm* frustrated. I'm playing like a Little Leaguer instead of a future MLB rookie. My pitches are uneven. My pacing is off. I've let more batters hit tonight than any other game of the season.

The stakes are too high for these kind of mistakes. Everything is riding on my ability to deliver consistent wins in front of the scouts.

My future.

My way out.

My dream.

Get it together, Archer.

Perhaps sensing my nerves, the crowd roars encouragement from the bleachers. If I search the blur of faces, I know I'll see my parents out there somewhere. Pa munching Cracker Jacks, cursing under his breath each time I mess up a pitch; Ma clutching her rosary, praying for a miracle.

But I won't see the one person I need to the most.

I grip the ball tighter, summoning focus. No matter how I try, I can't seem to locate it. I don't know what the hell is wrong with me tonight.

Actually... I do.

My head is a downright mess — even worse than it was on Tuesday, after Rico and Barboza's unexpected visit. I think I was still in a certain amount of shock when they walked out of my house. Because instead of freaking out, falling apart... I simply tossed my duct tape bindings deep in the garbage pail where my parents wouldn't see them, changed into my baseball uniform, and drove to the field.

I played, but my heart wasn't in it — throwing pitches on autopilot, just trying to make it through each inning without thinking too much. And... trying not to notice the blonde head missing from its normal spot in the bleachers.

We squeaked out a narrow victory, thanks in no part to my efforts. Coach assured me everyone has an off game, now and again. The guys on the team slapped my shoulders in the dugout, telling me to let it roll off.

Little did they know, baseball was the last thing on my mind.

That night, I lay in bed feeling unsafe in my own home for the first time, flinching in the darkness at each creaking floor board and falling tree branch. I held my aluminum bat beneath the sheets, finding some small solace in the makeshift weapon.

But what good is a bat against a gunshot?

I couldn't bring myself to close my eyes, afraid of what I'd find when they opened again. Instead, I prowled the house, checking the locks a hundred times. As if any lock could actually keep the danger out.

They got in before.
They can do it again.

A room away, my parents slept on, blissfully unaware.

As the night marched onward toward dawn, my eyes grew as heavy as the heart inside my chest; my soul as exhausted as my body. The only thing in the world that I truly needed... the only thing that might offer some reprieve from the encroaching darkness... was the one thing I couldn't risk reaching for.

Jo.

All I wanted was to run to our spot in the boathouse. Straight to her. To wrap my arms around her warmth, pull her against my chest, and let her absorb all my pain and fear and hopelessness. To take comfort in her soft whispers.

It's okay, Arch.
We'll figure it out.
Together.
Like we always do.

But I couldn't. The thought of what might've happened if she'd been with me when those assholes were here... if they'd laid a hand on her instead of me...

You seem pretty tight with that girl, Rico's voice haunts me. *The blonde with the legs.*

My mental state only devolved as the week went on, sleeplessness and stress driving me to distraction. At school, I was edgy. Irritated. Snapping at anyone stupid enough to come near me. At practice, I was so preoccupied Coach Hamm called it quits early, telling me to rest up before the big game against St. John's Prep.

Not that it did much good.

Here we are, final inning, and the score is dangerously close. 7-6 — a meager one point lead over our rivals. Which is laughable, really. This should be an easy victory. A walk in the fucking park. The Exeter Wolves are ranked first in our division; St. John's didn't even qualify for playoffs. And yet, they're handing me my own ass on a silver platter with each play. Hitting balls that any other day should be strikes.

There's only one person to blame.

Myself.

I'm off my game.

If I can just manage to keep St. John's from scoring any points this last turn at bat, Exeter will win — by a sliver, sure, but I'll take it if it means salvaging our undefeated record.

Normally, striking out their final batters would be a simple task. Tonight, it feels more than daunting. The fastballs I'm throwing are sluggish in comparison to my normal speeds. My jaw clenches tighter as the final inning ticks on, tension twisting my insides into knots.

Hit.

Hit.

Hit.

The first three batters send my pitches soaring into the sky. Before I know it, the bases are loaded. Primed for a home run, which will easily bring them into the lead.

God damnit.

They're going to score.

They're going to win.

St. John's beating us would an unimaginable upset. For the team, for the town, for me. When the next player steps up to the plate, a confident smile on his face, an unfamiliar sensation ripples through me.

Fear.

Fear that I won't be able to halt their momentum and give us a last minute victory. Fear that I'm not half the player everyone in the crowd seems to think I am.

I've never been insecure in my abilities before. Baseball has always been the one thing I could depend on. Whatever else life threw at me — family teetering on the edge of poverty, pretentious classmates, brother with a penchant for fucking up everything he touches — it didn't matter. Because I always had baseball.

My ace in the hole.

My ticket out of this life.

I don't know who I am if I'm not standing on the pitcher's mound, ball in my hand, crowd cheering madly at my back. The thought that it could all disappear is more frightening than a gun in my face. It shakes me down to the very core.

I throw again — a curveball, this time.

It's a foul, nearly hitting the batter. He jumps back to avoid being slammed in the leg, glaring at me from beneath his helmet.

Shit.

The crowd groans their disappointment.

The umpire looks at me warningly.

Coach Hamm calls for a time out.

My teammates gather in a huddle by home plate, the outfielders panting from their long jog. I can't quite meet their eyes, afraid I'll see disappointment there.

I'm letting them down.

I'm letting myself down.

"Reyes, what's up with you this week?" Coach asks bluntly. "I've never seen you play like this."

I blow out a breath. "I'm sorry, Coach. Guess I'm a bit distracted."

"Then find a way to focus. I don't care how." His hand clamps down on my shoulder. "You have to strike him out. It's our only shot, here."

"I know, Coach."

"I don't need to remind you that there are scouts in the

crowd tonight, son. Half the town's out there. They expect a win. So do I. So do your teammates."

"I know."

"Maybe we should put in the backup pitcher," Snyder suggests from across the huddle. "Just because Reyes has his period doesn't mean the rest of us should suffer the consequences."

Several of my teammates snigger.

My jaw clenches in fury.

God, I'd like to punch that smug smile right off his face.

"Why don't you leave the calls to me, Snyder," Coach scolds. "Focus on your own plays. You haven't made a single out this entire game."

Snyder snorts. "No disrespect, Coach, but it's tough to do that with Reyes giving up more hits than a battered housewife."

"You want to see a real hit?" I hiss, starting forward with full intentions of punching him in the face. That would put a stop to his trash-talk.

Thankfully, Chris steps in front of me, blocking my path before I can do something that would get me tossed from the game.

"Not worth it, dude," he mutters through the cage of his catcher's mask. "Let it go."

"Look, we're getting out asses handed to us out there!" Coach says, exasperation plain in his voice. "The last thing we need is infighting. I don't want to hear the words *backup pitcher* again. Is that clear?"

My teammates are silent.

"Win or lose, the final score doesn't rest on Reyes' shoulders alone." Coach Hamm glares at each player in turn, his brow furrowed beneath the brim of his emerald green cap. "This is a team. So get back out there and start showing me some damn teamwork."

"Yes, Coach!" we all bark in unison.

"Tag them out. Hold the score. Win the game."

"Yes, Coach!" we repeat, louder.

He holds out his fist. "Wolfpack on three."

We all extend our mitts into the center of the huddle. As a group, we chant, "One... two... three... *WOLFPACK!*"

My head hangs low as I walk back to the pitcher's mound. Restless energy radiates through my every nerve ending. Taking my position, I stare at the dirt caked on my cleats. There's so much pressure resting on my shoulders, it's difficult to straighten them back to full height.

The crowd has gone silent, waiting for the game to resume. Waiting for me to throw again. I can feel the weight of their eyes, the density of their anticipation thickening the warm summer air. The sun is starting to set, basking the entire stadium in gold. Behind me, in the outfield, the scoreboard looms menacingly, an irrefutable reminder of the stakes.

HOME: 7

AWAY: 6

Final inning.

Zero outs.

Bases loaded.

I grit my teeth and try to shut out the background noise. Ryan Snyder's smug presence at first base. Coach's furrowed brow. My teammates watching from the dugout. The scouts lined up along the fence. My parents' worried faces in the crowd.

It all fades into a distant hum.

But no matter what I do, I can't quite eradicate the noise inside my soul. I can't erase the constant feeling that my life has spiraled so far out of control, I might never get it on track again. It's the sort of distraction no amount of deep breathing can soothe.

My grip tightens on the ball. My eyes narrow on Chris' mitt behind home plate. I'm about to throw when, in the hush that's fallen over the field, I suddenly hear it — a voice, ringing out into the night, clear as the water in the shallows of the cove beyond the boathouse.

"YOU'VE GOT THIS, ARCHER!"

My head snaps up, whipping toward the bleachers. I scan the crowd. It takes a minute, but I find her. Everyone else is sitting down, but she's on her feet, standing tall in the front row. Her long blonde hair hangs loose around her shoulders. Her legs stretch on for a mile in those skimpy cut-off shorts. And her eyes...

They're locked on mine.

She's here.

She came.

Even after I was such an asshole.

Even though I don't deserve it.

When our gazes meet, a slow smile spreads across her face — one reassuring enough to warm me from the inside out. One that seeps into the marrow of my bones and undercuts every bit of anxiety churning through my system.

"YOU CAN DO THIS!" Jo yells across the distance, not seeming to care that the people around her are turning to stare. I know how much she hates to be the center of attention. But that doesn't stop her tonight. "SHOW 'EM WHAT YOU'RE MADE OF, REYES!"

God, I miss her.

She's standing right there, but I miss her so much I can barely breathe. My throat feels like it's about to close up. I can't yell back to her; I manage a nod, so she knows I'm listening.

She nods back, her smile stretching wider. Beside her, the Wadell twins shoot to their feet, two platinum bookends.

"*Ah-woooo!*" they howl in unison. "*Go Archer! Go Wolfpack!*"

Before long, the entire Exeter section of the bleachers is cheering. Howling like wolves. The sound swells as everyone joins in. I'm sure my parents are somewhere in the mob, screaming their heads off, but I can't take my eyes off Jo long enough to look.

"*AH-WOOO!*" she howls, loud as anyone.

When I turn away to face home plate, it's with a refreshed sense of purpose. I feel steadier. In control of myself for the first time since Tuesday. My attention hones in on the catcher's mitt, pinpointing the precise spot where I need the ball to break. Tracing up the leather seams, finding my target.

One solitary stitch.

My grip tightens.

My arm cocks back.

My knee hikes up.

A perfect fastball blasts into Tomlinson's glove.

"Strike!" the umpire calls.

Then another.

"Strike two!"

One more.

"You're out!"

The crowd roars.

A smile twists the corners of my lips as the next batter moves into position at the plate.

Time to take back what's mine.

CHAPTER FIFTEEN

JOSEPHINE

AFTER THE WOLVES win the game, the senior class is ready to celebrate. For good reason: it's been years since Exeter has had an undefeated season; even longer since we've been headed into the playoffs with strong odds favoring a State Championship title. And it's all because of rockstar pitcher Archer Reyes.

I can't control the pride that swells my heart nor the stupid smile that tugs at the corners of my mouth as I watch him walk off the field surrounded by his teammates, the crowd roaring his name at top volume. The urge to run to his side is so strong, I have to look away.

Hundreds of shoes clank against the metal bleachers as spectators flood toward the exits. Ophelia and Odette walk behind me, chattering excitedly about the party. I don't pay much attention; I'm lost in a daze, my thoughts distracted. I can't stop thinking about the way Archer looked at me during the final inning. The way his slumped shoulders went straight. The way his face lit up when he saw me there, in the crowd.

I called his name and he came alive.

If I had any sense of self-preservation, I would've kept silent. I'm under no obligation to cheer him on. Not after last weekend. He made it quite clear he wants to fight his battles without any help from me.

And yet...

Watching him struggle inning after inning... Watching him begin to lose faith in himself with the entire town there to witness it...

Torture.

No matter how angry I am at him, no matter how much he's hurt me, I can't stand to see Archer in pain. I'd break my own heart a thousand times rather than watch his shatter.

Is that what it is to love someone? I wonder. *Sacrificing your own feelings to protect theirs?*

I'm so caught up in my thoughts as I cross the parking lot, I don't notice Miguel and Flora until I've bumped straight into them. They're parked one row over from the Range Rover.

"Josephine!" There are tears in Flora's eyes, but she's smiling. "Isn't it just wonderful? Undefeated!"

I smile back. "You must be so proud."

Miguel's eyes are red-rimmed. He manages a choked grunt. "Hell of a season they had, huh?"

Reaching out, I squeeze his arm. "Hell of a son you've got."

He looks up at the sky, blinking rapidly.

Flora grabs me in a warm hug and whispers in my ear. "Thank you, for what you did — for calling out to him. You're always there whenever he's struggling."

I clear my throat awkwardly. "What are friends for?"

"I don't know what he'd do without you."

"I'm sure he'll be just fine."

Pulling back, she peers into my eyes. As usual, I'm sure she sees far more than she lets on, but she doesn't say anything. She merely pats my cheek and murmurs, "Don't stay out too late celebrating, *mija*."

"I won't."

With a nod, she turns back to Miguel. He winks at me before they turn to leave. He slides his arm around her shoulders, steering her gently through the crowd toward their junky old truck — stunningly out of place in an ocean of designer vehicles. My heart pangs as I watch them. They fit perfectly together, their edges aligned like two puzzle pieces.

"Were those Archer's *parents*?" Odette asks from behind me, her voice laced with incredulity.

I jolt in surprise as I turn back to the twins. I'd forgotten they were there. "Oh. Um... yep, that's them."

"Huh." Ophelia's eyes are narrowed on Miguel's truck. "Not exactly what I expected."

My spine stiffens. "What exactly did you expect?"

Odette giggles. "Personally, I always assumed Archer was the son of Mexican drug lords or something."

"His family is Puerto Rican."

"Whatever." She rolls her eyes. "I'm just saying, I was picturing Pablo Escobar... not the guy who cleans Pablo Escobar's pool. You know what I mean."

"*No*, actually," I say with overt enunciation. My rage is boiling to the surface, threatening to spill over. "I really don't know what you mean, Odette."

Her lips twist into a pout. "*Whatever.*"

"Don't get your panties in a bunch, Josie." Ophelia sweeps her bangs out of her eyes and starts walking. Her voice drifts back over her shoulder. "By the way, Ryan texted me earlier — he can't drive you to the party anymore. Apparently, he wants to do shrooms with Andy beforehand or something. So you're coming with us."

"Oh." I take a steadying breath. "Then maybe I should just go home. As long as you guys don't mind dropping m—"

"Don't be crazy!" Odette cuts me off. Her arm loops through mine as she drags me toward the bright pink SUV. "You're coming to the party. Everyone is going to be there!"

"*Everyone*," Ophelia echoes.

My teeth grind together as I climb into the backseat. We wind through the tiny downtown area, blasting music as we cruise past the railroad station and circle the harbor. Behind the wheel, Ophelia puffs her vaporizer and bobs her head to the beat. In the passenger seat, Odette chugs a spiked lemonade and howls out the windows until her throat is hoarse.

I try to muster some of my earlier excitement, but it's vanished on the wind. I stare at the twins, seeing them in a different light than I did mere moments ago.

Ophelia's judgmental stare.

Odette's offhand racism.

No matter how many times I tell myself they don't mean anything by it... that they're not bad people, merely products of their own privileged upbringing... I can't shake the apprehension that's blossomed within me.

I stare resolutely out my window, wishing I was home in my room, sketching out a new sewing pattern instead of on my way to a kegger with people I'm not sure I have anything in common with anymore.

The party's pounding bass is audible two full blocks before we turn onto Chris Tomlinson's street. There are at least ten cars already outside, spilling out of the driveway onto the lawn. The second we're parked, the twins bolt for the house, disappearing inside in a cloud of smoke and perfume. Clearly, they're eager to locate cold beverages and cute boys as soon as humanly possible.

For a while, I hover on the front porch, staring at the door like a little kid mustering the courage to enter a haunted house. People arrive in an endless stream, carrying cases of beer brazenly across the lawn. No one is worried about underage drinking tonight. Chris' father is the Chief of Police; his parties never get busted.

I don't see Archer's truck anywhere. I suppose it's possible he caught a lift with one of his teammates and is already inside chugging beer with the rest of them... but I doubt it. I know him too well. Archer Reyes enjoys being in control. He doesn't like to rely on anyone, for anything.

Not even me.

My lungs feel so tight, I can barely pull in air. I'm overcome with the desperate urge to run — away from this party, away from the complications of my own life. I'm about to turn and bolt down the stairs when a voice startles me into stillness.

"Not thinking of bailing on me, are you?"

I flinch in surprise as an arm slides around my waist. "Ryan! You scared me."

"Sorry. Didn't mean to sneak up on you."

He grins and takes a long sip of the beer in his hand. His long blond hair is still damp from a locker-room shower. He's ditched his muddy uniform in favor of a white button down and a pair of navy shorts. He looks like he's on his way to a casting call seeking an 'All-American boy-next-door.'

"What are you doing out here by yourself?" he asks. "I've been looking for you inside."

"Just getting a little fresh air, I guess."

His brows arch doubtfully. "Hiding is more like it."

"Fine, so, maybe I was hiding." I make a small gap between my thumb and pointer finger. "Just a *little* bit."

"No more of that. We're celebrating!" He pounds his chest with his free hand. "WOLFPACK! *Ah-wooo!* Undefeated, baby!"

I laugh. "A momentous occasion."

"I'm rolling on shrooms right now, so I can't tell if you're teasing me or not." He grins wider. "But I've decided I don't really care. Get your ass inside the house, girl. We have beer pong to play and memories to make."

Before I can protest, he grabs my hand, laces his fingers with mine, and tugs me through the front door.

FORTY MINUTES LATER, my buzz has completely worn off and I'm ready to go home. Ryan, on the other hand, has gone from tipsy to trashed in a remarkably short span of time thanks to the six beers he chugged during our singular game of pong. Either that, or the mushrooms are taking full effect.

It's hard to say for sure.

"You're so hot," he breathes against the shell of my ear as he steers me down a short hallway, deeper into the house. With his chest pressed to my back, his steps weave a jagged course. He keeps is hands tight on my hips. "So hot."

"Thanks," I mutter, looking around for the twins. They're nowhere to be seen. Probably off somewhere, flirting with cute boys. I wish they'd resurface. I want to leave. Though, at this point, even if Ophelia would agree to drive me, I'm not sure she's sober enough to get behind the wheel.

I could always walk. It's only five miles...

At the end of the hallway, we pass the bathroom. There's a line of six girls waiting to use it — fixing their lipstick, taking selfies, scrolling social media. One of them is wiping tears, her mascara pooling in muddy streaks at the corners of her eyes. The sound of someone throwing up reverberates beneath the gap in the door.

I grimace and keep moving. Behind me, Ryan's body presses closer. His fingers stroke the denim of my cut-off shorts.

"Where are we going, Ryan?"

"*Shhh.* You'll see."

His hands grip my hipbones tighter as he guides me across a threshold, into the sunroom on the side of the house. It's all glass walls and wicker furniture, designed to overlook the terraced yard and topiary. This time of night, the lawn outside is pure black — an ebony canvas stretching toward the tree line.

The sunroom is both quieter and emptier than the rest of the house. Only a handful of other people are in here — couples, mostly, hooking up against the walls, their hands roving in the darkness. I feel my cheeks heat as Andy Hilton slips his hands down Candi Ciccirelli's pants. She throws her head back as he sucks on her neck, moaning without a hint of self-consciousness.

I glance sharply away.

On the far side of the space, a group is huddled around the coffee table, snorting lines of something. They're totally in shadow, their faces indiscernible in the darkness. Every so often, the flare of a lighter sparks a bong back to life. Their conversation is a hushed, indecipherable murmur.

"What are we doing in here?" I whisper to Ryan.

"I just wanted to be alone with you for a second."

"I think we should go back to—" My words break off as he pulls me down onto a built-in window seat in a small alcove in the corner. I land on his lap. He's breathing hard as his arms fold me against his body. He's warm as a furnace.

"Ryan—"

"God, you're so hot," he tells me for the third time. His right hand slides around to cup my ass, his fingertips grazing the bare skin below the hem of my shorts. His left reaches for the bottom of my t-shirt and begins to slide up my stomach, toward my breasts.

I start to squirm. "Ryan, wait—"

"I can't wait." His lips skim my earlobe. "I can't think straight around you."

"You can't think straight because you're drunk."

"So are you."

"I'm not, actually." I grab his wrist to stop him from feeling me up. "Let's go back to the other room, Ryan."

"But I like it in here."

"Well, I don't." I struggle to extract myself from his arms. He's holding me too tight. My heart starts to pound as his fingers wander toward the button of my shorts, panic hijacking all my senses.

I shouldn't have let him lead me in here.

The belated realization does little to help me.

"Come on, baby..."

"Ryan, I think you have the wrong idea—"

"Don't be a tease, Valentine. These tight little shorts are driving me crazy. Here, I'll prove it to you..." He grabs my hand and presses it against his crotch. Through his shorts, I can feel the firm length of his erection. "See how much I want you?"

"*Stop!*"

I wrench my hand from his grip and elbow him sharply in the stomach. When he gasps, his hold loosens enough for me to wriggle free. I find my feet and start for the door, pulse thudding far too fast inside my veins.

"Valentine! Come back!"

I don't stop moving.

"Are you shitting me right now?" Ryan's on his feet, following me in large, staggering strides. He grabs my arm and yanks me backward, hard enough to make my eyes water.

Before I know it, I'm pinned against a wall with his body caging me in.

"Let me go!"

"Let you go?" He snorts, a sound of utter disbelief. His expression is full of rage. "You've been leading me on all week!"

"I have not." My cheeks heat with hurt and humiliation. I can't believe things have gone so wrong, so fast.

I can't believe I ever thought this guy actually liked me.

"Give me a break, Valentine. You're not as innocent as you look. I'm sure you and Reyes have been doing the nasty for years—"

I flinch as if he's struck me. Craning my neck, I look for an escape route to the door but I'm trapped on all sides. Everyone else in the room is either too stoned to notice what's going on or too selfish to intervene.

"I don't understand why you're being like this." Ryan's voice has gone cold, stripped of all its earlier charm. He presses against me, driving my spine into the wall. He's still hard. "Stop blue-balling me, baby."

I plant my hands against his chest and shove, desperate to keep him at arm's length. "Leave me alone, Ryan. I mean it."

"You don't really want me to leave you alone... I know you don't..."

"You're being an asshole."

"And you're being a cock-tease!" He steps back a stride, scowling. "You know what? You're not even worth this much effort. You're *nothing*. Nothing but Reyes' sloppy seconds."

I don't even think about it; my hand moves of its own accord, slapping him across the face hard enough to leave a mark.

He reels backward, fury overtaking his expression. "You fucking *bitch!*"

He's so angry, I'm certain he's going to strike me. Unable to escape, I steel myself against it. My eyes shut, waiting for the blow.

It never comes.

Instead, Ryan's body jerks backward, a puppet on pulled strings. In the darkness, I hear a stranger's voice. Low. Intent. Cold enough to make every hair on my neck stand on end.

"Here's a tip, kid. When a girl asks you to stop..." The stranger pauses. "You fucking stop."

When I open my eyes and see the man standing there, holding Ryan in a chokehold with tattooed arms, his face etched in lines of pure, unadulterated wrath... my mouth falls open in surprise. Because my savior isn't a stranger at all. I haven't seen him in almost three years... but I'd recognize those eyes anywhere.

Burnt caramel.

Burning with fury.

Just like his younger brother's.

Jaxon's mouth twists in greeting as our gazes tangle together. "Long time no see, Josephine."

CHAPTER SIXTEEN

ARCHER

WE ROLL up to Tomlinson's house two hours after the game. The detour to pick up the keg from Jason Samborn's older brother took far longer than expected. From the looks of it, we're the last people in the whole goddamn town to arrive.

Four guys pile out of the bed of my truck the second I shut the engine. Lee Park helps Samborn hoist the keg toward the front door, staggering beneath its weight. George Massey and Steve Abbott follow, shoving each other playfully on the front walk.

The Tomlinson residence looks like a 'single family home' stock photo, built in a cookie-cutter, upper-middle-class style. There's a white picket fence and a tree swing in the front yard, for god's sake. Everything is color-coordinated in safe neutral tones; the camouflage of suburbia.

Nothing Baby Boomers enjoy more than a nice beige.

Inside, half the senior class is already in full party mode. Translation: half the senior class is already well on their way to wasted. Music blasts from the speakers — some antiseptic pop song I don't recognize. Sienna and two of her minions are standing on the coffee table, shaking their asses to the beat, putting on a show for anyone willing to watch.

Several of my teammates appear more than willing. They ogle from their spots on the sectional, sipping frothy cups of beer, their eyes glued to Sienna's body. When she sees me walk in, she winks one heavily-lashed eye in my direction and blows me a kiss.

I keep moving.

"Yo!" Tomlinson yells from the kitchen as we make our way deeper into the house. "You guys finally made it! Bring the backup keg in here, will you? The first one is already tapped."

I scan the scene, eyes sweeping from one dark corner of the party to the other. It's the standard crowd — thirty or so jocks and cheerleaders, the odd band geek or student council member mixed in for extra flavor. A small group is playing flip-cup on the kitchen table. A few couples are making out against the walls. Several people have already spilled out onto the patio, stripping down to their underwear and jumping into the hot tub.

I spot the Wadell twins shooting pool in the adjacent billiards room, a flock of boys surrounding them. Their platinum bobs practically glow in the dark as they drape themselves across the green felt, short skirts flashing hot pink underwear every time they bend over. They're firing balls into pockets with remarkable precision, given the fact that there's a snowflake's chance in hell either of them is sober enough to see straight.

The twins party harder than most guys twice their size.

"Archie!" they squeal in unison as I step into the room. Promptly shoving their pool sticks into the nearest onlookers' hands, they bounce over to me. Each hooks an elbow with one of mine, so I'm fully sandwiched.

"Don't call me that," I grumble.

"Oh, *you*." Twin A swats me on the arm. "Always so very *grouchy*."

"Seriously, downright *grumpy*," Twin B concurs.

I fight the urge to jerk away from them. I need their intel. "Where's Jo?"

"What's it to you?" Twin A asks.

"Yeah, why do you even care?" Twin B adds.

I glance from one to the other. Frankly, I haven't the foggiest idea who's who. I've never been able to tell them apart, even after six years of classes together.

Directing my gaze at Twin A, I take a shot in the dark. "Odette, where's Jo?"

"I'm Ophelia!"

"Sorry. *Ophelia*, where's Jo?"

"She's busy."

My brows lift. "What the fuck does that mean?"

They shrug in perfect sync.

Annoyed, I extract myself from their arms and back up a pace. "Look, I'm not interested in whatever game you two are playing here. Just tell me where my friend is."

Odette's face scrunches into a prissy expression. "From what we hear, calling the two of you *friends* is no longer accurate."

I stiffen. "Excuse me?"

"Josie told us you two are barely speaking, these days," Ophelia informs me with a bit too much satisfaction. "So why would we tell you where she is? I doubt she wants you showing up, ruining her night."

Odette harrumphs her agreement. "Apparently, you've ruined quite enough already."

"Since when does Jo confide anything in the two of you?" I ask skeptically. It's hard to imagine Josephine Valentine has a single thing in common with either of them.

"Since *now*." Ophelia smirks. "What are you, like, jealous she's finally got someone besides you to hang out with?"

"More like concerned. I know how much trouble you get yourselves into."

Last summer, Odette had her license revoked within weeks of receiving it after she totaled two cars while high on Adderall; in the winter, Ophelia got caught cheating on the SATs and had to bribe her way into Wesleyan with an astronomical donation, courtesy of her parents. They're the kind of kids who grew up with so much money, '*struggle*' was just a word in the dictionary.

I guess mistakes don't really have repercussions when your father is a billionaire.

Ophelia rolls her eyes. "Oh, please, Archer. Just because you've spent your whole life putting Josie on a pedestal doesn't mean we're required to."

They're calling her Josie? I bet she hates that.

"She's not some fragile relic to be viewed from six feet away. She is entitled to have some fun." Odette runs a finger down my chest. Her glossy lips are slightly parted as she holds my stare. "Maybe you should try it sometime." She glances coyly at her twin. "We can be *really* fun. Isn't that right, O?"

I grab her wrist and fling it away from me. "Knock it off."

"Touchy, touchy."

"Josie's our friend. And you'd better get use to it." Ophelia pulls a compact vaporizer pen from her cleavage and takes a puff. "Because we protect our friends from douchey boys who don't appreciate them."

My patience is wearing dangerously thin. "How much I appreciate Jo is really none of your business."

They shrug in unison. "It is if you want to know where she went."

Oh, for fuck's sake.

"I do appreciate her," I growl. "More than you'll ever know."

Odette leans in. "Then why have you been ignoring her existence the past few weeks?"

"And why didn't you ask her to prom?" Ophelia jumps in. "Now she's totally dateless on extremely short notice!"

My brows furrow in confusion. Jo doesn't care about school dances. She once told me she'd rather gouge her own eyes out than attend one. Last month, she said the very sight of ticket stands popping up around the halls gave her — and I quote — *worse nausea than a drunken cheerleader swaying to tacky slow songs on a party cruise around the Atlantic.*

Needless to say, the news that she wants me to ask her — badly enough to mention it to the Wadell twins, of all people — is making my mind spin.

"But..." I shake my head to clear it. "Jo doesn't care about prom."

"You idiot!" Odette smacks my arm. "Of course she does! Every girl cares about her senior prom. She's just playing it cool. Probably because the person she wants to go with hasn't asked her yet."

Ophelia shoots me a pointed look. "That would be *you*, dumbass."

I rub the back of my neck and exhale sharply. "I didn't realize."

"That you're a dumbass?"

"That she wanted to go," I grunt.

Odette giggles. "So... does that mean you're going to ask her?"

"Not sure how that decision concerns anyone except Jo."

"Um, because if you *aren't* asking her, we're going to find her a different date," Ophelia informs me, waving her phone in my face. "A hot one. We've already texted her picture to, like, ten potential guys from Pingree and St. John's Prep."

I glance up at the ceiling, wishing like hell I'd never started this conversation. I speak through clenched teeth. "I can't ask her anything if you don't tell me where she went."

The twins look at each other. Finally, Ophelia rolls her eyes and mutters, "We don't know where she went. She left with some guy."

"She *left*?"

"Mhm. She said he was giving her a ride home."

My pulse kicks into higher gear. "When?"

"Like... thirty minutes ago, maybe?"

"What guy? Snyder?"

Odette shakes her head. "No, Ryan got wasted within, like, five minutes of getting here. Bad batch of mushrooms, I guess. He's passed out on a patio lounger."

The relief I feel is short-lived. "If she's not with Snyder, who the fuck is she with?"

"We already told you, we don't know! We've never seen this guy before." Ophelia puffs on her vape. Her eyes are bloodshot. "He was pretty sexy, though."

Christ.

"You two claim you're friends with Jo now," I snap. "If that was actually the case, you'd be looking out for her. Not letting her leave with some random guy."

"We're her friends, not her mother." Odette rolls her eyes. "Loosen up, Archie."

"Fuck you, Odette."

"*Rude!*" Tossing her hair dramatically, she turns her back on me and stomps over to the pool table.

Ophelia lingers a moment longer, staring at me. Her head tilts in contemplation. "The guy she left with... he looked a lot like you, now that I think about it." She pauses to take another hit of her JUUL. "Do you happen to have a brother?"

The air vacates my lungs in a panicked gust.

———

I RACE HOME as fast as I can. I don't worry about getting pulled over. All my thoughts are reserved for Jaxon.

Jaxon and Jo.

Together.

If he lays a finger on her, I swear to God...

Five miles has never felt quite so far.

My foot presses harder against the accelerator. With a white-knuckled grip on my steering wheel, I blow through a stop sign. I take turns on two wheels, ignoring every speed limit and school zone.

At the front gates of Cormorant House, my brakes screech to a stop with a shower of pea stone. Leaning half out my window, I punch in the access code with impatient fingers. As soon as the wrought-iron swings wide, I floor it once more, barreling onto the property like my life depends on it.

Like Jo's life depends on it.

Beneath my boiling anxiety, a deep rage simmers. I'm so furious, I can barely see straight. After all I've done to keep her out of harm's way... Jaxon comes along and drags her into it without thinking twice.

I shouldn't be surprised — he's never given much thought to anyone's interests except his own. Never given much thought to anything, really, except where his next fix is coming from.

Don't get me wrong, I do love my brother. I never blamed him for his addiction. After all, he was no more aware than any of us that a shoulder injury at a JV soccer game would wind up being the gateway to a world of pharmaceuticals. He had no idea, as he swallowed down his doctor-approved Vicodin, that he'd crave the high it delivered long after his prescription ran out and his pain was gone.

The problem is, addicts don't take drugs for physical pain. They take it to soothe something deeper inside, where no one else can see.

I know that.

I don't judge him for it.

I would forgive him almost anything.

I would absolve him of whatever he did to hurt me.

But not to her.

Because if he harms a single hair on Josephine Valentine's head... I'll kill him with my bare hands.

First, though, I need to find him.

My parents are at the cottage; I doubt he'd go there. I head for the main estate, slowing only slightly as I round the first bend of the circular driveway. Cormorant House comes into view, a dark silhouette in the distance.

My eyes move automatically to Jo's suite on the second floor. Her window is dark. In fact, every window in the mansion is dark. Even the porch light is off. The stairs sit in shadow when I pull up before them.

Maybe he took her somewhere else.

When I spot the empty maroon sedan parked beneath a tree on the side of the house, its paint chipping into patches of rust, I know that's not the case. It belongs to Jax; I'd stake my soul on it.

My pulse is erratic when I shut the engine and bolt from the truck. I bound up the steps in three giant strides. I can't think clearly enough to form a real plan. All I know is, I need to find Jo. To make sure she's all right. Whatever happens after that is a secondary concern.

I'm barely breathing as my hand closes over the front door handle and tugs.

Locked.

I begin to knock — tentatively, at first, then louder when a minute passes without answer.

"Jo!" I call, resting my forehead against the thick wood. I strain to hear any signs of life inside. "Jo, open up! It's me." My voice breaks. "It's Archer."

She's a light sleeper. She'd hear me knocking, I'm certain of it. So she's either ignoring me... or she's not here.

Where the hell did he take her?

Cursing under my breath, I pull out my phone and call her again. Like the last three times, it goes straight to voicemail. I jog around the terrace to try the back door, but it's locked as well. Cupping my hands around my eyes, I peer through the glass, into the dark kitchen. I can't see a damn thing.

"She's not in there," a voice says casually from behind me.

I go tense, my muscles turning to stone.

I know that voice.

Sucking in a deep breath, I spin around to face my brother. My hands curl into fists at my sides as I take in the sight of him. There are a few more tattoos decorating his arms than the last time I saw him, but otherwise he looks exactly the same.

Tousled hair. Furrowed brow. Sharp gaze.

"Jaxon."

"What — no welcome-home hug?" His lips twist. "Thought you'd be happy to see me, *hermanito*."

"I doubt that very much, seeing as last time you were home, I threw you out on your ass."

The memory of that night — when I caught him stealing money from our parents' stash of petty cash and tossed him out the front door, into the dirt — hangs heavily in the air between us. It always will. That's not the kind of encounter you ever truly move past.

"Oh, I remember." He takes a step closer. His eyes never shift from mine. "How could I forget such a moment of brotherly bonding?"

"Cut the shit, Jaxon. Where is she?"

"Your precious Jo? Why?" He laughs. "Don't tell me you think I'm capable of hurting her."

"I don't know what you're capable of, Jax. I don't know you anymore. I haven't for a long time."

"By all means, don't dance around my feelings."

"Do you have feelings?" My brows lift. "Forgive me. I wasn't aware that a guy like you was capable of feeling anything."

"A guy like me?"

"Yeah. You know — one who'd endanger the lives of his entire family to save himself."

"I warned you," he snaps. "Last month, when I came home—"

"To steal money."

"—to pack my clothes, I told you things were messed up. I told you to be careful."

"Messed up? *Messed up?!*" I step forward and grab him by the shirtfront, my fingers fisting in the fabric. "Two gang members have been following me for weeks. They ambushed me after practice last week and almost shattered my pitching hand." My grip tightens. I want to physically shake some sense into him. "Four days ago, they broke into our house, knocked me unconscious, tied me to a chair, and threatened my life. *Our parents' lives.* All because they're determined to get to you, Jax." I drop my arms to my sides, disgusted. "That's far more than just *messed up.*"

He grimaces, but offers no response. Not even an apology.

"You don't seem surprised to hear any of this," I point out.

He shoves past me and starts to pace. "The guys who came here... Did you get their names?"

"Rico. Barboza."

Jaxon nods. His skin is wan in the moonlight, his face bloodless with fear. He continues to walk tight loops around the terrace. "They're top enforcers for the Latin Kings. Not the kind of people you want to fuck around with, Archer."

"Since when has what I *want* ever been a factor here? I didn't exactly invite them over for tea and crumpets."

"I know! I know." He runs a hand through his hair. "It's complicated, all right? I owe their boss a debt. I thought when I got out, I could pay it off gradually. Or, if I couldn't get the money, I'd just... disappear for a while."

Rage swells inside my chest. "That was your grand plan? You thought you could just go off the grid until a goddamn *gang* forgot about you? Jesus Christ, Jaxon! Did you really believe, if these guys are as dangerous as you say they are, they'd let you skip into the sunset without coming after your family?"

"Don't yell at me." He presses a hand to his temple, his movements jerky. "I can't think when you're yelling."

Suspicion stirs to life as I watch him. The jerkiness of his movements. The erratic speech pattern. I've seen it all before — far too many times. It's hard to tell in the dark, but I'm certain if I looked close enough, I'd find his pupils constricted to pinpricks.

"Are you high right now?"

He glowers. "Fuck you, Archer!"

"That's not an answer."

He's tellingly silent.

I step forward, feeling hollow. My voice is stark as I ask again, "*Are you high?*"

"Look, just... lay off me, okay? I'm under an insane amount

of pressure right now." His eyes dart around the yard, avoiding mine. "You don't understand what I'm going through."

I do understand, though. All too well.

He's using again.

Oxy. Vicodin. Whatever he could get his hands on.

"God fucking damnit, Jax!"

I'm overcome with the urge to hit something. Hard. I clench my fingernails into my palms instead, scoring rows of half-moons across my flesh. Past experience tells me there's no use in reasoning with him — not while he's high. Using logic on a junkie is like speaking Latin to a toddler.

An experiment in frustration.

Jaxon shakes his head rapidly. "You don't understand. You've never understood."

"Then explain it to me."

"Prison!" he shouts. "You have no idea what it was like, being locked up in a place like that. Surrounded by the worst sort of people. Falling asleep at night behind bars, wondering whether the next day will be your last. Knowing you've got to do something, *anything*, to protect yourself — even make an alliance with monsters." He stares at me, his face a mask of scorn. "How could you possibly understand that, Archer? Look at your life!"

"My life?"

He gestures around at the beautifully manicured lawn, sloping down toward the sea. "Look at this place! Every day, you wake up in paradise. You grew up in a fucking fairy tale, Archer. Don't pretend otherwise."

"Last I checked, you spent your childhood here too, Jax."

"Yeah, but it was different for you."

"You're rewriting history. I might've grown up in a castle, but we both know I sleep in the servants quarters. I'm the fucking *help*, not heir to any throne." I glare at him. "Don't act like I've lived some life of privilege. Don't act like I had any more opportunities than you."

"But you did. You still do!" He turns his face away, but I can hear the resentment in his voice. "You have private school. You have baseball. You have scholarships. You have a way out."

"A way out I fucking earned, Jaxon! You may not want to hear it, but our lives are a reflection of our choices. You made yours; I made mine. Don't resent me for taking a different path, just because yours led somewhere you don't like anymore."

"Here we go again. Perfect Archer, the golden boy, the good son. Pointing out all my fuck-ups."

"Me, the golden boy?" I scoff. "That's rich. You're all Ma and Pa ever talk about. You're the subject of every conversation, even when you aren't there. The more poison you put in your veins, the more determined they become to save you from yourself. And as for your fuck-ups? I don't need to point them out, Jaxon. You do that all on your own, every time you break their hearts by lying, cheating, or stealing from them."

He rolls his eyes. "Yeah, yeah. I've heard it all before. I'm the big bad wolf, ruining the Reyes family name. Spare me the lecture, will you?"

"This isn't about our family name. This is about you putting everyone in your life in the crosshairs of violent criminals."

"I'm figuring it out! You just have to give me more time!"

"More time isn't going to help, Jax. You knew about this when you got out of Cedar-Junction. As far as I can tell, the only thing you've done in the two months since then is get high and go into hiding. Not necessarily in that order."

"I'll talk to Rico. Okay? I'll get them to back off."

"How? Enlighten me. Because they didn't give the impression they'd back off for anything less than your full cooperation." I pause, my mind spinning a million different directions.

"Maybe if you talked to your parole officer, the police could get you some kind of deal as an informant. Witness protection or—"

"No. I'd be dead before I opened my mouth."

"The police could protect you."

"There's no protection from this! Don't you understand?" He runs his hands through his hair until it's sticking up in several directions. "These guys will kill everyone. Me. You. Ma. Pa. *Everyone*."

Rico promised me as much; clearly, he wasn't bluffing.

"Fine. No police." I take a deep breath. "What's your backup plan?"

Jaxon is no longer meeting my eyes. He stares toward the tennis courts, his face pallid. "The Kings mostly circulate heroin and fentanyl. They make a killing in more rural parts of the state, but they don't have a strong foothold this far north of Boston yet. Most kids up here stick to the basics — shrooms, ecstasy, molly, pot. Whatever's floating around the party scene." He shifts his weight from foot to foot. "If I can create demand for the more intense product... get fentanyl flowing freely in these circles... I think it'll be enough to clear my debts."

My brows furrow. "So you're going to deal for them? Get a whole generation of my classmates hooked on drugs that will ruin their futures? Sign them up for a lifetime of misery and pain, just to save your own skin?" I can't keep the utter disdain out of my voice. "Jesus, Jaxon. You've made some questionable decisions in the past, but I thought you at least had a moral compass. This is... beyond awful. Even for you."

"It's either deal for them or pay them off! And I don't know about you, Archer, but I don't have that kind of capital." His eyes move toward Cormorant House, lingering on the glass panes of the back door. "There's only one person I know who might."

"So that's why you went after Jo tonight. You think you can extort money from her? Somehow convince her parents to pay off your debts?"

"No! *No*. It was just pure chance, seeing her at the party tonight. I was catching up with a few old friends, smoking a little weed... She was with some Ken Doll douchebag who wasn't taking no for an answer, if you know what I mean. I stepped in. Made sure he got the message, loud and clear."

"Snyder," I hiss under my breath, seeing red.

He's a dead man.

I struggle to rein in my emotions.

"You should be thanking me, not yelling at me," Jaxon prattles on, his words running together. "If I hadn't been there, things might've gone very differently for Josephine."

I take a step toward him. "I think I'll save the appreciation parade for after you tell me what you've done with her."

"Who says I did something to her?"

"Past experience."

Jaxon looks even more jittery than before. He's a hairsbreadth away from a full-fledged breakdown. "I told you before — I helped her tonight! I saved her! I'm the good guy here, Archer."

Maybe he's telling the truth.

Maybe not.

I can't bring myself to care. An all-consuming rage is rising inside me, blotting out every other emotion. For the first time in my life, I understand the term *blind rage*. My anger has sharpened to such an extreme, the rest of the world is blurry in comparison.

"Oh, spare me," I snarl. "You're no saint. You saw an opportunity and you took it."

Jax fidgets. "I don't know what you're talking about."

"Sure you do." I take a step into his path, forcing him to meet my eyes. "Tell me — did you think you could kidnap her? Hold her for a hefty ransom?" I tilt my head. "Or did you plan to hand her directly over to the Kings and let them do the dirty work for you?"

"No..." he says weakly. "That's not true..."

"As long as your scorecard is clear, who cares what they do to her, right?" I take another step, my every atom vibrating with rage. "Even if they kill her..."

He flinches.

"Torture her..."

He flinches again.

"Rape her..."

And another.

"That's just collateral damage, right? A justifiable cost of your freedom."

"No, Archer!" Jaxon's voice breaks on my name. "You've got it all twisted. I wasn't going to hurt Jo. I'd never give her to them. I just... I thought maybe she could get the cash for me. The Valentines have more money than Zuckerberg! Fifty grand is pocket change to people like that."

Before I'm conscious of moving, I've crossed the terrace, grabbed him by the throat, and pinned him up against the stone wall. Leaning forward, I bring my face within an inch of his. My grip around his throat tightens until he's gasping for air.

"You will never touch Josephine Valentine again," I say, each word crystallizing in the night. "Do you understand me?"

Jaxon wheezes something indecipherable. The whites of his eyes flash with panic.

"Sorry, what was that?" My brows lift. "I didn't quite hear you."

"Won't—touch—her," he gasps. "*Swear.*"

"Good. I'm glad we've got that settled."

The instant I release him, he doubles over, desperately sucking oxygen into his lungs. When he's breathing normally again, he looks up at me with an expression that's almost smug.

"Seems I'm not the only Reyes who can't control his temper," he rasps. "Maybe you're more like me than you thought, little brother."

"I'm nothing like you."

"Is that so?"

With effort, I get ahold of myself, tamping down the boiling rage to a bubbling simmer. Lashing out again won't do me any favors. To Jaxon Reyes, life is one long game of poker. A series of bluffs and discards. He plays people like hands of Texas Hold'Em, using whatever he's dealt to win. Adapting his strategies for maximum personal gain.

I've already revealed far too many of my own cards by letting my temper get the best of me. I should've played it cool. Kept my vulnerabilities hidden.

"You've changed, Archer. You're much more violent than I remember." He pauses, head tilting in thought. "Or is this rage only triggered because I threatened your pretty little girlfriend?"

My muscles tense, but I manage to keep my expression empty.

He thinks he can wield Jo against me like a weapon?

I'll just have to take that weapon away.

"She isn't my girlfriend." I force a laugh. "Don't tell me that's why you thought she'd help you? You're even dumber than I thought."

He stares at me for a long beat. "Dating or not, that girl will do anything for you. Anything."

"Maybe back when we were kids. You've been away a long time, Jaxon. Things change. People grow apart."

"Bullshit," he mutters. "I was gone two years, but I haven't forgotten the way you look at that girl."

"How's that?"

"Like she's the light at the end of a very dark tunnel."

"God, you really must be high." I roll my eyes, selling the lie with every fiber of my being. "You think I actually like being her friend? I tolerate her for exactly one reason: her parents paid my tuition to Exeter. As soon as I walk across that graduation stage, I plan to keep on walking, right out of her life."

Jaxon's eyes flicker back and forth across my face, attempting to discern fact from fiction. I make sure to keep my expression clear of every emotion but one.

Indifference.

Inside my chest, my heart pounds twice its normal speed. My voice is eerily level as I speak the greatest lie of my life.

"Jo Valentine means nothing to me. *Nothing.*"

There's a long moment of silence. Jaxon weighs my words, doubt scored deeply across his features.

"If she's nothing to you, why did you come here looking for her?" he asks slowly. "Why did you just throw me against a wall for coming near her?"

Damn it.

He may be high, but he's not a total idiot.

I shrug. "I heard you took her from the party. I thought I might be able to intervene before you did something to land yourself back in jail — not to mention, get our family tossed out on the streets." I pause. "You realize Vincent Valentine is close friends with the State Police Superintendent and more than a few members of foreign intelligence, don't you? Kidnapping his only daughter isn't a smart move if you want to stay on the right side of the law. And what do you think will happen to Ma and Pa if you piss off their employers?"

Jaxon pales. "I didn't think..."

"Of course you didn't. You never think." I shake my head. "I just hope you didn't do anything to harm her. For your sake."

"I didn't touch her! I swear!"

"Then where did you take her?"

"She's down at the boathouse. She said she wanted to look at the stars for awhile." He sucks in a jagged breath. "I walked her there to be nice. I was on my way back to my car when I saw you up here on the terrace."

Relief floods me; I'm careful not to let it show. But deep inside my heart, where Jaxon cannot see, two words chase one another back and forth through every chamber — a thudding underscore to every beat.

She's safe.

She's safe.

She's safe.

CHAPTER SEVENTEEN

JOSEPHINE

THE MOON CRAWLS across the sky in slow degrees. I lay on the dock, flat on my back, staring up at it as waves roll gently beneath me. Trying to sort out my thoughts.

They feel as unfathomable as those distant stars; a lightyear away from reality.

It's been a strange night, to say the least. I'm not sure what's a greater surprise — Ryan Snyder turning out to be the biggest asshole on planet earth, or Jaxon Reyes swooping in as my unexpected knight-in-tattooed-armor.

I haven't seen Jax since he went to prison. I didn't even know he was out on parole. Apparently, Archer didn't feel the need to inform me of his early release. I'd be lying if I said it doesn't sting to realize I'm no longer the person he confides in.

There was a time he told me every thought inside his head, every secret of his heart, every longing within his soul.

After Jaxon came to my rescue at the party, he drove me home in a beat-up maroon sedan I've never seen before. It's bumper hung so low, it scraped the curb with a shower of sparks every time we went up a hill.

He was mostly silent as we wound through the dark streets toward Cormorant House. I was equally quiet, caught up in my own head, too consumed by the memory of Ryan's reaching hands to make much small talk. I tried not to glance too often in his direction, feeling somewhat awkward in his presence despite our long history.

I've known Jaxon since I was an infant. He's Archer's older brother — and his spitting image, surplus a few tattoos. But we've never been particularly close. Four years is a big age gap when you're young. And by the time we were all teenagers, Jaxon was already heading down a very different path. One of overdoses and rehab stints and, eventually, a three-year sentence at Cedar-Junction.

Despite his time behind bars, Jaxon doesn't seem any worse for wear. He still has that sly smile, that darting gaze that never lingers long enough to get a proper read on his thoughts. When he walked me to the boathouse, he ruffled my hair like a little sister as we said our goodbyes.

Like old times.

That was almost an hour ago. It's nearly midnight, now. I shiver against the wood planks, chilled to the bone. The warmth of the day has long since faded. My shorts and t-shirt offer little protection from the wind whipping off the water. Goosebumps break out across my skin; I rub my arms to subdue them, a futile task.

I should go inside. Climb into bed, shut my eyes, reset the day. But, looming emptily behind me, Cormorant House feels just as cold as the night. An inhospitable specter, devoid of life. I don't want to walk its vacant halls alone. Doing so makes me feel like a ghost. As though, at any given moment, I could simply...

Disappear.

The sound of raised voices drifts to me on the wind. I sit

up, glancing around for the source. Straining my ears, I realize it's coming from the house.

Two men, speaking rapidly.

They're too far away to make out any of their words. I should probably feel fear as I climb to my feet, but I'm too numb from cold to feel much of anything. Bested by my own incorrigible curiosity, I move quietly down the dock, toward solid ground.

I follow the voices up the path to the estate, my footfalls silent against the grass. My hand curls tightly around my keys, the only weapon at my disposal. Their metal edges dig sharply into my palm.

I keep to the shadows — an unseen eavesdropper in the dark. The argument grows louder as I approach the house. I'm nearly to the terrace when one of the voices becomes identifiable.

I stop in my tracks.

"She isn't my girlfriend." I hear Archer scoff. "Don't tell my that's why you thought she'd help you? You're even dumber than I thought."

I duck instinctually behind a maple tree, my heart hammering against my ribs.

Who is he talking about?

I strain to catch more of their conversation. My eyes widen when I recognize Jaxon's voice, responding. "That girl will do anything for you. Anything."

"Maybe back when we were kids," Archer volleys back. "You've been away a long time, Jaxon. Things change. People grow apart."

"Bullshit. I was gone two years, but I haven't forgotten the way you look at that girl."

How's that? I think hopefully.

"How's that?" Archer asks flatly.

"Like she's the light at the end of a very dark tunnel."

My heart lurches into my throat and lodges there. Breath becomes an impossibility.

"God, you really must be high." Archer's cold laugh sends shrapnel into the fabric of my soul. "You think I actually like being her friend? I tolerate her for exactly one reason: her parents paid my tuition to Exeter. As soon as I walk across that graduation stage, I plan to keep on walking, right out of her life."

My eyes are stinging from the wind. That's why I'm crying. *The wind.*

Just the wind.

I brush the tears off my face, but they keep coming. The pain inside my chest is crippling. My knees threaten to buckle beneath me. I reach for the tree trunk to steady myself.

"Jo Valentine means nothing to me," Archer tells Jaxon. There's not an ounce of hesitation in his voice. "*Nothing.*"

A fissure erupts beneath my ribs, tearing through the fragile cartilage. Breaking me open, into fragments.

I can't listen anymore. I can't bear to hear another word from his cruel, contemptuous mouth.

Tears blind me as I dodge into the dark. I don't bother wiping them. Stumbling sightlessly through garden beds, I circle around to the front door, shove my key into the lock, and fall across the threshold. A pained sob chokes out of my throat as I hit the floor, echoing back at me in the vaulted atrium.

Lying there on the cold marble, the estate's vastness presses in at me from all sides... it's empty rooms a perfect reflection of the hollow panging inside my heart.

THE FOLLOWING MORNING, I stagger into the kitchen after a sleepless night and stop cold at the sight that greets me. Surely, I must be hallucinating from sheer exhaustion. Because sitting at the island countertop, sipping mugs of coffee and swapping sections of *The Boston Globe*, are my parents.

They glance up when I walk in, matching smiles spreading across their faces.

"Good morning, Josephine," Vincent says casually. As though he's just come back from an hour-long trip to the grocery store, not a monthlong walkabout through Sub-Saharan Africa.

"You're back early."

"Are we not allowed to return to our home without advanced notice?" A light laugh titters out of Blair's mouth. "We wanted to surprise you, so we moved up our flight plan by a few days."

"Best part of having a private jet." Vincent grins. "No airline fees for changing your itinerary."

My eyes dart back and forth between the two of them. "When did you arrive?"

"About an hour ago. We decided to let you sleep in. Though I must say, it doesn't appear to have done much good. You look tired, Josephine. A wrinkle appears between my mother's brows as she examines me. "Did you sleep well?"

"I'm fine."

"There are circles under your eyes. Maybe I should make a call to my dermatologist. There's a wonderful cream he could give you to—"

"*Mom.*" My teeth grind together. "I said I'm fine."

"Well, then get over here and give us a hug. It's been two weeks since we've seen you!"

"Three," I murmur under my breath, crossing the room to them.

Neither stands up. From their stools, they half-turn and extend their arms out for an embrace. I step forward like a good soldier and allow them to enfold me in a group hug. In my head, I count out exactly five seconds before they disengage.

"Have you lost weight?" Blair asks, leaning back to examine me with a critical eye. "You look thinner."

I take a deep breath and swallow down the useless words that claw at the back of my throat. Walking around to the other side of the island, I sit on a stool and try not to slouch beneath the weight of their stares.

"You know, darling..." My mother folds her hands on the countertop — a practiced move I recognize from press junkets and publicity tours. "You don't seem very happy to see us."

"Of course I'm happy to see you." I pause. "It's just... June 5th isn't for another week. Remember?"

They trade a bewildered glance.

A fissure of concern shoots through me. "You are planning to be home for my birthday, aren't you?"

"Ah! Right. Your birthday." Vincent nods. "Of course. Wouldn't miss it."

Blair is giving me her most soothing smile — the one she uses on frazzled employees. "Things have just been so busy at VALENT lately, we wanted to make sure we got a chance to see you before your graduation. Can you believe, in just three short weeks, you'll be done with high school?"

"Two weeks, actually. The ceremony is June 10th. I already reserved your tickets."

"Of course, of course. That's what I meant to say." She presses a hand apologetically to her temple. "Jetlag."

"Mmm."

"How are your classes going?" Vincent steeples his fingers in front of his mouth. "GPA still holding strong?"

My lips tug up at the corners. "Strong enough to make me the Valedictorian of my class."

"With the intelligence we passed down to you, I'd expect nothing less." My father grins. "You were predisposed to brilliance."

My lips flatten.

Blair's expression turns quizzical. "That means you'll give a speech, doesn't it, darling? At the commencement?"

"Yes."

"Have you finished writing it yet?" She tucks a strand of chestnut hair behind her ear. "I'd be happy to run my eyes over it for you. Offer some constructive critique. I've given my fair share of speeches over the years."

"Your mother truly is a gifted public speaker." Vincent glances warmly at his wife. "An inspiration to hear."

"Actually..." I chew on my bottom lip. "I haven't started writing it, yet."

"Josephine!" Blair gasps. "That is *inexcusable.* What on earth have you been doing with your free time?"

"I've been busy studying for the AP exams." I try not to sound defensive. "They start on Monday. I want to do well."

"That's no excuse. Your mother is right. A speech isn't something to be whipped together overnight." My father's eyes, blue like my own, narrow sternly. "Your words will be embedded in the memories of your peers for the rest of their lives. Whenever they think back to their graduation day, they'll recall whether you were inspiring or insipid. You owe it to them to deliver a message worth remembering."

"I'm just..." I clear my throat. "I'm struggling a bit with selecting the right topic."

Vincent's eyes narrow even further. "Then I suggest you stop joyriding around town in my Porsche and start prioritizing your academics."

"I'm not joyriding," I grumble. "I only use it to get to school."

"So Miguel said."

"Because it's the truth! Why would he lie about something like that?"

"He'd better not." Vincent chortles. "Not when I'm the one signing his paychecks."

I inhale sharply, trying to remain calm. "It's not like you're even around enough to drive the Porsche, Dad. I could steer it off a cliff, shatter it to bits, and have it rebuilt from scratch without you ever noticing."

He's silent for a tense beat. "Are you back-talking, right now?"

"I'm sorry." I drop my gaze to the countertop, studying the glittery facets in the black marble; flickers of light in the darkness. "I promise I won't embarrass you at the commencement. I'll work on my speech tomorrow."

"*Today*, I think," Blair murmurs, picking up her newspaper again. "No time like the present. Don't you agree, Vincent?"

His eyes are already scanning the international news bolded across the front page in his hands. "As they say... procrastination is the enemy of progress. You're nothing if you're not producing."

I don't say another word. I know from experience that this conversation has reached a stopping point as far as my parents are concerned.

Decision: made.

Discussion: over.

I shift uncomfortably on my stool, watching them read. Five minutes tick by with agonizing slowness. The silence in the kitchen is absolute, except for the occasional shuffling of pages as they switch sections.

Sports.

Politics.

Entertainment.

Classifieds.

Gaze downcast, I start in surprise when a coffee cup slides into my view. My eyes flicker up to Flora's face as I curl my hands around its warmth.

"Thank you."

"My pleasure, Josephine." She speaks softly to avoid disturbing my parents. "Do you want breakfast? I can make pancakes. There are fresh blueberries from the garden."

"That sounds go—"

"Flora! *There* you are." Blair cuts me off with a shrill exclamation. "I've been meaning to talk to you about the gardens. They are completely unruly. I walked around the estate earlier and was simply mortified by the state of our mulch-beds. Miguel has always been a solid worker but I'm afraid, if he can no longer keep up with the demands of such a large piece of property, perhaps we will need to make some changes around here."

"*Mom!*" I hiss, appalled.

"My apologies, Mrs. Valentine," Flora whispers. Her eyes are locked on her shoes. "I will speak to him about it immediately."

"Very well. I don't think it's too much to ask that Cormorant House be kept at the same standard to which we've become accustomed." Blair sniffs delicately. "That said, I also feel the linens in the master bathroom don't possess quite their usual crispness. Did you perhaps change our brand of detergent? You are aware, I'm certain, how strongly I feel about using only organic products..."

I can't stand to sit here anymore. Can't stand to hear my mother doling out verbal lashes to the woman who raised me, referring to the man who's guided my every step as nothing but hired help.

Unnoticed, I slide off my stool and slip out of the kitchen, retreating to the safety of my bedroom.

If it wasn't so upsetting, it would almost be funny: as empty as this house feels when my parents are gone, somehow, it feels even emptier when they finally come home.

I TYPE three words into the Google search engine, feeling more like a gum-smacking Valley girl than the Class Valedictorian.

Graduation speech ideas.

I click enter with low expectations. Apparently, they weren't low enough. The results that populate the screen are utterly useless — an endless list of laughable clichés and time-worn tropes. Certainly not an address fit to impress my parents.

Though, in all honesty, they'd probably be happiest if I used my stage time to talk about their life-saving efforts at VALENT.

My parents, Blair and Vincent Valentine, are a constant source of inspiration...

Spare me.

I click away from the useless search results and check my social media pages instead. A tagged photograph taken at last night's game pops up — me and the twins. The three of us grin into the phone screen beneath the orange-toned stadium lights.

Was that only yesterday?

It feels like a lifetime ago. That girl, sandwiched between the twins, smiling happily... she's a stranger to me. A naive little fool who still believed that, occasionally, life is more than merely a series of heartbreaks and disappointments.

A girl who existed before Ryan.

You're nothing. Nothing but Reyes' sloppy seconds.

Before Archer.

Jo Valentine means nothing to me. Nothing.

Before Vincent.

You're nothing if you're not producing.

I brush tears off my cheeks. After all the crying I did last night, I'm surprised there's any moisture left in my body. If only I could turn some internal faucet to stop my eyes from leaking.

A ping from my laptop draws my attention. At the bottom corner of my screen, a chat window pops up. Odette's face pouts at me from her small, circular profile photo.

Bitch! 😒 **Why aren't you answering my texts?**

I sigh and type back.

Jo: I lost my phone last night. It must've fallen out of my pocket at the game.

Odette: That sucks! 😟 *When are you getting a new one?*

Jo: Not sure yet. I want to check the bleachers, first.

Odette: Who was that hot guy you left the party with last night?

Jo: Jaxon Reyes.

Odette: Archer's older brother?!

Jo: Yep.

Odette: The one who went to prison?

Jo: Yep.

Odette: OMG! 😲 *Details, please!*

Jo: Nothing to tell.

Odette: 😶😶😶

Jo: He drove me home. That's it.

Odette: Boooooring.

Jo: That's my middle name.

Odette: LOL. 😂 *In other news… We found you a date for prom!*

Jo: ???

Odette: His name is Charlie. Plays lacrosse at Deerfield. Total hottie.

Jo: ???????

Odette: Hold on a sec.

A link appears in the chat box. When I click on it, I'm taken to a new window, featuring the profile of one Charlie Sears. Age 18. Marblehead resident. Deerfield Academy Senior Class President. Three-sport athlete. Certified scuba instructor.

I scroll through his pictures, taking in the chiseled jawline and dark auburn hair. The broad shoulders and bright eyes.

Odette wasn't lying: he is, in fact, a total hottie.

The chat window pings again.

Odette: SEE?! Perfect, isn't he?

Jo: Are you sure he wants to go with me?

Odette: Duh. We sent him your picture. 😇 *He thinks you're a babe.*

Jo: ……

Odette: I think the words you're

> *looking for are THANK YOU ODETTE AND*
> *OPHELIA! YOU'RE FANTASTIC!*
>
> *Jo: Thank you Odette and Ophelia.*
>
> *Odette: That's the spirit. LOL.*
> *Gotta log off now. But message us*
> *this week if you want to go dress*
> *shopping! We'll help you find*
> *something fab… even if we have to*
> *hit every outlet mall in*
> *Massachusetts.*
>
> *Jo: Thanks.* 🖤 *I mean it.*
>
> *Odette: xoxoxo*

I close the laptop with a soft click. My mind spins, trying to recalibrate to this new information.

I'm going to the prom.

With a boy I've never met.

I suppose he can't be worse than any of the boys I *have* met. He doesn't appear to be a serial killer — at least, not from my quick perusal of his profile.

What's the worst that could happen?

The thing is, I don't have any real reason not to attend the stupid dance-slash-dinner-cruise our student council's planned. Lame as it may be to admit… in my head, prom has always seemed like the true culmination of high school. A milestone more important than walking across a graduation stage to accept a diploma or tossing a cap into the air.

I guess that's why I made the dress.

Walking slowly toward my closet, butterflies stir to life in the pit of my stomach. I push aside the hangers holding my most recent design projects and reach all the way into the back, until my fingers brush against soft cloth. Pulling the garment out, I can't help admiring the way it shimmers in the low light.

Honestly, it was never my intention to make my own prom dress. But several months ago, while wandering the aisles of my favorite craft store, I stumbled across a bolt of fabric that stole my heart in an instant. The dark blue-gray silk had a natural fluidity that reminded me of the ocean at wintertime, when the sky is overcast and the surface has gone wild with ripples. I had no plan to go on, no pattern to work from... but I tossed every yard of it in my cart anyway, unable to leave it behind.

As soon as I got home, I set to work like a woman possessed — first sketching out a design, then draping the fabric over my mannequin. Pinning it into precise, elegant lines. Cutting and trimming and stitching.

For two days straight, I hunched over my machine like a poor seamstress sewing for her supper, all my attention fixated on the dress in my tired hands. My life dwindled to the most basic of elements.

Thread.

Needle.

Hem.

Seam.

I worked until my fingers were swollen; until my eyes were bleary with exhaustion. And when it was finished... when the dress appeared complete even to my hyper-vigilant eyes... I finally put it on.

Standing before the mirror, twirling around like a princess in a fairy tale, I could see it so clearly.

My perfect prom night.

In the perfect dress.

With the perfect date.

I dreamed of how I'd walk down the grand staircase of Cormorant House — a corsage on my wrist, a limo waiting in the driveway. I dreamed of the boy waiting at the bottom of those stairs — a modern Prince Charming in a tailored tuxedo, his bright caramel eyes fixed on me with wonderment.

Now, in the harsh light of reality, that feels more like a fantasy.

My fingertips trail across the whisper-thin silk of the dress I made for a boy who was never mine. And my heart aches for a dreams turned to dust.

Life is not a fairy tale.
I am not a princess.
I am nothing at all.

CHAPTER EIGHTEEN

ARCHER

THE DARK LORD and his Mistress of Doom have returned — a week ahead of schedule, no less — and brought with them a perpetual cloud of tension that hangs heavily over Cormorant House.

I, personally, don't have much occasion to interact with Vincent and Blair; I can count the number of conversations I've ever had with them on one hand. But I grind my teeth as I watch my parents tiptoeing around the estate on eggshells, doing their best to remain invisible while they complete their tasks. They'd never admit it aloud, but we're all thinking the same thing.

Please let this visit be a short one.

The only silver lining is that so long as they're here, Jo will be safe. Sure, she's probably going insane stuck inside the walls of that house, subject to her parents' constant scrutiny... but at least she isn't wandering around, a target for my brother and his many enemies.

After talking to Jaxon, I'm strangely calm. I shouldn't be — the situation is more dire than ever, seeing as he's disappeared again, leaving me with no more than a weak assurance that he'd quote-*handle everything* -unquote. Perhaps, after a month of living in fear, I've simply become numb to it.

I walk the halls of Exeter, anesthetized to the end-of-year chaos exploding all around me. With just over a week of classes left, my classmates are ensconced in a cloying charade of nostalgia. They pass yearbooks back and forth. They wipe tears at their lockers. They hug people they've barely spoken to since freshman year, declaring false intentions to keep in touch.

Class itself is an endless stream of group projects and boring thesis papers. Most teachers are either unwilling or unable to fight against the so-called "senior slide." They hand out plentiful As, more than ready to see us move on — into adulthood, out of their hair. Several of them take me aside after class and tell me not to worry about my final exams at all.

Focus on pitching.

You've got a title to win.

Go Wolfpack!

I disappear into baseball, grateful for the distraction of playoff games and long practices. There's a new game every night, a fresh team to conquer. As the week trudges on, the Wolves advance steadily through the bracket, defeating Lowell and North Andover, then BC High and Braintree. Our eyes are fixed on the State Championship trophy — the crown jewel of an undefeated season.

If Coach Hamm notices Ryan Snyder's fresh set of black eyes, or the fact that his first baseman and star pitcher refuse to look at one another, he chooses to ignore it. For what it's worth, the beating I gave Snyder in the parking lot on Monday morning was less about inflicting pain than it was delivering a promise.

Touch Josephine again and you will live to regret it.

Much as I'm loathe to admit it, Jaxon was right about one

thing. There is a new violence birthed inside me; a burning anger I find myself unequipped to contend with. At any given moment, it's liable to lash out — a solar flare off the surface of the sun, destroying everything in close orbit. The longer I suppress it, the more the sensation heightens.

Monday.

Tuesday.

Wednesday.

Thursday.

By the time my birthday rolls around on Friday... I am a supernova, primed to combust.

———————

FRIDAY MORNING, I jerk awake when my parents throw open my bedroom door. They step inside the room, paper party hats sitting lopsided atop their heads, and start singing in off-key voices.

"*Feliz Cumpleaños a ti. Feliz Cumpleaños a ti. Feliz Cumpleaños a Archer! Feliz Cumpleaños a ti.*" They grin in unison. "We love you!"

I sit up, rubbing bleary eyes. "Thank you, thank you. Though, if you really loved me, you would've let me sleep in."

"Hush!" Ma swats at me playfully.

Pa reaches out to squeeze my shoulder. "Happy birthday, son."

"My baby is eighteen already!" Ma sniffles. "How time flies."

"Ma, don't cry."

"I'm not!" she lies, dabbing at her eyes with a handkerchief. "I just can't believe you're so grown up. Before I know it, you'll be off at college..."

"Here we go again." I sigh. "Ma, Bryant is only a two hour

drive from here. I'll be home so much, you won't even miss me. I promise."

The air goes still. They glance at each other.

"Bryant?"

I grin devilishly. "Did I not mention that I'd made my decision? I'm planning to announce it after the Championship game tomorrow night. But I wanted to tell you guys first."

"*Mijo!* We are supposed to be giving you gifts today, not the other way around." Ma abandons her handkerchief, full-on crying now.

Pa looks like he's not far behind. His eyes are red-rimmed as he pulls me into a bone-crushing hug. "I'm so proud of you, Archer."

My own eyes are prickling. My voice comes out thicker than usual. "I couldn't have done it without you guys. I hope you know that."

Ma closes in on my other side, wrapping her arms around us both. I don't shrug them off or pull back. For nearly a minute, I allow them to hold me, like I'm five years old again.

"I suppose we need to get some Bryant t-shirts," Ma murmurs against my hair. "Now that you're officially going to be a Bulldog."

I smile. "I've already got that covered, actually..."

Extracting myself from their arms, I walk to my dresser. In the bottom drawer, there are three identical sweatshirts. Gold letters spell out BRYANT against the black fabric.

"Here." I pass one to each of my parents. "These are for you. The Bryant coach gave them to me when I met with him last night."

As they pull them excitedly over their heads, I turn back to shut the drawer. My fingers linger on the third sweatshirt waiting inside.

Size XS.

I got it for Jo. Despite everything... I desperately want to give it to her; to watch her face light up when she realizes I'll be attending school only a half hour away from her at Brown.

I must be insane.

If I put it in her hands right now, she'll probably hurl it straight into the sea. I've pushed her so far away, I'm not sure I'll ever be able to get her back.

Tomorrow is June 5. Her birthday. Since she always spends it with her parents, we usually celebrate together on mine — trading presents in the boathouse rafters at dusk. Last year, I gave her a vintage sewing machine I stumbled across in a thrift shop; she bought me front row tickets to see the Red Sox at Fenway.

Beside Jo's Bryant sweatshirt, there's a small jewelry box. Inside it, a necklace sits on a bed of plush velvet. It's not particularly fancy; not studded in diamonds or crafted from the finest platinum. It's rather plain, in fact. But when I saw it in a shop window, I knew it was meant for Jo.

The pendant is made up of thin cords of gold, overlapping in the shape of a simple knot. Looking at it, most people might think it's nothing special — just a cluster of lines, looped together. Only someone who spends time on the water would understand the true meaning.

A fisherman's knot.

Sailors call it the true love knot. They say it's unbreakable. That, tied correctly, it won't ever come apart. Stress only makes it stronger. The more you tug, the tighter it grows.

Before I can question my own motivations, I tuck the small box inside the front pocket of my sweatpants. My parents are too busy examining their new Bryant attire to notice.

"Come on, *mijo*," Ma says, linking her arm with mine. "I made breakfast."

They lead me into the kitchen. My favorite foods are

stacked high on the table — blueberry pancakes, pan de mallorca, fresh-squeezed orange juice.

"Wow." I grin, pulling out a chair. "Thank you."

"Looks perfect, Flora," Pa says, taking his seat.

"I only wish your brother was here." Ma places several pancakes on my plate. "Then it would truly be perfect."

I gulp my orange juice.

"Have you heard from him this week?" Pa asks quietly.

Ma shakes her head.

He deflates a bit, shoulders slumping in his sweatshirt. "I called the auto shop where he's been working. His boss said he hasn't come in for his shifts the past two weeks."

Her hand reaches for the cross around her neck. "Maybe he's found another job..."

"It's possible. Try not to panic, Flora. We don't know for sure that he's gotten himself into trouble again."

Their anxiety is palpable. I place my hands on my lap beneath the table, so they won't see them tightening into fists.

"I'm sure he's okay. It's just... I worry." Ma sighs. "Maybe we should call his P.O. to see if he's heard anything—"

"No," Pa interjects. "If we do that, we might as well send Jaxon straight back to prison. He's supposed to be staying with us, remember?"

My mother grips her cross harder. "I only wish we knew where he was."

"Maybe he met a girl. Two years is a long time... "

"*Miguel!*"

Pa shrugs. "It's true! Now, eat your breakfast and try not to worry so much. I'm sure Jaxon will come home soon. He wouldn't risk violating his parole."

"If he fails his drug test—"

"He won't! I know my son. He's sober and he is going to stay that way."

"But Miguel—"

Before my mother can finish, I rise to my feet, slamming my hands down on the tabletop hard enough to make the dishes jump.

"*Mijo!* What on earth—"

"You know what I want most for my birthday?" I growl, glaring from one face to the other. They're both wearing stunned expressions. "To not think about Jaxon. To not talk about Jaxon. To not have *every fucking minute of every fucking day* revolve around the selfish prick also known as Jaxon!" I lean forward, eyes narrowing. "You truly think he's off somewhere being a productive member of society? You're delusional. Jaxon is capable of one thing: self-destruction. And no matter how many times you try... you can't save him from himself."

"*Mijo...*"

Exasperated, I run my hands through my hair as I mutter, "You can't even save yourselves."

They say nothing.

My angry words seem to have sucked every ounce of air out of the room. In heavy silence, my parents watch as I storm across the kitchen and shove open the front door. It slams behind me with a bang that makes several birds take flight from a nearby tree.

The guilt I feel is a faint trickle in comparison to the flood of rage and resentment swirling inside me. I'm too worked up to get behind the wheel. I walk the property instead, the grass dewy against my bare feet.

This early on a Friday morning, the grounds are even quieter than usual. I can hear the Tesla's tires rolling down the driveway from across the lawn — Jo's parents, heading into the VALENT headquarters in Boston bright and early.

Even when they're home, they're barely here.

I give the main house wide berth as I walk down toward the water. Jo is probably inside, getting ready for school. All week, I've seen her only from a distance. She walks the halls with her nose buried in a book, rushing between AP tests.

Biology, Physics, Chemistry, Calculus.

I'm sure she'll ace them all. Good grades are the only way to capture her parents' attention. They trade affirmations for straight-A report cards, expressions of love for academic excellence. And Jo complies, working herself to the bone for a condescending pat on the head.

It's sickening to witness.

When I reach the boathouse, I jog down the steps to the dock. My thoughts are a mile away — zig-zagging between a dozen pressing concerns. Which is probably why I don't see the girl lying flat on her back at the far end of the dock until I'm a handful of paces away.

My steps falter.

She's fast asleep, snoozing in the sunshine like a cat in a picture window. As soon as I see her, all the anger I've been harboring bleeds out of me in a rush, pooling in a puddle at my feet.

For a moment, I can only stare — at the morning light on her face, slanting across the upturned bridge of her nose. At the billowed length of blonde hair, pillowed beneath her bare shoulders. At the glow of her skin, kissed by the start of a summer tan.

I barely breathe, not wanting to disturb her slumber. I'm not sure how long I stand there watching her. Probably long enough for it to be creepy.

I don't give a shit.

These unguarded moments with Jo are precious to me now. *Who knows how many more I'll get?*

I wish I could stretch each fleeting second I spend in her

presence into an hour, a day, a lifetime. I wish I could hold her soft exhales in the palms of my hands, cradle their warmth against my chest to ward off the cold realities that have taken up residence inside my heart.

Her effortless beauty grabs me by the throat. That smart-talking mouth, currently slack with sleep. Those ridiculous dimples, dents of joy in rosy cheeks. I study her intently. Every freckle, every eyelash. Every perceived flaw she sees when she looks in the mirror.

I want to run my fingertips over them. To trace her imperfections with my hands until she realizes they were never imperfections at all.

God, I need to kiss her.

It's an impulse I've had forever. One I've spent a lifetime tamping down, trying to ignore. Unsuccessfully, as it turns out.

I can't help it. Since the moment I first learned what kissing was, I've wanted to do it with Jo. I've dreamed about it. Ached for it. Just once, I want to feel the press of her mouth on mine. To lose myself in the riptide of her lips until I'm lost at sea, too far out to ever turn back.

Her blue eyes blink open without warning.

Shit.

I barely have time to wipe the longing look off my face, to reassemble my features into an indifferent mask before she sits up and spots me standing there, ten feet away.

"*You.*" She starts, eyes widening. "What are you doing here?"

I swallow roughly. "I didn't know you were here."

"Clearly." She climbs to her feet, brushing sea-salt off her bare legs. Her dark blue pajama set perfectly matches the color of the cove surrounding us. "If you'd known, you wouldn't be standing there, would you?"

I don't react; I don't say a word in my own defense.

Unfortunately, my silence seems to piss her off even more, judging by the way her brows pinch together. "I saw Jax the other night," she says, an accusation in her voice. I didn't even know he was out."

"Sorry," I mutter. "I should've told you."

She takes a step toward me. Her whole frame is shaking — not with cold, but with fury. "No. You don't owe me anything. We aren't even friends. We're *nothing*. Right?"

My mouth opens. "Jo—"

"I heard you," she snarls. "The other night. I heard exactly what you said to Jaxon. *I tolerate her for exactly one reason: her parents paid my tuition.*" She steps even closer. "*As soon as I walk across that graduation stage, I plan to keep on walking, right out of her life.*" Another step. We're only a pace apart, now. "*Jo Valentine means nothing to me.*"

The blood drains from my face. "Jo—"

"Don't bother." Her mouth twists. "I don't need to hear whatever excuse you're going to come up with to justify your behavior. I don't want to listen to whatever lie you'll use to make me feel better about this."

"But—"

"No! *No.* Don't you understand? I don't care anymore, Archer. I can't. I don't have it in me. For weeks, I've done everything I can think of to reach you, to make things better between us..." She blinks rapidly, fighting back tears. "Silly me for thinking we were ever something worth fixing."

I flinch.

She takes a shaky breath. "So I'm done now. Done caring. Done trying. Just... *done.*" There's a loaded pause, stretching in the space between us. "But before I go, I need you to tell me one thing. I think you owe me that much."

My heart is pounding so hard, I'm sure she can hear it. Still, my voice comes out remarkably level. "What is it?"

"If you were truly just pretending to be my friend for all this time... Why did you have to do it so damn convincingly?" Her voice cracks, and I feel my heart crack right along with it. "Why did you let me believe it was real for all this time?"

Right now, even if I had an answer for her, I wouldn't be able to give it. My throat is so blocked with emotion, speaking is impossible.

Her eyes hold mine for a small forever. They are infinitely blue, unfathomably blue. The kind of blue that can't be captured. It's the same hue you see at the point where sea meets sky on a distant horizon.

Forever out of reach.

"Happy birthday, Archer," Jo whispers haltingly. "I hope you got everything you wanted."

She darts around me and walks away — down the dock, up the lawn, into the house. I stand there like a man carved from stone, listening as her footsteps fade, staring out at the ocean. I don't bother reaching up to brush away the tears that drop like rain onto my cheeks.

There's no one around to see.

Before I finally go, I reach into my pocket and place the jewelry box at the end of the dock — like an offering left to the sea gods of olden times. I can't bear to throw the necklace out. Better to let it be swept away by the wind or swallowed up by a rogue wave.

"You're not nothing, Jo," I whisper thickly as my fingers stroke the small velvet box one last time. "You're the only thing."

CHAPTER NINETEEN

JOSEPHINE

JUST AS IT has for the past seventeen years of my life on this particular day... at 8:00AM on the dot, the song begins to play.

"Joesphine" by *The Wallflowers*.

I burst out of bed when I hear the opening strains and run down the stairs in my pajamas, barely slowing my pace as I race across the first floor. Excitement churns inside my veins. I wonder what my parents have planned for me this year.

A picnic on the Hinckley out at Misery Island? Lunch at my favorite restaurant in Rockport, with a harbor view featuring the famous Motif #1? A drive down the coast, into the city, for dinner and a show?

Frankly, I don't care what we do. I'm just eager for a full day with them.

A day not about work.

A day only about their daughter.

In light of recent events, I've never felt more in need of their love. Perhaps they can fill a sliver of the chasm Archer has opened up inside my chest.

Skidding to a stop in the entrance to the kitchen, my head

swivels around in search of them. Except... I only see Flora and Miguel standing by the marble island, smiling at me as The Wallflowers whisper their final refrain.

"Happy birthday to you, happy birthday to you," they sing together, their voices off-key. They're each wearing a cheap paper party hat. "Happy birthday, dear Josephine. Happy birthday to you."

"Thanks, guys..." My brows are arched. "But... where are my parents?"

Miguel and Flora glance at each other. "The thing is, *mija*—"

"They're gone, aren't they?" I ask, even though I already know the answer.

Miguel scratches the back of his neck. "They left this morning."

"Ah."

Flora wrings her hands. "There was an urgent issue with VALENT."

I try to smile, but can't quite manage it. The excitement inside me had deflated like a week-old birthday balloon. "Urgent. Of course. It always is, when it comes to their company."

Never to their daughter.

"They left you a note." Flora gestures at the piece of paper sitting on the countertop. "I'm sure it explains everything better than we could."

With a nod, I walk forward and snatch up the stationary. It's a thick, creamy cardstock, embossed with the name BLAIR VALENTINE at the top. Honestly, I'm surprised she didn't use the company letterhead; this feels more like an internal memo from Management than a love note between mother and child.

My eyes scan the handwriting — an immaculate, sloping

script, each letter crafted with utmost care. Almost like calligraphy. If Blair had been the kind of mother who'd left cute notes in my school lunchboxes, they'd surely have been the envy of the elementary cafeteria.

I was always fascinated by the kids whose mother's tucked colorful post-its beside their sandwiches and thermoses, desperately curious about the messages scribbled there. Probably something trivial, I assured myself.

Have a great day, sweetie pie!

I love you to the moon and back!

Those who were lucky enough to receive notes would roll their eyes in exasperation, but they could never quite conceal their smiles. An undeniable glow of security seemed to emanate from their pores as they bit into peanut-butter and jelly sandwiches with the crusts thoughtfully cut off.

I am loved, their posture broadcasted smugly. *My parents love me.*

At the end of every lunch period, I'd watch those same kids crumple up their post-its and toss them away along with their granola bar wrappers and empty juice boxes. The temptation to fish them out of the garbage, simply to understand what I was missing, only faded as I moved on to middle school.

No one packs their lunch at a private academy.

Dearest Josephine,

By the time you read this, your father and I will be at 35,000 feet, halfway across the Atlantic. Though it pains us to leave you, we had no choice in the matter. A catastrophic packaging issue has arisen at our distribution center in Geneva. We must deal with it at once, otherwise risk delaying next month's relief shipments.

I am certain you understand the importance of our trip, for we have raised you to value the lives of many over the happiness of one. On this, the first day of your eighteenth year, may you step into adulthood with all the poise and purpose we have instilled in you since your birth.

We will make every effort to return in time for your graduation next week. Until then, know we are in a state of utmost suspense, awaiting the brilliance of your valedictorian speech.

Happy birthday, darling.

Hugs!

Blair & Vincent Valentine

PS: There are several gifts awaiting you on the dining room table. We do hope you put them to good use in our absence. xx

---

My mother always signs her notes with their full names. It's as though she's preparing them for a future museum exhibit chronicling their lives, or perhaps a PBS special on the glorious existence of two modern-day saints.

Here, you'll see correspondance between Blair Valentine and her daughter, written on Josephine's eighteenth birthday. A tireless human rights advocate, Blair prioritized her work above even her own family obligations.

I hope I'm long dead by the time the powers-that-be determine our family's historical relevance should be displayed behind glass.

When I set down the stationary, I'm immediately enveloped in a double embrace. Flora and Miguel hold me tight for far longer than five regimented seconds. Trying not to cry, I allow myself to bask in their warmth until my pulse slows its furious pace.

"Are you okay?" Flora asks when I finally pull back.

I wipe my eyes with the sleeve of my shirt. "Of course."

"If you want, we can spend the day with you," Miguel offers. "Maybe take you out for lunch at that pizza place you like—"

"No, that's all right." I force a stiff smile. "If anything, I should be grateful they were here as long as they were. Five full days, this time — that's practically a record. And they'll be back for graduation next week."

I'm not sure whether I'm trying to convince them or myself.

Flora frowns. "But, *mija*—"

"I'm okay. I promise." I take a deep breath. "Who cares about a stupid birthday, anyway? It's just a regular old Saturday, as far as I'm concerned."

Miguel crosses his arms over his chest. "You're sure you don't want to do anything to celebrate?"

My lips twist. "I have a speech to write."

"You can't sit alone, doing schoolwork on your birthday." Flora's brows pull together. "At least say you'll come to the baseball game with us tonight."

"State Championship." Miguel nods. "Should be an intense game. Xaverian is also undefeated this season."

"Oh, um..." I trail off, not knowing how to explain that seeing their son is the last way on earth I want to spend my birthday.

"Can you believe it's Archer's final high school game?" Flora plops down onto a stool, shaking her head in disbelief. "Next time he steps onto a pitching mound, he'll be a collegiate athlete."

"Go Bulldogs!" Miguel cheers.

"Bulldogs?" My eyes go wide. My breath catches. "As in... the Bryant Bulldogs?"

They glance at one another.

"Surely, Archer told you?" Miguel asks hesitantly.

"No." I shake my head. "No, he didn't."

"*Dios mío*, we've ruined his surprise." Flora smacks her palm against her forehead. "I'm sure he was planning to tell you tonight. Oh, Josephine, promise you'll act like you don't know when he tells you."

"*If* he tells me," I mutter.

"Of course he will." Miguel waves my words away. "You're his best friend."

Flora is staring at me, her eyes brimming with curiosity. "Is everything okay between you and Archer?"

"Sure," I lie brightly. "Why wouldn't it be?"

I'm not upset at all by the fact he didn't tell me about his college decision. I'm not remotely confused that he's chosen to attend a school mere minutes away from mine, despite having offers from better baseball programs across the country. And I'm certainly not still reeling from our confrontation yesterday.

Nope.

Not at all.

Not one bit.

"You just seem..." Flora trails off.

"Leave the girl alone." Miguel shoots her a look.

"Fine, fine." Flora lifts her hands in surrender. "Josephine, would you like your presents, now? They're in the dining room."

I heave a sigh. "Might as well get it over with..."

Walking into the adjacent room, I can't help thinking that Blair and Vincent's presents are a perfect reflection of their parenting style — practical, impersonal, and unadorned. No shiny wrapping paper or frilly bows. No oddly-shaped boxes to build anticipation. The gifts sit on the table, laid out in an orderly row.

A fountain pen.

A moleskin journal.

A box of dermatological cream.

A book titled *Global Nutrition*.

How perfectly pragmatic.

I carry the stack of gifts up to my room, telling myself to be grateful. So what if the notebook and pen serve as a not-so-subtle nudge to write my speech? Who cares about Blair's slightly off-putting determination to erase my under-eye circles? What does it matter that Vincent's idea of father-daughter bonding involves a book report on world hunger?

Be grateful, Jo.

Some kids don't get any presents at all.

I TRY to write the speech. I swear, I do. But the words simply will not manifest. The longer I stare at my laptop screen, the emptier my mind becomes. After a full hour of frustration, the walls of Cormorant House seem to press in around me, an ever-tightening vise.

In desperate need of fresh air, I back the Porsche out of the garage and head for open roads. The wrought-iron gates swing closed behind me with a loud clang that reminds me of a prison cell.

Free at last.

Beneath the lingering disappointment at their departure, a small part of me is undeniably glad my parents are gone again. I'm not sure I could've survived another dinner of stilted conversation, putting on a brave face as they questioned me about my AP examinations. I don't know how many more breakfasts I could've spent deflecting their inquisition into the status of my speech.

Frankly, the burden of their disappointment made it difficult to swallow down my food.

I've always found it annoying how Hollywood movies push the bullshit idea that your parents are supposed to love you unconditionally. (Maybe that's why I prefer to watch reality baking shows.) Blair and Vincent made it crystal clear from day one that their fondness for me would rise and fall in direct proportion to my achievements.

It's a lesson I was glad to learn.

Love is not a fixed constant in the equation of life, even if we treat it like one. Expecting anyone to love you invariably is foolish. Emotions are at best vacillating, at worst volatile. And always, always, always conditional.

The summer sun beats down, warming my shoulders as I meander through town. I buy an iced macchiato at the Starbucks drive-thru, taking cooling sips at every stoplight. The picturesque June weather has brought with it the first tourists of the season. They wander in small family units, purchasing kitschy, nautical-themed knickknacks from overpriced boutiques. Couples hold hands as their children chase after ice-cream trucks, dollar bills outstretched. In the park, a caricature artist sketches portraits for passerby while a local guitarist busks for tips, his guitar case spread wide.

I drive for about twenty minutes, selecting streets at random, and eventually find myself on the far side of town, not far from Exeter. I pull into the parking lot. It's empty now, but in a few hours it'll be jammed with tailgaters, their faces painted green for the big game against Xaverian Brothers High School.

I park near the bleachers. I've already searched them once for my missing iPhone, but I figure it can't hurt to check again. I was in a rush on Monday morning, with only a few minutes to spare before my Physics exam. I didn't have the chance to be thorough. If my phone fell through the gap, there's a good chance it's still sitting there.

The world is dim below the ascending seats. Sun slants through the rows at odd angles as I step into the dark. I weave around metal suspension poles, keeping my eyes on the ground. Cigarette butts are scattered every so often, along with crushed beer cans — evidence of more than one post-game celebration. My sandals crunch on discarded peanut shells and pieces of litter as I walk the shadowy length.

It's eerily quiet and cramped beneath the bleachers. Chain link fencing forms a cage at the back end, metal hangs close overhead.

Lucky I'm not claustrophobic.

Still, I increase my pace as the search continues, keen to return to the plentiful sunshine in the parking lot. The few belongings I stumble across don't belong to me — a man's empty wallet, a child's pink stuffed bear, a baby's dirty pacifier. Against the fence, a metallic glint momentarily gives me hope. Upon closer examination, it turns out to be nothing but a piece of aluminum foil.

I sigh, defeated.

No sign of my iPhone anywhere.

Doubling back, I retrace my steps toward the parking lot. The sun-drenched asphalt is a welcoming light at the end of a shadowy tunnel. I'm so relieved to be out of the dark, I don't notice I'm not alone until I'm halfway to my car.

"Pretty sweet ride you've got there."

Startled, I whirl around toward the voice. Two unfamiliar men are standing on the bleachers, staring down at me. I squint against the bright sky, trying to bring them into focus. It's difficult to make out their faces in silhouette.

"Thanks," I murmur, backpedalling a step. I'm not in any explicit danger, but for some reason my heart has kicked into high gear.

"Is it for sale?" The man asks. "Our boss has a pretty sweet collection of vintage cars. I'm sure he'd love to add a classic Cabriolet to his fleet."

As he's speaking, he starts walking down the bleachers. His companion follows in silence.

"No, sorry." Shaking my head. "It's not for sale."

"Shame." The man sighs. "If you like classic cars, you should take a look at our Bronco." He points behind me. "She's a beaut, huh?"

Not wanting to appear impolite, I dutifully glance over at the boxy black vehicle, parked beneath a tree on the other side of the parking lot.

"Cool," I murmur, not knowing what else to say. "Looks vintage."

"Built way back 1970 — long before you were born, huh? What are you, seventeen?"

I glance back just in time to see the men step off the bleachers, onto the asphalt. Without the sun shining into my eyes, I'm able to see their faces clearly for the first time. Nervous butterflies burst into life in the pit of my stomach. Between the copious tattoos, stacked muscles, and vaguely menacing demeanors, they're not at all what I was expecting.

I'm probably being irrational, but there's something unsettling about the way they're watching me. Like two cats eyeing a field mouse, moments before the pounce. I back up another few steps, trying to keep a safe margin of space between us. The car is still a dozen paces away.

"Eighteen," I blurt nervously. "Today, in fact."

"Happy birthday."

"Thanks." When I bump into the side panel of my car, I

reach blindly for the door handle, not wanting to take my eyes off the men still walking toward me in slow strides. "I, uh... I have to go, now. My parents are expecting me. Have a good day."

"Where are you running off to so fast, sweetheart?" His eyes slide to his friend and he gives a small nod. "We have some things to ask you about..."

I yank at the handle, no longer caring about looking rude. Before I can get the door fully open, someone reaches out and slams it shut again. I scream as the man grabs me, but the sound is quickly silenced as his right hand clamps down over my mouth. His left wraps around my waist and lifts me straight off my feet.

My teeth sink into his palm; he barely even flinches. Thrashing against his hold, my legs pedal uselessly at empty air. The man holding me might as well be made of stone; his chest, pressed against my back, is solid granite.

My eyes scan our surroundings. The parking lot is totally deserted. Even if I could scream, there's no one around to hear me.

I'm on my own.

The scrawnier man — the one who's been doing all the talking — steps into my view. He's smiling at me like we're old friends.

"Okay, then. I'm Rico. This is my associate, Barboza. If you're a good girl and you answer our questions, this birthday won't be the last one you celebrate. Understand?"

It's difficult to breathe with the massive palm pressing down over my face; speaking is not an option. I stare at him blankly, trying not to cry. My heart is beating so hard, I'm worried it might combust.

"Nod if you understand me," Rico says flatly.

Somehow, I manage a small nod.

"Good girl. Now, we know you're tight with the Reyes boys. Personally, I don't care if you're dating the younger one or the older one. Hell, for all I know you switch back and forth between the two. Whatever. I don't judge."

Rage flares inside me.

"Look at that fire in your eyes!" Leaning closer, he brings his pockmarked face within inches of mine. "No wonder those boys keep you so close. White as snow, but I bet you're *en fuego* in the sheets. Am I right, mami?"

My glare intensifies.

"You ever get the urge to try out a real man, you let me know." He sticks his tongue out and wags it rapidly at me.

I go stiff as a board. Fear burns through me, a hot current.

This situation could get a lot worse for me.

Rico laughs, enjoying himself. "Oh, lighten up. The only thing I want from you today is information. Think you can you help me with that?"

I give another small nod.

"Excellent. Where is Jaxon?"

Eyes going wide, I shake my head. My response is muffled.

He jerks his head at his partner, and the pressure loosens enough for me to gasp out a few ragged words.

"I don't... know anything... about Jaxon."

"That's not what I want to hear, sweetheart." Rico sighs. "We saw you leave that party with him last weekend. But he's a sneaky bastard. He managed to slip our net after he dropped you off."

I try to get my breathing under control. "I haven't seen him since!"

"You sure about that?"

"I swear. I haven't seen him."

"Did he say where he was heading?"

I shake my head. "No. He just dropped me off."

"You notice anything inside his car? Maybe a receipt from a motel or a restaurant? Any clue about where he's hiding out?"

"No, I didn't notice anything. But I wasn't really looking."

Rico leans in and stares at me for a long beat, studying my face for signs that I'm lying. Eventually, he heaves an annoyed sigh. "Next time, pay better attention."

"O-okay," I bleat. "I will."

"If he shows up again — and he will show up, make no mistake — we want to know about it. You understand?"

"Y-yes."

"Good. Your little baseball star boyfriend knows how to get in touch."

He jerks his chin at his partner. Barboza releases me instantly. I drop like a rag doll, crumpling to the pavement in a pile of limp limbs. A heavy boot stomps down, directly beside my head.

I flinch into the fetal position — curling my knees to my chest, shielding my head with my arms. Trying to make myself as small as humanly possible.

Rico chuckles. "See you soon, sweetheart."

I don't dare move until the sound of their footsteps has retreated across the parking lot, until their engine has rumbled out of earshot. When I finally find my feet, the men are long gone.

I pick up my keys, climb into my car, and start the engine. I'm halfway home when I have to pull over again.

My eyes are too full of tears to see the road.

CHAPTER TWENTY

ARCHER

THE CAMERAS FLASH from all sides, a blinding strobe. I grin as I lift the State Championship trophy over my head. My teammates are a blur of motion around me — jumping into the air, pounding their chests, howling at the top of their lungs.

"WOLFPACK! *AH-WOOOOO!*"

"STATE CHAMPS!"

"UNDEFEATED, BABY!"

The Xaverian team trudges off the field, disappointment ebbing off them in waves. They gave their best effort, but it wasn't enough to beat us.

To beat *me*.

Tonight, I brought my A-game. I channeled every ounce of rage and fear and self-loathing into my arm; let it coil in my muscles like electrical charges in a storm cloud. Each pitch was a lightning strike, a bolt of pure power flying out with unstoppable force.

No batter stood a chance.

Inning after inning, they stepped up, determined to land a

hit. Inning after inning, I sent them back to the dugout, unsuc-
cessful in their efforts.

A no-hitter.

A massacre.

HOME: 10

AWAY: 0

A perfect end to a perfect season.

After the final score is called, Exeter fans flood onto the
field — a mix of family members and significant others, alumni
and school staff. I briefly catch sight of my parents in the mob,
jumping up and down like enthusiastic teenagers. I lose track of
them when Chris Tomlinson and Andy Hilton hoist me into
the air. The whole team begins to chant my name.

"*REY-ES! REY-ES!*"

My body shoots higher toward the sky with each syllable.

"*REY-ES! REY-ES! REY-ES!*"

Aloft on Chris and Andy's shoulders, I hold the trophy over
my head for the world to see. The crowd yells their support.

"*AH-WOOO!*"

"*WOLFPACK!*"

"*AH-WOOOOO!*"

I know it's stupid, but I find myself searching their faces for
Jo. Seeking her out, despite every instinct in my body shouting
at me to stop.

She's not howling with the Wadell twins.

Not jumping with my parents.

Not anywhere.

My smile is slightly strained as I'm brought back down to
solid ground. I fight the urge to pull my hat brim down over my
eyes when a reporter with a *Boston Globe* press lanyard
hanging from his neck shoves a microphone into my face. A
cameramen stands beside him, filming the celebration.

"Archer!" the reporter yells over the din. "Congratulations

on your undefeated season. How are you feeling right now, after leading Exeter to a State Championship title?"

"This trophy doesn't just belong to me — it belongs to every guy on this team. I'm proud of the work we've done together. We had an unbelievably talented roster this season. Not to mention an amazing coach."

I turn toward Coach Hamm. His eyes are glassy with emotion as he holds out his hand for me to shake. I clasp his palm firmly against mine as cameras flash all around us.

"Coaching you, Reyes..." His chest swells. "It was an honor."

"Honor was mine, Coach." My Adam's apple bobs as I work to clear the lump in my throat. "I'm going to miss being an Exeter Wolf."

The reporter leans in, microphone extended. "Archer, you are currently the top-ranked high school pitcher in the country, but you have yet to confirm where you'll be playing next year. Do you have any plans to announce your decision? Or are you going to leave us in suspense all summer?"

Dropping Coach Hamm's hand, I turn to look directly into the cameras. "I consider myself supremely lucky to have had so many amazing offers. It would be an honor to play for any collegiate team. But I'm ready to announce my decision."

A hush falls over the crowd.

People jostle closer, straining to hear.

"Have you signed your National Letter of Intent?" the reporter asks.

I nod. "Signed, sealed, delivered this morning."

"Where are you headed, Archer?"

I take a breath, conscious of the many eyes on me. Trying to savor the moment — cameras rolling, press waiting breathlessly for an answer.

One day, in the not too distant future, they'll be taking my statement for the Globe's Sports section after I pitch a no-hitter at Fenway.

"Come next spring, I'm proud to say I'll be putting on the black and gold Bulldogs uniform at Bryant University."

Everyone applauds, clapping and cheering for me in a wave of sound that makes my eyes sting.

"Any reason you chose Bryant in particular, Archer?"

I swallow hard. "I want to be close to the people I love most."

***

AS SOON AS the fans clear out, we break out the keg. Chris and Andy hoist it onto the field and place it on home plate. The entire varsity team huddles around, waiting for their chance to pump the tap into a red plastic cup.

I've never been one for hazing rituals or cult-like team bonding exercises, but this one Wolfpack tradition feels like a fitting send-off to our season — and, for some, to the game in general. Most of these guys won't play at the collegiate level. Certainly not in the minor or major leagues. Which means, as of tonight, their baseball careers are effectively over.

When all eighteen of us have full cups, we gather in one final player huddle.

"Wolfpack on three!" I yell, holding up my cup toward the sky, where a full moon is rising.

A chorus of voices joins in, cups lifting to join mine. "One... two... three... *WOLFPACK!*"

We chug until our cups are dry.

Then we fill them up again.

And repeat... and repeat... and repeat... until I've lost track of how many beers I've consumed. Until the world has turned into a tilt-a-whirl, spinning madly all around me.

For one night only, I don't worry about repercussions or responsibilities. I allow myself to be just another one of the guys, laughing at stupid jokes, reminiscing over our best plays, celebrating the end of something that, in many ways, defined my teenage years.

My eyes sweep around the empty stadium. Without the bright overhead lights blazing, it's lit only by moonlight. The bases glow in the dark, white squares shining in a perfect diamond formation. The pitcher's mound is a dark hill at the center.

There are many things I will not miss about Exeter Academy of Excellence. The god-awful green uniforms, for one. Don't get me started on the demanding teachers. The pretentious students. The utter lack of diversity in the student body.

But I will miss this. Being a Wolf. Screaming my lungs out with my teammates on a dirt patch three nights a week, knowing we're about to send our rivals home with wounded pride.

I never feel quite myself during the off-season. Without baseball, I am utterly unexceptional. Just like any other guy on the street. For months on end, I walk around with restless hands, waiting for the day I'll finally pick up my glove again. It's as though I've pushed the mute button on the most vital part of me.

I still haven't quite wrapped my head around the fact that the next time I play, it'll be in another stadium entirely. Another state. Another chapter. But for tonight... for one last night... I am still a Wolf. I push the future aside as I howl up at the full moon with the teammates who've become unlikely friends.

At some point, someone discovers that The State Championship trophy — shaped like a massive chalice with ornate gold handles — makes for a perfect drinking goblet. Lee Park shoves it into my hands, filled to the brim with frothy beer.

I laugh as I lift it to my lips, already regretting the headache I'm going to have in the morning but far too buzzed to argue.

"REY-ES! REY-ES! REY-ES!"

The entire team chants, their volume growing to a roaring crescendo as I begin to chug the contents. I don't stop until the chalice is completely empty.

"Hell yeah!" Chris pounds my back, grinning ear to ear. "That's how it's done!"

"Yo! Reyes!" Andy calls, picking up a bat and giving it a few lopsided swings. "Let's see if you can still strike me out when you're blackout drunk."

"Hilton, I could strike you out blindfolded."

He tosses the bat at me. I dodge it, stumbling slightly. My reflexes are slower than usual, sloshing around beneath a layer of foam.

"Ah yes. The great Archer Reyes." Ryan Snyder scoffs sarcastically, shooting me a scathing look across the keg. Even in the dark, his double black eyes are apparent. "A hundred bucks says he crashes and burns before his first collegiate season. Any takers?"

There's a collective intake of air as silence falls over the rowdy group.

Snyder isn't done. His slurred voice booms into the night like a thunderclap. "Two hundred bucks says he never even makes it off the bench!" He smirks. "Archer Reyes is nothing but a flash in the pan."

In the suffocating quiet that follows, I set down the trophy with deliberate slowness. Screwing up my face in faux-confusion, I glance around the group, then back at Ryan's twin black eyes.

"Sorry... could someone translate what he just said?" I ask. "I don't speak raccoon."

Chris snorts beer out his nose.

Snyder takes two steps toward me, tossing his empty cup to the ground. His fists swing up into a fighting stance. "You want to go, asshole?"

"*Go?*" My brows shoot upward. "Go where? The prom? I'm flattered. Thought you already had a date, but if you insist..."

"Shut up!" Snyder hisses, still advancing on me with violence etched across his face.

I don't move an inch. My voice is bored. "I've punched you out twice now, Snyder. You keep coming back for more, people will start thinking you've got a crush on me."

"I said *SHUT UP!*"

"And I said I don't speak halfwit, raccoon-eyed rich boy. Keep up, will you?"

Charging forward, Ryan really looks like he might kill me. Right now, I'm feeling reckless enough to let him try. Thankfully, Chris and Andy are less keen on bloodshed. They step forward to block his path, forcing him back with unyielding grips.

"Let me go!" Ryan growls.

"Would you two kiss and make up already?" Andy snaps, his muscles straining. "No girl is worth this."

My reply is instant. "Depends on the girl."

"Whatever. I'm over this," Snyder mutters, finally backing off. In his first wise move maybe ever, he walks over to the dugout where Carl MacDonald is drinking, swearing under his breath the whole way.

Chris looks at me and Andy. "Let it be known: I will miss you two goons, but I will not miss some of our teammates."

"I'll drink to that," Andy says, raising his cup.

By midnight, the keg is empty and we're all completely wasted. The bleachers are scattered with unconscious bodies. Red cups litter the infield like confetti. Steve Abbott is using first base as a pillow. Jason Samborn is slumped against the batting cage, snoring like a freight train.

Chris, Andy, and I are lying in the outfield, staring up at the stars. They swim around like fireflies before my eyes.

"Guess I should call for extraction," Chris says, fumbling for his phone to text the JV team — tonight's designated drivers. "Gotta get everyone out of here before the sprinklers turn on at 2AM."

He stumbles off toward the bleachers to rouse the fallen soldiers.

"I can't believe it's over," Andy murmurs when it's just the two of us.

"Aren't you trying out for the team at San Diego State?" I turn my head to look at him. "You'll have a chance to play again."

"I'm not talking about baseball, man. I mean... *this*. High school." He shakes his head. "Took my last final on Friday. Playoffs are over. Yearbook is signed. All that's left is prom and graduation."

"Just graduation for me."

"You're not going to prom?"

"Nah."

"What the hell, man?"

"No date."

"Dude, I barely have a date. I'm taking June Woods. The girl has zero personality. If she were a genre, she'd be hold music."

I snort. "She can't be that bad."

"Trust me. She is." He grimaces. "What about Valentine?"

"What about her?"

"I always assumed…"

My tone flattens. *"What?"*

"Don't give me that death-stare! Jeez, you're so touchy when it comes to her."

Gritting my teeth, I glance back at the stars. "Sorry."

Andy is silent for a long stretch, then clears his throat. "Look, it's none of my business, man. I don't know what went down between you and Snyder, or why he'd bother trying to start something with your girl when it's clear to anyone with eyes that you two are star-crossed lovers or some shit like that. But I do know one thing. If you're so crazy about her, you should tell her. *Soon.* Before everything changes. It might be your last chance."

I offer nothing in response. But as I stare up at the night sky, his words churn over and over inside my head, stirring up unwelcome emotions. Making me want things I can't have.

After a few minutes, the JV players begin to arrive, their headlights flashing brightly in the parking lot as they herd the uncooperative drunkards into their back seats. Andy and I start walking toward the parking lot. Our gaits are both a bit staggered.

"It's because I'm so crazy about her," I say haltingly as we pass home plate.

"What?"

I look at him. "The reason I can't risk telling her how I feel. It's because I'm so crazy about her."

"Dude… that makes no fucking sense."

"Welcome to my life."

CHAPTER TWENTY-ONE

JOSEPHINE

THERE'S a giant hornet flying around inside my head. Burrowing between my ears with a relentless drone. Pushing me toward consciousness.

Bzzzzzz.

Bzzzzzz.

Bzzzzzz.

I sit up in bed, the dream fragmenting into fuzzy images of incandescent wings and yellow stripes. It takes a moment to register that the sound I'm hearing is not happening inside my head. It's coming from the front door access panel, downstairs in the atrium. Someone is ringing the guest buzzer at the outer gate.

What the hell?

It's the middle of the night — the world outside my windows is a grayscale painting, awash in strokes of ebony. The clock on my bedside table reads 1:35 AM.

Who would come here this late?

My stomach turns to stone as memories of yesterday morning come rushing back. Those men, in the parking lot...

Is it them?

Are they here?

Somehow, I doubt they'd bother ringing the bell.

It took me ages to fall asleep, even with a state-of-the-art security system to alert me to any intruders. I'm actually surprised I managed to nod off at all. Every time I closed my eyes, I saw a pockmarked cheek and cold black eyes. I heard a voice, chill with malice.

See you soon, sweetheart.

My mental exhaustion must've finally outweighed my anxiety. I wore myself out with worry all afternoon, going back and forth over my options a million and a half times.

Should I call my parents? Tell them what happened? Ask for help?

I quickly tossed that idea to the curb. Blair and Vincent are a world away, dealing with their so-called packaging crisis. There's nothing they can possibly do to make things better.

Should I call the police? File a report? Give a written statement about the men who attacked me?

Not without setting off a chain reaction of events out of my control. More than likely, the second I utter the name 'Reyes,' the officer in charge will haul Flora and Miguel into the station for questioning. Jaxon could wind up in trouble again. And as for Archer...

He has far too much to lose, right now. His future, his dreams, are finally within his grasp. I refuse to be the one to drag him further into... whatever this is. Not after he's worked so hard to distance himself from his older brother's reputation.

The more I think about it, the more convinced I become that what happened to me yesterday has something to do with how he's been acting these past few weeks. Rico basically confirmed it with a single offhand comment.

Your little baseball star boyfriend knows how to get in touch.

It's like someone's finally handed me the missing pieces of a puzzle. I turn them over in my hands, trying to fit them into a picture that no longer makes any sense.

My frustration is almost as strong as my fear. I may not understand exactly what's happening here... but I know in my bones that Jaxon is the root of it. Any problem the Reyes family has ever endured is a direct result of his poor choices. And it surely cannot be a coincidence that Archer started pushing me away as soon as his brother was released from jail.

His cold indifference, his cruel treatment, his sudden avoidance... I replay it all with fresh eyes, consumed by a desperate sort of hope. A fool's hope, perhaps. But hope is a funny thing. It can ensnare all logic, can break apart the most convincing of lies.

Maybe it was all an act.

I cling to that possibility like a naive little girl, clutching her teddy bear to ward off the monsters under her bed. It's pathetic how acutely I want to believe there's an alternate explanation for the seismic shift in the boy I love.

Bzzzzzzz.

The gate rings again. I grab the large knife off my beside table — the one I took from the kitchen earlier, just in case — and make my way downstairs. The access panel glows in the dark, its buttons a faint row of illumination. I press one to enable the microphone and outside camera. The screen flickers to life, revealing a black Jeep Wrangler waiting at the gates.

I'm so relieved it's not a Ford Bronco, I nearly fall over.

"H-hello?" I bark into the intercom, trying to sound assertive. "Who's there?"

The driver sticks his head out the window, pressing his nose practically against the lens. Despite the slight fishbowl effect of the camera, his face is vaguely familiar to me. I'm almost positive he's one of the JV baseball players. Justin Some-thing-Or-Other. A junior at Exeter.

As for why he's at my home at two in the morning, I have no earthly idea.

"Oh, good, you're here!" he bleats nervously. Beneath the rim of his baseball cap, his acne-peppered cheeks are flushed with embarrassment. "I'm sorry to bother you so late, but I'm the designated driver tonight. I'm supposed to drop off Reyes, but he won't give me his address..." The boy darts a look at his passenger seat. "He just keeps telling me to take him here... to you..."

I press a hand to my temple.

Of course.

"I'll take him somewhere else if you want," the boy says. "It's just... he's pretty insistent—"

"*Jo!*" Archer shouts suddenly, his voice garbled. His head appears out the open roof of the Wrangler as he stands up in his seat. "It's me, Jo..."

He looks unsteady, swaying in the wind. Even through the camera, his eyes are visibly bloodshot.

"I forgot the code," he tells me, laughing like it's the funniest thing in the world. "Can you buzz us in?"

I bring my lips close to the two-way speaker. "Why should I help you, Archer? You're a total jerk."

"I know. I know I am. But..." His hands press together in prayer. "*Pleaseeeeee*, JoJo. Let me *innnnn.*"

His voice is slurred and full of static, but it still slides over me like a drug, triggering goosebumps across my skin. I hate myself for being so affected by him. I hate that, even when he's treating me like crap, he owns every beat of my stupid heart.

"Fine." I sigh deeply. "Not that you deserve it."

Before I can second-guess myself, I jam my finger against the button, allowing the gates to swing wide.

I STAND on the front steps in my fuzzy slippers, shivering against the cold. My pajama set is painfully thin.

Thankfully, I don't have to wait long for the Wrangler to make its way up to the house. My eyes lock on the beam of its headlights arcing around the circular driveway. It stops at the bottom of the steps with a crunch of gravel.

Stomach twisting with nerves, I descend to it slowly. I'm nearly there when the passenger door swings open. Archer practically falls out onto the pea stone. It seems, in the time it took to travel from the front gates, he's slipped even further into the clutches of inebriation.

"Fuck!" he exclaims as he falls.

I react instinctually — darting forward to catch him before he can face-plant. I grunt as we collide, struggling to hold his not-insignificant weight upright. His arm slings heavily across my shoulders. His head lolls toward the crook of my neck.

"Hi, Jo."

"Jesus, you're heavy," I rasp.

"*You're* heavy."

"Good comeback."

His whole body starts shaking with laughter. "I personally thought so."

"I'm glad you find this so amusing." Despite my best intentions, my lips twist. I've never seen him this hammered before. "Come on, big boy. Let's try to walk. That's it. Nice and easy. Lift your feet."

Blessedly, Justin materializes at my side and takes half of Archer's weight. Just in time, too — Archer is fading fast, his arms hanging limply at his sides, his eyelids fluttering closed.

Together, we manage to get him up the steps, onto the terrace. I'm panting by the time we maneuver his prone body onto one of the chaise loungers in the nook that overlooks the side garden.

My features twist into a scowl as I examine him. "How much did you drink?"

"Half a keg," Archer mumbles. "Give or take."

"Great."

"Is it okay that he sleeps here?" Justin asks, wringing his hands. "You won't get in trouble with your parents or anything, right?"

"They aren't home."

"Oh." His cheeks are red. He can't quite meet my eyes. "I'm really sorry about this. You probably think I'm an idiot for bringing him here, but I didn't know what else to do and—"

"The only idiot here is Archer Reyes. Don't worry about it." My brows lift. "Let me guess — they all got blasted after the big win and made you JV guys their personal chauffeurs for the evening?"

"I don't mind, honestly! It was cool to hang out with him, even for a little while." There's hero worship in his eyes as he stares at Archer — splayed out on the lounger in his grass-stained uniform, hair sticking six directions, mouth slack with sleep. "He's an incredible player. I'll miss watching him pitch. But I'm sure in a few years I'll seen him again... probably on the big screen at Fenway." His mouth tugs up at one corner. "And someday, when he's really famous, I'll be able to tell my kids about the night I drove Archer Reyes home, back in high school."

My heart gives a little pang. I press a hand to my chest, trying to subdue it. "Well. I appreciate you getting him here safely."

"It's the least I could do. Really." Justin's expression grows sheepish as his gaze darts up to mine. "I didn't know you two were dating."

"We aren't."

"Really?" His brow furrows. "He talked about you the whole way home."

I suck in a sharp breath. "He did?"

"Yeah. He was pretty worked up that you weren't at the game, to be honest." His lips flatten into a frown. "He said a State Championship title didn't mean anything without you there to celebrate with. And that..."

My heart is pounding. "And *what*?"

"Oh. Um." His cheeks flush even redder. "You know what? I probably shouldn't have said anything. It's not my business."

"But—"

"I should get going." He starts jogging down the steps. Halfway to the driveway, he turns back. His voice carries up to me. "Don't be too mad at him, when he wakes up. You may not be his girlfriend, but the way he talks about you..." He shrugs again, avoiding my eyes. "Maybe you should be."

With that, he hurries down the rest of the steps, slides into the front seat, and speeds off. I watch his taillights disappear before I pivot around toward the idiot passed out on my terrace. His handsome face is slack with sleep — thick eyelashes fanned out against his cheeks. His chest rises and falls in a steady rhythm.

Moving with utmost care, I lower myself gingerly onto the edge of the lounger. My hipbone presses against his side. He's warm as a wildfire, despite the chill in the air. I resist the urge to lean into him, to absorb his heat.

"What's going on in that head of yours, Archer Reyes?" I whisper, reaching up to brush the lock of hair off his forehead. I'd like to take a crowbar and pry his thoughts into the open. Brute force may be the only way to get some honest answers out of him.

When I pull back my hand, his arm whips up from his side,

quick as a wink. His eyes never open, even as his fingers encircle my wrist in a tight manacle. I barely have time to suck in a surprised breath when he yanks me forward with a sudden burst of force. I fall onto his chest, my head landing in the hollow where his shoulder meets his neck.

"*Hey!*"

He ignores my sharp exclamation, wrapping his arms around my back. Pulling me tight against him. Aligning my curves against the firm planes of his chest.

I stop breathing.

For years, I've wanted this — to be so close to him, it's impossible to tell where his body ends and mine begins. His hands on my back, his scent invading my senses. Our mouths a scant inch apart.

As I stare at his face, a million emotions flash through me. Confusion, anger, joy, pain. I'm half-convinced I'm still upstairs in my bed; that this is all a dream...

Or maybe a nightmare.

"You should go," he says softly. So softly, it lands like a punch to the stomach. "You should leave me."

Even as he says it, he tightens his hold, his body acting in direct contradiction to his words.

"Archer," I whisper, voice trembling. "What are you doing—"

"Jo," he breathes back, his mouth in my hair. "*My* Jo."

I go still.

How long have I waited to hear those words?

How dare he say them now, when I can't be sure he means them?

Planting my hands firmly against his chest, I shove out of his hold and spring to my feet. Tears fill my eyes in the space between one heartbeat and the next. I'm breathing hard, my pulse a sharp staccato.

"No, Archer."

He sits up, startled by my abrupt departure. His eyes are slivers, half-hooded with the effects of alcohol, staring blearily at me across the space I've created between us.

"Jo—"

"No," I grit out, my entire frame quaking with rage. "I am not *your* Jo. I'm not some plaything you can keep in your back pocket for emergencies, then toss aside whenever you get bored of me again. I'm a *person*. I have *feelings*. There was a time you used to care about hurting them."

He drops his head into his hands. He's silent for a very long time. So long, I think maybe he's passed out again. When he finally speaks, his voice is full of anguish.

"I still care."

He does?

He looks up at me, and my heart splinters at the look of pain on his face. "I care so much, it's killing me."

I'm afraid to breathe — afraid, if I move one single muscle, this moment will shatter into dust and be swept away on the wind.

"Then *why?*" A tear leaks out my right eye. Archer watches it slide down my cheekbone and fall to the terrace with a tiny splash. "Why are you being like this? Why have you been lying to me?" I take a step closer, my tears picking up speed. "There's nothing you could tell me the would make me turn away from you, Archer. *Nothing*. So just let me in. Let me be part of whatever is going on."

Shaking his head rapidly, he staggers to his feet. "No. No, I can't be here." He lurches sideways, stumbling off balance. "I can't talk to you about this. It's not safe."

"Stop!" I cry, chasing him across the terrace. Grabbing him by the arm. Tugging him around to face me. "I'm not going to let you push me away again! I know you're in some kind of trouble. I know you only told Jaxon you don't care about me to keep me out of whatever he's dragged you into. But if you'd just explain what's happening, I'm sure I could help "

Archer's expression darkens into the same cold mask I've grown accustomed to, lately. "I don't want your help. Don't you understand that? How many more times do I have to say it?"

I fight the urge to smack him. "You are the most stubborn human alive!"

"And you're the most annoying!"

"I hate you!" I scream into his face.

"Good!" he roars back. "I hate me too."

Losing my battle with self-control, my hands fly out, shoving his shoulders roughly. "God damn you, Archer! You *asshole!*"

He doesn't even try to deflect my hit. He absorbs it like water into a sponge, rocking back with a slight wheeze.

For a silent beat, we glare at each other — our rising tempers colliding like two broadswords. His voice is a soft timbre, grating against my frazzled nerve-endings.

"You feel better, now?"

"Yes, actually." My nostrils flare on a sharp exhale. "I do."

"Then do it again," he eggs me on. "Go on. I deserve it."

Without stopping to consider how twisted this whole thing is, I shove him again, lashing out with all the wounded pride pent-up for weeks inside my heart.

"*Jerk!*"

He nods in agreement, accepting the blow.

"*Coward!*"

I shove him once more — harder.

Too hard.

He stumbles back into the wall of the house, cracking his head with a painful thud.

Shit.

I fly forward, concern sparking through me at the thought that I've actually wounded him. But he doesn't look injured. He merely leans against the stone, moonlight slanting across the chiseled angles of his face. He's breathing like he's just run a marathon, his mouth slightly parted. And he's looking at me as though... as though...

I freeze.

His gaze is half-lidded, tracking my every infinitesimal movement. Reading me almost by memory, a book whose pages he's turned a thousand times. His face is stripped clean of the indifference he's been wearing like a shield, empty of all his earlier anger. And I'd swear on my life, the emotion simmering in his eyes isn't hate.

It's something far scarier.

Something that electrifies the very air we're breathing in uneven gasps.

I take a faltering step toward him, bringing us within arm's reach of one another. A dangerous proximity for two people balanced as we are on the edge of a razor-blade. Which way it's about to cut, I can't say.

Friend.

Enemy.

Or... perhaps something else entirely.

"So you hate me, huh?" he whispers in a hollow voice.

I take another step.

The final step.

"I really do," I breathe.

"That's a relief."

My lips part to respond, but I don't manage to get a single word out. In one great stride, Archer closes the gap between us, hauls me up against his chest, and crushes his mouth against mine in a heart-stopping kiss.

A kiss eighteen years in the making.

The brush of his lips sets off a seismic shift within my heart. Shakes the solid earth beneath my feet. Renders everything I've ever believed about love completely null and void.

There is nothing friendly about the way his mouth moves over mine. Nothing platonic. Nothing remotely safe.

He devours me.

Drags me under the surface.

Drowns me in passion.

I never want to come up for air.

His hands shove impatiently into my hair, twisting in the thick strands. He yanks my head back so he can deepen the kiss, his tongue spearing into my mouth with a moan that turns my bones to water. All I can do is hold on for dear life, clinging to his shoulders, letting him lay seige.

Since I was a little girl, I've dreamed of the day Archer Reyes would finally kiss me. I've spent countless hours wondering what it would be like. If he'd be tender or frenzied, hesitant or forceful.

Somehow, he is both everything and nothing like I imagined. A perfect medley of anticipation and expectation. He kisses me like I belong to him. His lips claim mine with both unflinching authority and acute familiarity.

I respond in kind, just as desperate to stake my claim.

He is mine as plainly as I'm his.

I make damn sure he knows it. Make sure he will never forget the way my hands feel as they slide over his shoulders; the way my breasts brush up against his chest; the way my tongue strokes his in harmony.

Our touches are filled with so much passion, we shake with it. Tears spill down my cheeks, falling onto our lips. He kisses them into oblivion.

We lose ourselves. There, in the shadows of Cormorant House with the moon shining down and the waves breaking along the shore, we disappear for a small infinity into one another, sacrificing all sense of self for a stolen moment of combined bliss. Putting aside our uncertain futures for one, shattering instant of unadulterated happiness.

We are not Josephine and Archer.

Not best friends.

Not sworn enemies.

We are merely two souls, spiraling deeper and deeper, like smoke from separate wicks on a single candle. We burn both for and in spite of each other, inextricably bonded by a foundation far deeper than attraction, far stronger than friendship, far bigger than fear.

This kiss...

It changes everything.

It's me, who breaks away first.

I pull back, creating enough space between our faces to gasp for air. Archer's breaths are just as uneven as mine. He's looking at me with an expression I've never seen before.

Desire.

His eyes blaze so brightly with it, they could scorch the flesh from my bones. But when he sees the pain written across my features... when he recognizes what's about to happen... his face becomes a mirror of my agony.

He knows me too well.

He's memorized my lines before I've ever spoken them.

"Jo..." His voice cracks. His hands are still in my hair — his fingertips pressing against the back of my head, as though he can't quite bring himself to let go.

I don't want him to.

But I need him to.

"We can't do this, Archer," I whisper, tears slipping down my face in an endless stream. "Not this way."

He sucks in a jagged breath.

I reach up and take hold of his wrists, tugging them gently from my nape. I hold on for a few seconds longer than strictly necessary before I release him.

His hands fall limply to his sides.

"I've wanted this for so long — longer than I've ever wanted anything in my whole life." I make myself take a step back, even though every atom in my body is screaming at me to stay pressed against his warmth. "But it finally happens and... it's all wrong. It's all messed up. *We're* all messed up."

A muscle leaps in his cheek as his jaw locks. He doesn't speak. Not a single word.

I force myself to go on. "The Archer I want — the one I've spent years dreaming about — is a version of you I'm not sure exists anymore. Because that guy? He was a good guy. He never lied to me. He didn't keep secrets. He didn't push me away." I suck in a breath, trying to keep my voice level. "He protected me. He made me laugh. He held me when I was sad. He was my best friend."

His eyes close and I know he's holding his emotions on a tight leash.

"*That's* the Archer Reyes I want to kiss," I murmur softly. "That's the Archer Reyes who owns my heart. That's the Archer Reyes I'm desperately in love with."

A tear slides out beneath his lashes, onto his cheek. He shakes his head, unable to respond.

"If you're still that guy? Then I'm in. I'm all in." I reach forward and wipe the droplet off his cheek. He shudders under the featherlight brush of my fingertips. "But if you aren't... if you can't be, anymore... then I'm walking away. I have to. Because having half of you would be worse than none at all. "

His eyes open. They're almost amber in the starlight. The haze of pain in their depths tells me, even before he speaks, that he's about to break my heart.

"I can't give you the answer you're looking for." His Adam's apple bobs. "I can't be the guy you're looking for."

I step back, gasping for breath like I've just been sucker-punched. There's an anvil on my chest, compressing my ribs, flattening my heart to useless pulp.

"I'm sorry," he tells me, his voice devoid of feeling. "I wish I could explain—"

"*Don't.*" The word tastes like blood in my mouth. "Don't say any more. I'm begging you. Just... don't."

I turn and walk into the house, leaving him alone in the dark — along with my mangled, traitorous heart.

CHAPTER TWENTY-TWO

ARCHER

I NEVER SHOULD'VE KISSED her.

There's a reason people say that ignorance is bliss. For years, I've wondered what it would be like to yank her into my arms. To finally, *finally*, take something I've wanted for as long as I can remember. But as torturous as the not-knowing was...

Knowing is infinitely worse.

Because now that I've felt the billowy soft skim of her mouth on mine... now that I've experienced the way her curves fit perfectly against my chest... there's no going back.

I can't unsee.

I can't unfeel.

The memory of her is embedded in my DNA, scored into my skin like a hot brand. Kissing Josephine Valentine was like coming up for air in a moment I hadn't even realized how badly I was drowning. And the second she pulled away from me...

My head slipped back beneath the surface.

And I began to sink once more.

Without the distraction of baseball to focus on, my mind is on fire with thoughts of her. She is everywhere I turn — in the sun-dappled light on the waters of the cove, in the sound of the waves crashing against the rocks at night, in the sweet summer breeze that rustles through the trees. Her voice is a ceaseless melody, haunting me.

Having half of you would be worse than none at all.

She was right to walk away from me. I don't deserve her. Not now. Not like this. I had no business crossing that line in the first place. Now that I have, there's no taking it back.

I'd blame the alcohol for my actions, but that would be a lie. Sure, being wasted lowered my inhibitions. But those intentions were there all along, clawing toward the surface like a wild thing. It was only a matter of time before they broke free.

I've always been an active person — running six miles nearly every morning, lifting weights in my spare time, spending every free minute outdoors. In the aftermath of the kiss, I find I can barely drag myself out of bed in the morning. In the rare instances I actually leave the house, I glower at anyone who even glances my direction.

My parents watch me with worried eyes, trading glances in the kitchen when they think I'm not looking.

Mijo, let me fix you something to eat, my mother suggests gently. *You're looking pale.*

Come for a ride with me, son, my father proposes. *Some fresh air will do you good.*

But I have no appetite — not for food, not for activity. Not for anything except sitting in my bedroom, staring at the ceiling, wondering what the girl I love is doing at this exact moment in time. Wondering if she's as consumed by thoughts of our kiss as I am.

After three full days of avoiding all human interaction, the door to my bedroom flies open. I look up from my phone to find my father standing there, glaring at me.

"Get up," he says flatly.

"Pa—"

"Get. Up."

I look back down at my phone. "I'm really not in the mood for a lecture."

"And I'm not in the mood to watch my son impersonate a sloth."

"I was going for *slug*, actually."

"Well, mission accomplished." Pa crosses into the room, grabs the phone out of my hand, and tosses it into the wastebasket.

"What the hell!"

"Three days, I've watched you mope around here like a lovesick schoolgirl. Enough is enough."

"I haven't been moping," I grumble.

"You have. I know, because I've been where you are. Believe it or not, I've done my fair share of moping, in my day."

My brows lift. "But you and Ma have been together... forever."

"Your forever and mine are not the same." My father sighs. "There was a time when we were young and life was hard and nothing seemed certain — least of all our future as a couple. Whatever you and Josephine are going through right now..."

I stiffen. "Who said anything about Jo?"

"Give me a little credit."

I scoff. "You certainly picked a stellar time to start paying attention to my relationships."

"I've always paid attention. I just don't shove my opinions down your throat unless I really need to. I trust that, when it comes to your love life, you know your own heart best. Most of the time, at least." He punches me lightly in the stomach. "Seems to me, what you could use right now is a bit of perspective."

"I don't need perspective. I need to be alone."

"In my experience, a man only craves solitary confinement when the person he'd like to spend his time with isn't an option." He shoots me a look. "Don't give up on her just yet, son. The road to enduring happiness is never smooth."

"What, are you working for Hallmark now? *If it's meant to be, it will be.*" I roll my eyes. "You sound like a cheesy greeting card."

He smacks me upside the head.

"*Ow!*"

"True or false: the best things in your life — your spot on the varsity team, your college offers, your pitching skills — were simply handed to you, no strings attached."

"False," I mutter, rubbing the back of my skull.

"Exactly. You had to earn all those things. You had to work for them." He pauses. "Why do you think love would be any different?"

"I... Well..." I trail off.

"Son. Love, like all the best things in life, is not a free hand-out. It takes effort. Time. Patience. Commitment." He holds my stare, his eyes steady. "If you really want to be with someone... you have to *earn* them."

"Is that what you did? With Ma?"

He nods. "Your mother was not an easy nut to crack, as they say. Stubborn as they come, with a temper to boot. Not only that, her family was adamantly opposed to her marrying me. They wanted her to stay in San Juan forever, marry her neighbor, live one street over from the house she grew up in... It was not easy to convince her to leave behind everything she knew and start over with me in a strange new place, owning nothing but the shirts on our backs. For a while, the odds seemed stacked so high against me, I thought them insurmountable."

"So how did you make it work?"

"I told her that a comfortable life with another man would not make her half as happy as an adventure with me. And then, I set out to prove it, every day." A smile spreads across his face. "I don't think she's ever regretted her choice."

"But what if..." I swallow hard. "What if being with you had put her in a situation where you couldn't ensure her safety? What if her life would've been worse off for loving you? Would your decision have been the same? Would you still have taken her away from the security of that simple life in her hometown?"

Pa is silent for a long time. "I'm not sure I like your question. It makes my mind turn in uncomfortable directions."

I glance sharply at the wall.

I've probably said too much.

He runs a hand through his hair, his expression contorted in deep thought. "It's hard to say what I would've done. I would never knowingly put your mother in harm's way. But, selfish as it sounds, I'm not sure I would've chosen any differently." His lips twist. "I can't live without her, you see."

I do see.

All my life, I've seen how they are together. Flora and Miguel. A perfect match. Complementary in every conceivable way. They possess that rare kind of co-dependence seen most often in fiction.

"Archer."

I look at him. "Yeah?"

"I know you. I know you would never put anyone in danger. Most especially Josephine. It's clear as day how you feel about her, even if you can't admit it yet."

"Is it really that obvious?"

"Yes and no. Obvious is the wrong word. It's more like... *inevitable.* Since you were no more than babies, the two of you have had a special connection. The way you move together —

it's like two planets sharing the same orbit. There's a certain gravitational pull when you're in the same room. It's so strong, anyone who comes between you looks vastly out of place." He laughs lightly. "Your mother and I have had a front-row seat for years. We knew it was only a matter of time before your planets collided."

"But if it's as you say — *a collision* — that's not exactly a good thing, Pa. Two planets slamming into each other sounds like a recipe for disaster. I believe scientists would classify it as an *extinction event*, actually."

He shrugs. "They'd also tell you that's how Earth wound up with the moon. That beautiful floating thing in our night sky is just a byproduct of two planets colliding in space a few billion years ago."

I stare at him. "Do you have an answer for everything?"

"Of course not. I'm just a handyman." He winks. "Remember: sometimes, the only way to make something new is to break down what you have and start from scratch." He pushes to his feet. "Now, come out to eat. Your mother made enchiladas."

I'M HELPING Ma with the dishes when the cottage door swings open. We all turn at the sound, eyes widening.

Jax steps across the threshold. "Honey, I'm home."

"Jaxon! Thank god you're back." Ma races to his side, wrapping him in a hug. "Where have you been? I've been so worried. You look thin. Have you been eating? I'll fix you a plate. I've just put the enchiladas away, they're still warm..."

"Give the boy a chance to speak, Flora." Pa is staring at his son with narrowed eyes. "I think we'd all like to hear how he's been spending his time, these past few weeks."

Jaxon shifts his weight from foot to foot. "I just needed a bit of alone time."

I scoff.

His eyes cut to mine, a warning in their depths.

"Alone time?" Ma's nose wrinkles. "We spent two years without you, *mijo*. We missed you every day. You must understand how hard on us it is to have you back for such a short time... to watch you walk out again without warning..."

"Sorry, okay? I should've called."

"What about work?" Pa asks bluntly. "Your manager at the tire shop said you haven't shown up for your shifts."

"I... uh." Jaxon swallows. "I got another job."

"What job?"

"An old friend of mine set it up."

I scoff again. "*Right.*"

"Shut the fuck up, Archer."

"Jaxon!" Ma cries. "Language!"

Pa's voice drops low. "Don't speak to your brother like that, Jaxon."

"He's disrespecting me!"

I roll my eyes. "To disrespect someone, they have to be worthy of respect in the first place."

"Archer!" Ma turns to me with a shocked look. "Apologize."

"No," I say flatly, never shifting my eyes from my brother. I'm so fed up with him — with his lies, with his habits, with the way he keeps hurting my parents again and again. "Why don't you tell them the details of your new job, Jax? Explain to them exactly what these *old friends* of yours have you doing."

Silence falls over the room.

"What is he talking about, Jaxon?" Pa asks, stepping toward his eldest son.

"He's just trying to stir up trouble!" Jax scratches at his ear, looking jittery. "He's jealous I'm home. He wants to make me look bad."

"*Mijo*," Ma murmurs, examining him more closely. Awareness is creeping into her gaze. "Your brother loves you. We all love you."

"If that's true, then you'll lay off me!" he yells. "You'll cut me a little fucking slack while I try to get my life back on track!"

My parents trade a glance.

Jaxon starts to pace, nervous energy rolling off him in waves. "I had to ditch my car, okay? I need to borrow your truck, Pa. Just for a few days. It's for a job."

"I need my truck for my own work." My father's voice is steady, brooking no room for argument. "Perhaps we can find this car you... *ditched*... and get it fixed. I know a good mechanic in Rockport—"

"No! God, why are you always like this?" Jaxon exclaims. "Why can't you ever just help me out?"

"We have *helped you out* —" My mother makes air-quotes with her fingertips. "—many times in the past, *mijo*. You know we would do anything to make your life easier."

Jaxon's eyes are darting around the living room, not landing on anything for longer than a heartbeat. "What about your truck, Archer?"

"You must be joking."

"Fuck you!"

"Jaxon," Ma whispers. "Please..."

He sucks in a breath. "Look... maybe you could spot me a little cash. Not much — just enough for me to get by for a week or so."

I laugh. I can't help it — the sound bubbles up from my stomach and explodes out my mouth, filling the room like the rapport of a gun. "Of course that's why you're home. It all makes sense, now. You need money."

"You've got a fresh mouth, little brother. Someone ought to shut it for you." Jaxon strides toward me, his fist cocking back.

I don't duck. I don't even lift my hands to defend myself from the impending blow.

My mother screams as Jaxon swings at me. Before the punch lands, my father steps between us, palming Jaxon's fist like a basketball. Absorbing the strike with impressive ease.

"Enough," Pa grunts, squeezing Jaxon's hand until he gasps in pain. "This is my house. While you are under my roof, you will not act like this. Do you understand me?"

Jax gives a shaky nod.

"Good."

Pa is still holding Jaxon's fist. Yanking on it, he pulls his son close enough to peer directly into his eyes — searching his pupils for the telltale signs of drug use. After a long moment, he leans back. His tone is impassive.

"You're using again."

"Let go of me," Jax hisses, ducking his gaze. "You don't know what you're talking about."

My father's face is carved from stone as he releases his first-born son. My mother looks like she's about to cry.

"This was a waste of time," Jaxon mutters, heading for the door. "Don't know why I bothered coming here. You people don't care about me."

"Jaxon!" Ma calls as he steps outside, her voice full of pain. "Don't say that!"

The slamming screen door is his only response.

She starts after him, but my father stops her with a gentle touch on the small of her back.

"Flora. Let him go. You have to let him go."

When her tears begin to flow, he folds her against his chest.

She sobs into his shirt as he strokes her hair, making soothing noises.

Over her head, our gazes meet. His eyes hold a new awareness — and new questions.

Later, he mouths sternly at me. *We need to talk.*

I swallow hard and give a small nod of agreement.

Maybe it's time I finally told my parents exactly what kind of trouble Jaxon is in.

Maybe they're finally ready to listen.

AN HOUR LATER, Pa and I lean against the sit-atop lawnmower, staring across the expanse of lush green grass. The grounds of Cormorant House are always pretty, but now, on the cusp of full summer, they're glorious.

"You knew," Pa says after a long beat of silence.

I nod. There's no use denying it.

"How long?" he asks.

"Officially? About a week. But I've suspected since he first disappeared last month."

"Why didn't you tell us?"

"You were so happy to have him back." I stare down at my shoes. "I didn't want to be the one who took him away from you again."

"That's not your call to make, Archer." Pa shakes his head. "We are your parents! We are supposed to protect *you*, not the other way around!"

"I'm sorry."

"Don't apologize. This isn't your fault. I'm just..." He blows out a breath. "This situation is difficult. For me. For you. For your mother, most of all."

"Is she going to be okay?"

"In time. But not today. She is taking your brother's relapse very hard. She blames herself, you know. If she'd told the doctors not to prescribe those pills, all those years ago when he was injured, maybe—"

"That's ridiculous."

"I agree. But emotions are rarely logical."

We're both quiet for a stretch.

"I hate to see her cry," I say finally, my throat thick. "When he went to jail, she cried for months. I thought she'd never stop. So, when he came back and started to spiral again... I figured, if I could keep her from finding out... maybe she'd never have to know. Maybe she'd stay happy." I pause. "I didn't realize how serious the situation was until later."

"I know you have a protective streak, son. It's one of your most honorable qualities. But sometimes you get so caught up in trying to protect the people you care about, you wind up doing more damage in the long run."

My eyes press closed.

If only he knew how right he is.

A hand clasps my shoulder. "We love your brother. We will always love your brother. But we are not blind to his faults. It's better for us to know all the information, so we have a chance to help him. Really help him."

"You mean rehab."

"If that's what it takes."

Neither of us says what we're both thinking.

If it even works.

In the past, rehab has never been more than a temporary fix. We have no reason to believe this time would be any different. And the cost alone for a six-week detox program...

It's far more than our family could ever afford.

Jo's parents were generous enough to cover Jaxon's two previous stints, back when he was a troubled teen living on their property. There's no guarantee they'd do so again, now that he's an adult — and an ex-con, at that.

"Would Vincent agree to—"

My father cuts me off with a stark whisper. "I don't want to take more charity from the Valentines. Especially since I'm not fully convinced rehab is the best place for your brother, right now."

"What's the alternative?" I ask. "Send him back to prison? Lock him up for the rest of his life?"

"That's the last thing I want for him. But I think we both know, this is about more than just him using again." My father is watching me intently. "Earlier, in our conversation about Josephine... something you said caught my attention."

I avoid his gaze. "What's that?"

"You asked me if I'd have still pursued your mother, despite knowing I'd be putting her in danger. I can't help wondering if this danger you're so worried about dragging Josephine into has something to do with your brother."

My jaw locks down, holding the words at bay. After keeping them inside for so long, I'm not certain I know how to release them.

"Tell me, Archer," Pa orders. "The truth, this time. All of it."

I know, from his grave tone as much as the stern furrow of his brow, that there will be no evading my father's questions.

Not any longer.

I suck in a deep breath, trying to steady myself. And then, in as measured a voice as I can manage, I tell him. Everything. About Rico and Barboza. About their threats to me, to Jo, to him, to Ma. The parking lot ambush, my hand poised on a tailgate hatch; the afternoon break-in, a gun pressed against my cheek.

I describe their determination to bring Jax into the fold,

dealing dangerous product to his local connections. And, finally, I tell him the darkest of my suspicions: that Jax will comply with their demands, rather than risk his own neck.

An unforgivable act of self-preservation.

"No," my father breathes when I finally trail off into silence. "This cannot be true."

"I wish it weren't."

"How could you not tell me this?" he roars, making me flinch. His voice has risen to twice its normal volume. I've never heard him yell before; he's usually the epitome of calm. "How could you keep this a secret for so long?"

"I'm sorry," I whisper. "I didn't know what to do. I didn't want to put you or Ma in any danger."

"So you thought you'd put yourself in it instead? *Dios mio*, Archer, I could strangle you for being so stubborn."

"Get in line," I mutter, thinking of Jo's words to me last night.

You are the most stubborn human alive.

He begins to curse in Spanish, a rapid stream of profanity I can barely follow.

"I was trying to keep you safe," I tell him, exasperation stirring to life inside my chest. "Don't I get any points for that?"

"And who was keeping *you* safe? Huh? Who was protecting you when these men showed up? Or do you think you're invincible?" Without waiting for an answer, Pa pushes to his feet and begins to pace. "Of all my worst fears, I never thought... a *gang*... dealing again..."

The cursing resumes.

My eyes narrow in thought. "If he's caught again, he'll face a much harsher sentence. He could end up spending half his life in prison if we don't do something to fix this."

Pa stops in his tracks. When he turns to look at me, bewilderment contorts his features. "You think that's what I care about right now? Your brother getting in trouble?"

I blink. "Uh..."

"*Archer.*" My father falls to his knees in front of me. His eyes are rimmed with red. "I have two sons. I love them both. But it pains me deeply that you think I would ever value Jaxon's future over yours." He grabs my hand, his steely grip grinding my finger bones together. "I will not sacrifice one son to shield the other. I will not let you walk around in fear, paying the price for a sin you had no part in."

My eyes are stinging. "I... I just thought..."

"I know what you thought. But you're wrong." He stands and pulls me into a hug so tight, it squeezes the air from my lungs. "Your brother is the only one who should be held accountable for his mistakes. Not me, not your mother. Certainly not you. I'm so sorry for ever making you think otherwise."

I hug him back, trying not to break down. Hearing this — that I'm not second-place in my parents' hearts simply because I'm the second-born — is something I've waited my whole life for.

We both brush inconspicuously at our eyes as we break apart and lean back against the lawnmower. His shoulder presses tight to mine. It's quiet for a long moment.

"Tomorrow," he says finally. "We will go to the police station together and tell them what's been going on. Whatever happens after that, at least you will no longer be in danger."

"But Pa, the police in this town... you know as well as I do how they react when they hear the name Reyes."

"My mind is made up, son." He blows out a breath. "Just give me tonight to talk to your mother. I need to be the one to break this to her. It will not be easy for her to hear."

Relief surges through me. It's undercut by a fresh tide of

guilt when I think about my mother's reaction to this information. I stare at my shoes again, thinking dark thoughts.

"She won't blame you," Pa says, reading my mind. "Your mother loves you very much."

"I know she does. I just hate the idea of hurting her."

"Mmm. Not just her, I think. How much does Josephine know about all this?"

"Nothing. Not with any certainty." I rub the back of my neck, a nervous habit. "Though I'm sure she has her suspicions."

"In that case, I'm sure she's furious at you for keeping her in the dark."

"Furious is an understatement."

"Then tell her. Make things right."

I look over at him. "I don't know how. I've been terrible to her, Pa. The things I've done... the way I've treated her... I don't deserve her forgiveness."

"There you go again, making decisions for other people."

"I'm not—"

"*You are.* But you don't need to. Josephine is a smart girl. She is quite capable of making up her own mind about things. Whether she wants to forgive you or hold a grudge until her dying breath... that's for her to decide. But you'll never know for sure unless you give her the chance."

My heart is thudding fast inside my veins. I curl my hands into tight fists, feeling like I'm about to fly apart into a million pieces. "I love her," I whisper. "I love her so much, it terrifies me."

"Then go get her."

"I can't."

"Why not?"

"She's already on her way to the senior prom."

"Last I checked, you are also a senior."

"Yeah, but another guy is her date."

"And you're the love of her life." He laughs. "Go after her, son. If you really want her... prove it to her. Earn her."

My pulse skips a beat. My mind is churning ten different directions. And every one of them leads to one destination.

Jo.

I leap to my feet, suddenly frantic. "What time is it?"

He checks his watch. "6:50."

My stomach drops to my feet like a stone. "I'll never make it in time. The boat leaves at seven sharp," I say, crestfallen. "I'm too late. She's already gone."

Pa is silent for a moment. When he looks at me, there's an almost giddy gleam in his eyes. "That's not necessarily true..."

CHAPTER TWENTY-THREE

JOSEPHINE

JUST AS I imagined long ago, I float down the front steps of Cormorant House in my perfect dress, my eyes locked on my perfect date waiting at the bottom. He stands there, dashing in his dark blue suit. His smile is a mile wide. His auburn hair catches the rays of early evening light, turning to a copper halo around his head.

"Josie," he murmurs, offering his arm. "You look beautiful."

I slide my hand into the crook of his elbow. "So do you, Charlie." I redden. "Er... *Handsome*! I meant you look handsome."

He laughs with a flash of straight white teeth as he leads me toward the waiting Hummer limo.

"Wow," I breathe, taking in the sight of it. "It's so..."

"Pink?" Charlie finishes. "I'd expect nothing less from the Wadell twins."

Like a proper gentleman, he holds open my door and helps me into the backseat. Inside, Ophelia and Odette are sitting on their dates' laps, sipping champagne

"Josie!" They squeal when they see me.

I've barely settled in my seat when Odette passes me a flute. It's full to the brim with bubbles.

"Cheers!" She clinks her glass against mine. "Happy prom!"

"Happy prom," I echo, taking a sip.

Beside me, Charlie holds his glass out to mine. "Thank you for allowing me to be your escort tonight."

"Oh, uh," I stammer. "Thanks for agreeing to come. Hopefully it won't be a total drag."

His dimples become more pronounced as his grin deepens. "I seriously doubt that's possible."

We do a round of introductions. Ophelia and Odette's dates — a stunning pair of twins from St. John's — are, coincidentally, named Oliver and Orlando. There is little to no intelligence behind their vacant blue eyes. But they seem harmless enough.

"It's nice to meet you," I tell them, taking another sip of my champagne.

They both smile, then promptly resume snorting lines of cocaine off the glass tabletop.

"Your dress is absolutely killer, Josie." Ophelia's eyes scan my frame, taking in every scrap of blue silk with undisguised envy. "Where's it from? Vera Wang? MiuMiu? I know it's not McQueen — I scoured his formalwear collection for months, looking for *my* dress." She gestures down at her vibrant red frock — a stunning confection of ruffles and tulle that gives the illusion she's wearing a giant rose.

"It's amazing, Ophelia." I lean forward to get a better look. My voice drops to a whisper. "But how on earth will you pee?"

She tilts her head. "*Very* carefully."

Everyone laughs.

"You look amazing too, Odette." I turn my gaze on her gown — a black sheath with ornate gold epaulettes at the shoulders that give it a military vibe. "You look like a sexy cavalry officer."

"That's exactly what I was going for!" She grins.

"You never answered my question," Ophelia reminds me, her eyes still locked on my dress. "Who's the designer?"

"Oh." I take a careful sip of champagne. "I am, actually."

"Seriously?!" Both twins gasp.

"Seriously."

"Okay, well, next time we have a formal event, you're totally in charge of making our dresses," Odette says. "We can be, like... your first brand ambassadors!"

Ophelia nods. "Goodbye, Alexander McQueen. Hello, Josephine Valentine."

"I think you guys are getting a bit ahead of yourselves." I shake my head. "I've really only designed a handful of things... Most of them aren't any good."

"But by the time you finish your first semester at school, you'll have a full portfolio," Odette points out.

"You are studying fashion design, aren't you?" Ophelia asks. "If you aren't, you're insane."

"I'd like to. It's complicated, though." I take a breath. "My parents are determined to have me take over the family business."

"Can't really blame them," Charlie murmurs absently. "VALENT is valued at nearly a billion, as of last quarter. If it goes public, the projections are off the charts..."

All three of us turn to stare at him.

He has the good grace to blush. "Sorry," he says apologetically. "I'm a bit of a finance junkie. When I found out I was going to the prom with the daughter of Vincent and Blair Valentine, I figured I'd better brush up on my knowledge about the company."

"So you're a cyber-stalker," I murmur teasingly.

"Guilty as charged." He gives a light laugh that doesn't quite cover up his eagerness. "Your parents are fascinating. The work they've done is literally changing the world. I can't imagine what it was like to grow up in the same house as them. It must've been like... being raised by gods, or something."

I take a very large swig of my champagne. "They're mortals, trust me."

It's always fascinating to hear other people talk about my parents — especially those who've been denied the pleasure of actually meeting them. Without the benefit of personal experience to temper your expectations, it's easy to assume Vincent and Blair Valentine are earthbound angels. On paper, they make Mother Theresa and the Dalai Lama look like slackers.

Perhaps sensing my stiffness, Charlie reaches onto the seat beside him and retrieves a plastic container. "Here... I got this for you."

"Oh!" My eyes widen on the corsage as he lifts it free of its case. "That's very sweet of you."

"Beautiful flowers for a beautiful girl."

I study the corsage as he slides it around my wrist. It's beautiful — pale blue blossoms surrounding a stunning white orchid. I notice he's got a boutonnière with identical blooms pinned against the lapel of his dark navy suit.

"Thank you." I smile, rotating my wrist to study it from all sides. "Now we're coordinated."

His hand lands on my thigh, just north of the slit that runs up the right side of my dress, exposing a good stretch of leg. He runs a finger across the sensitive skin of my kneecap.

I fight the urge to squirm away.

"A perfect match," he whispers, leaning over to kiss my cheek.

We drive down the highway, heading for the ferry port, drinking more champagne and sharing more than a few laughs.

My date is everything a girl could possibly hope for — charming, thoughtful, well-mannered, easy on the eyes. And, for some unknown reason, he seems to like me.

I should be over the moon.

I should be with someone else.

Pushing aside the intrusive thought, I do my best to have fun. I laugh and I chit-chat and I play my part with surprising poise. But no matter how brightly I smile, I have a feeling it doesn't reach my eyes.

I know for a fact it doesn't reach my heart.

———

THE RIDE from Cormorant House to Gloucester Harbor takes under twenty minutes on a normal night. With the Hummer limo, it takes nearly twice that — in no small part because the twins keep asking our driver to pull over so they can pose for pictures in scenic spots along the way.

By the time we reach the cruise-port, the ship is blowing its departure horn. A uniformed attendant collects our tickets at the bottom of the gangplank that leads onto the elegant vessel.

"Cutting it close," he says with a smile. "Have fun, kids."

Laughing breathlessly, the six of us dart aboard. Our high heels and dress shoes clatter like a small stampede across the metal. The boat itself is beautiful — a luxury cruise liner, built specifically for private parties and corporate functions. With two sprawling decks and an exposed veranda area strung with lights, there's more than enough room to accommodate the entire senior class.

Charlie's hand intertwines firmly with mine as he leads me toward the cabin. A crush of voices spills out a pair of double doors.

Inside, nearly a hundred people are spread across a dimly-lit ballroom, making small talk as appetizers circulate on lofted cater-waiter trays. Floor to ceiling windows offer a panoramic view from every angle.

Still, it feels somewhat stuffy. This opulent barge sits so heavily in the water, it's barely stirred by the waves. I barely feel like I'm at sea at all. I much prefer the open-aired freedom of my small Alerion.

My eyes sweep around the room, taking it all in. There are dresses of every shade, length, and style. I catalogue them in my mind, noting the more interesting designs. Some of the gowns in this room are one-of-a-kind creations from the top fashion minds in the world, specially commissioned for this event by the daughter's of billionaires.

Anything for Daddy's little girl.

Sienna Sullivan is in a skin-tight, turquoise number so low-cut, her personal flotation devices are nearly exposed. She glares at me as I pass by, her eyes scanning me up and down.

I ignore her.

The ballroom is arranged with dozens of white-linen tables. We find a free one on the starboard side and take our seats.

"I'm already regretting this," Odette announces with a grimace. I lean sideways to see her around the massive floral centerpiece. "How long are we stuck on this stupid boat, again?"

"Four hours." Ophelia looks around. "Actually, make that three and a half. Looks like we missed the cocktail hour."

"Is it truly a cocktail hour if they don't serve cocktails?" Odette asks.

I shrug. "I think I saw cocktail shrimp in circulation."

"*So* not the same thing." She reaches into her small clutch purse and pulls out a compact silver flask. "Luckily, I decided to BYOB."

"Planning to spike the punch?" Charlie asks. Beneath the table, he reaches for my hand.

"As if I'd waste my Grey Goose on these peasants." She rolls her eyes and takes a discrete swig, using her date as a human shield from the prying eyes of the chaperones. Not that said chaperones are paying much attention. The two that I saw on the way in — both teachers nearing retirement age in low kitten heels and shapeless shift dresses — had their noses pressed up to the glass, peering out at the ocean like they'd never seen it before.

The ship horn blows again: one long blast, then three short ones. In the distance, I recognize the muffled metal sound of the gangplank unlatching from the lower deck.

The ship heads out of the harbor, into open water, passing Eastern Point Lighthouse. The sun is dropping steadily toward the horizon, a pink-gold backdrop to the dinner service. We pass around the flask, each taking small swings as we wait for our table to be called up to the buffet. The vodka burns unpleasantly at the back of my throat — a harsh chaser to the champagne bubbling in my stomach.

I need to eat something soon, or I'll be queasy from far more than seasickness.

As if she's read my mind, a server appears. Her uniform is stiff with starch. "The buffet is now open for this section!" she chirps. "Please serve yourselves."

Ophelia scoffs. "Seriously? All the money we spent on tickets for this crap-fest and we're expected to serve *ourselves*? What is this, Soviet Russia?"

The server's smile drops at the corners as she walks away.

Odette grabs her sister's hand. "Do shut up, O. It's not all bad. There's a chocolate fountain!"

"Whose genius idea was that?" Her twin snorts. "I can't *wait* until we hit a rogue wave and someone takes a bath in it."

I shake my head at their backs as we walk to the buffet. Sometimes, I wonder how we became friends.

"Do they ever stop talking?" Charlie asks under his breath.

A surprised laugh pops from my lips. "Not really, no."

"Hard to get a word in edgewise," he notes, handing me a china dinner plate. "Maybe later, the two of us can break from the pack. Find somewhere quiet and actually get to know each other a bit."

An involuntary bolt of panic shoots through me as I recall the last time a boy led me to a quiet corner at a party, under the guise of getting to know me better.

Charlie is nothing like Ryan, I tell myself. *He's sweet and polite and trying very hard to make sure I have a nice night.*

"Sure, Charlie." I swallow down my nerves and smile at him. "That would be nice."

Buffet or no, it's an impressive spread — chicken cordon bleu, king crab legs, lobster tails, a full salad bar. We load up our plates with food and carry them back to our table. I don't have much of an appetite, picking at my food out of necessity rather than real hunger.

My dinner mates chat animatedly, jumping from topic to topic, but my focus has slipped. I stare out the window as we pass the familiar waters beyond Great Misery Island, chugging south along the craggy Massachusetts coastline toward Boston.

Three more hours.

I'm not certain I'll last.

After dinner, everyone makes their way up the stairs to the upper deck. The open-air space is designed for dancing, with a polished oak floor, standing speakers, and string lights crisscrossing the air.

The hired DJ is already blasting music — a throbbing electronica song that's been dominating the pop charts for weeks.

Everyone on the dance floor is screaming the words at the top of their lungs, writhing to the rhythm with abandon.

Ophelia and Odette each grab one of my hands and tug me into the center of the mob. Our dates trail close on our heels. At the chorus, the twins twirl me round and round between them like a spinning top, until I'm dizzy.

I'm not sure if it's the champagne or the vodka or simply the infectious energy of tonight, but I'm definitely tipsy. My bloodstream feels made of stars. For the first time since that night, when Archer yanked me into his arms and kissed me breathless, he does not consume my every waking thought.

After a few upbeat songs, the DJ downshifts into a slow song. I allow Charlie to pull me against him, his hands sliding down to brush the small of my back through the whisper-thin silk. I loop my arms around his neck and rest my head on his chest, wishing they'd play something faster. Anything but this heartbreaking Adele ballad about a girl trying to move on from a boy who couldn't love her back.

Nevermind, I'll find someone like you.

"Are you having a good time?" Charlie whispers into my hair.

I press my eyes closed. My eyes are stinging with tears. "Yes," I lie. "I'm having a wonderful time."

I MAKE my excuses after Adele croons her final notes, beel-ining for the bathroom. The one on the upper deck has a line out the door, so I walk down the steps to the ballroom. It's prac-tically abandoned — only a few stragglers partaking in the chocolate fountain, and some chaperones taking goofy pictures in the photo booth.

The bathroom on this level is empty. I take my time —

fixing a pin that's falling loose from my hair, wiping the smeared mascara from beneath my lash line. The girl staring back at me in the mirror may look beautiful on the outside, but inside she's broken. There's a sadness in her eyes no amount of makeup can conceal.

It seems like I've been on this ship for an eternity. My buzz is wearing off and my feet are beginning to ache in my high heels. When I step outside, into the night air, I turn away from the stairs that lead back to the dance floor and start the opposite direction. The deck wraps all the way around the ship. I head for the stern, away from the lights and the music and the crowd, seeking out a bit of solace.

The back of the ship is technically off limits. I step over the velvet rope barricade anyway and make my way carefully down a spiral staircase, taking extra care not to trip in my high heels. At the bottom, the aft deck juts out over the dark water, separated only by a thin railing. The name ODYSSEY CRUISES is embossed across the back in letters as tall as my waist.

It's a calm night. The moon shines down, dancing across the rolling swells. We're not far off shore — a couple hundred yards, maybe less. In his quarters at the bow, the captain steers us past a small island I recognize as Egg Rock, making a slow loop around it before we turn back north.

I lean against the railing, looking down at the froth churning from beneath the boat. The engine is a low, humming vibration — soothing in comparison to the thumping beat on the upper deck.

I have little desire to return to the prom.

Archer's always teased me about my antisocial tendencies. But he's never tried to change them. When he'd find me at a house party, loading up a stranger's dishwasher or watering their flower boxes with the outdoor spigot, he'd merely shake his head at me in amusement, those caramel eyes crinkling up at the corners.

Let's get you home, he'd say, holding out his hand. *Before you start scrubbing toilets.*

I brush a tear from my cheek, telling myself it's only from the wind.

It's so bizarre that tomorrow is graduation. At noon, I'll be standing on a stage, delivering the speech I scribed onto small index cards yesterday. It's a mess of clichés; a sappy monologue of trite memories to make my classmates laugh and pandering metaphors to make the parents nostalgic, with a core message about the value of hard work and the responsibility of an exceptional education.

My parents are going to love it.

In the distance, I watch the persistent flash of Graves Lighthouse, warning ships away from the rocks. I wonder how many unlucky vessels sank to the bottom of the ocean before its construction — an underwater cemetery of wooden skeletons, their names lost to time.

The sound of an engine interrupts my melancholy musings. I glance up, my eyes locking on a light bobbing across the surface of the ocean. An approaching vessel. It's barreling toward us at top speed, a plume of water shooting up behind it in a massive wake.

At first, I think it's just someone out for a joyride, playing chicken with the prom cruise. But when it pulls up alongside us, slowing to a crawl, I straighten from the railing to get a better look.

Are we being boarded by pirates?

It's hard to make out the shape in the dark, but there's something familiar about the silhouette of the small vessel. When a crew member turns a spotlight on it, bathing the navy picnic boat in a brilliant beam, I realize why.

It's my father's Hinckley.

And, standing at the wheel dressed in a suit... hair blowing in the wind... face twisted into a devil-may-care smirk... is none other than Archer Reyes.

I just about fall overboard.

"THIS IS A PRIVATE VESSEL," a crew member shouts into a loudspeaker. "YOU ARE NOT PERMITTED TO BOARD!"

On the upper deck, the music cuts off with a screech. I hear a rising murmur of voices as my classmates rush to the railing, peering over the side to see what's going on.

"Isn't that Reyes?" someone shouts. It sounds like Chris Tomlinson.

The captain cuts our engine, slowing us to an abrupt stop. Archer pulls back on his throttle too, bobbing motionless beside us. Stepping more firmly into view, he squints against the blinding beam of the spotlight.

"JO!" he screams at the top of his lungs, cupping his hands around his mouth. "JOSEPHINE VALENTINE!"

A collective gasp moves through the crowd of students on the deck above me. I don't look up. My eyes are locked on the crazy boy in the Hinckley.

"I'M NOT LEAVING, JO!" His voice goes ragged on my name. "NOT WITHOUT YOU!"

The crush of voices above reaches a fever pitch.

Where is she?

Has anyone seen Valentine?

Someone peering over the side spots me on the aft deck. Of course, it's the twins.

"There she is!" Odette yells giddily.

"Down by the stern!" Ophelia adds.

The cruise lights, lowered for ambiance, abruptly flip on to full brightness, basking the entire vessel in a warm glow that illuminates the water all around us. I hear people calling my name in the distance; I pay them no heed. I hear the sound of running feet as crew members race toward me; I don't even spare them a glance.

Because, across the dozen or so feet of ocean separating us, Archer has finally spotted me on the aft deck. When our eyes meet, his mouth tugs up at the corners.

"Hey, Jo," he calls, turning the wheel so the Hinckley begins to drift closer. "I've been meaning to ask you something!"

"What's that?" I call back.

"Will you go to the prom with me?"

I laugh. I can't help it. "I think you missed the boat. Literally."

"Yeah. Seems like it." He's still staring at me. "So how about you ditch with me instead?"

"Why should I?"

"Because I was wrong."

My heart leaps. "About?"

"Everything." He pauses. "But mostly about not being the guy for you."

My throat clogs with unshed tears. My voice, when it chokes out, is barely coherent. "You're such an idiot, Reyes!"

"Is that a yes?" His eyes flicker to the rapidly-approaching crew members. "Offer is time sensitive."

"YES!" I yell, reaching down to slip off my heels.

His smile blooms into a full-fledged grin that makes my knees weak as he eases the Hinckley toward the Odyssey, bringing his side along the railing. "You're gonna have to jump for it."

I eye the narrowing distance between myself and the open cockpit of the Hinckley. It's about a five foot drop.

In shorts and Sperry topsiders, no problem.

In formalwear, a bit trickier.

"DO NOT ABANDON THE VESSEL!" the voice on the loudspeaker instructs me sternly. "I REPEAT, DO NOT ABANDON THE VESSEL!"

But it's too late. I'm already scampering over the railing like Rose in *Titanic*. When the Hinckley is directly beneath me, I toss my heels into the cockpit and take a deep breath.

"Now or never!" Archer yells.

I don't think.

I just jump.

There are three seconds of heart-stopping free fall... and then I slam against solid wood, landing in a graceless half-crouch.

At least I'm not in the ocean.

The upper deck breaks into cheers, screaming for us at the top of their lungs. Even from here, Odette and Ophelia's voices are the loudest.

A hand appears in my visual field. I slide mine into it, allowing him to help me to my feet. My heart is lodged so firmly in my throat, I'm not sure I'll be able to speak.

"Hey," he murmurs. He's still holding my hand. His eyes never shift from mine.

"Um," I squeak. "Hi?"

"Sorry I'm late." His grin widens. "There was traffic."

"Have you gone totally insane?"

"Probably." He reaches out and tucks a strand of hair behind my ear with so much tenderness, the breath catches in my lungs. "But... I'll be even more insane if I go another second without doing this."

He kisses me, then.

In plain view of the entire graduating class of Exeter Academy of Excellence, along with about a half dozen crew members of Odyssey Cruises. With so much passion, I'm surprised we don't set the boat aflame.

The catcalls from the upper deck are ear-splitting. So is the loudspeaker.

"PLEASE RETURN TO THE VESSEL!"

But we're already floating far out of reach, caught up in a current they cannot control.

Archer never lets go of my hand as he turns back to the wheel, pushes up on the throttle, and steers us off, across the glittering expanse of the Atlantic.

CHAPTER TWENTY-FOUR

ARCHER

I STEER us back toward home.

Jo stands in front of me, her back pressed to my chest, hair flying out of her updo into my face. She's stunning in the moonlight. Even more so in that dress. It hugs her body so perfectly, it should be a criminal offense. I can barely see straight when I think about all that soft, creamy skin of hers, millimeters beneath a scrap of silk.

She shifts against me, a small sigh sliding between her lips, and desire surges through me in a hot rush. It takes exceptional effort to keep the boat on a straight course. I shrug off my jacket and hand it to her, in part to keep her warm but mostly so I don't drive us into the goddamned rocks.

We race across the waves at top speed, sending up a huge wake behind us. I'm grateful for the lack of chop as we slice effortlessly across the ocean's surface. If it was rough, the trip would take twice as long.

I slow down as we approach the cove outside Cormorant House. It's difficult to see the bouys in the dark, but I've sailed these waters with Jo a thousand times. I guide us along the dock, beneath the stone archway, into the boathouse slip with ease.

It's dim inside. In silence, I shut the engine.

"Wait here," I whisper into Jo's ear.

She shivers. "Okay."

I scramble toward the bow to tie off our lines. All the while, my heart pounds inside my chest like a cavalry charge. By the time I return to the cockpit, where Jo is perched on one of the cushioned seats, I think I might be having arrhythmias.

I take a cautious step toward her. During my crazy stunt, when I stole her away from the prom, when I pulled her close and kissed her... I was running on pure adrenaline. Now, in the quiet aftermath, nerves skitter down my spine as she lifts her large blue eyes to mine.

What is she going to say?

Will she tell me to fuck off?

"I think I must be dreaming," she murmurs. "There's no way this can be real."

"It is real, Jo," I murmur back. "I promise."

"Maybe you should pinch me. Just to make sure."

Swallowing hard, I reach out and brush my knuckles lightly against her neck. I can't bring myself to pinch her. I never want to hurt her again, as long as I live.

She shivers beneath my touch.

"How's this feel?" I whisper as I stroke my fingertips slowly down toward her clavicle. "Still like a dream?"

She nods slightly, her throat muscles contracting. "Yes. But if it is... I don't want to wake up, Archer. Not ever."

That's all the encouragement I need.

My hands slide around her waist as I pull her up against me. My mouth is desperate as it seeks hers. She's just as desperate as she returns my kiss, her lips pressing hard against mine. Her hands wind around my shoulders, sliding under my shirt collar to stroke the hair at the nape of my neck. She moans as my hands slide down her body, cupping her ass through the fabric of her dress.

God, she feels amazing.

Mouths fused together, we stumble backward into the small v-shaped berth in the cabin. My hands find the lapels of the oversized suit jacket she's wearing. I push it off her shoulders; it drops to the floor with a soft whoosh.

For a moment, I can only stare. Even in shadow, she's so stunning, it almost hurts to look at her.

"This dress..." I murmur, toying with one of the thin straps. "Is driving me crazy."

"Then... maybe you should take it off."

Fuck.

My cock twitches against the zipper of my dress pants. I'm hard as a rock. Her teasing me isn't helping matters.

"Jo... if you're not serious about this... we should stop."

"I don't want to stop."

Reaching up, she guides my hand to the straps of her dress. Together, we tug them off her shoulders. I groan as the silk slides down her skin like water, revealing her naked body.

She's not wearing a scrap of underwear.

"Jesus Christ, Jo. You're going to kill me."

She stands there, fully nude, staring at me without a hint of self-consciousness. Her breasts are small and perfectly round. Her rosy pink nipples are hard with desire. I can't resist reaching out to touch them. They fit perfectly in the palms of my hands.

I lean down to kiss her, but she puts a finger against my lips, stopping me with a whisper.

"Now you."

My hands shake as I loosen my tie and slide it up, over my head. She undoes the buttons of my dress shirt. Her fingers are just as shaky as she reaches for my belt buckle. I'm barely breathing as her hands skim over my zipper. She doesn't touch me — not yet — but her eyes track my every move as I push my pants to the floor, followed by my underwear.

My cock springs free, hard and ready.

I hear Jo's sharp intake of air.

A second later, I feel the faint brush of her fingertips against my abs. Sliding down the indentations. Stopping just shy of my hips.

My pulse is roaring between my ears. I can barely formulate a coherent thought. All I can think about its getting my hands on her skin, touching every conceivable part of her until I've memorized them by heart.

Stepping closer to her, I bring our bodies flush. In my eagerness, I smack my head against the low ceiling of the cabin.

"Fuck!"

Jo giggles at me.

"Oh, you think that's funny?"

"Yeah," she laughs. "I really do."

Growling playfully in retribution, I toss her onto the bed and follow her down. Our laughter is quickly forgotten as our bare bodies collide. I brace myself on top of her, staring down into her face.

"Jo," I breathe. "My Jo."

This time, she doesn't pull away.

This time, she brushes her lips against mine, wraps her arms around my back, and pulls me closer.

"My Archer," she echoes, kissing me again.

In the dark bunk, we explore each other like adventurers discovering new lands, using all our senses to drink each other in. I kiss her everywhere, reveling in the sound of her moans as I bring her to the brink of pleasure with my mouth between her legs. Feeling a thrill while I watch her hands fist in the crisp white sheets as her first ever orgasm rocks through her like an earthquake.

The more we touch, the more the need to be inside her grows. I'm panting hard when she retrieves the condom from the pocket of my discarded pants. As she rolls it onto my shaft, she keeps her eyes locked on mine.

"Are you sure about this?" I grit out between clenched teeth. "If you're not, if this is moving too fast—"

"It's not too fast," she breathes, pulling me on top of her. "I've been waiting for this moment for eighteen years."

"Me too."

My mouth brushes hers lightly. "This might hurt, Jo. If it does, just tell me to stop."

"I trust you, Archer."

Our eyes never shift as I push slowly inside her. We both gasp as our bodies join. She's so tight, it makes my eyes water. Pleasure shoots through my veins. I wonder if this is what it's like to do heroin — this sudden rush of extreme elation, this incomparable joy.

She cries out in sudden pain. Instantly, I go still. It takes all my strength not to move; to fight against the urge to drive inside her, burying myself to the hilt.

"Jo?"

Her voice is tight. "I'm okay." She takes a deep breath. "I'm good. Just..." She's looking up at me with so much trust, it slays me. "Just go slow."

I nod. "Okay. *Okay*. I can do that."

For Jo, I can do that.

It's not my first time, but it might as well be. This, now, is nothing like I experienced with Sienna. It's not even in the same realm of existence.

As the pain subsides and we begin to move together in earnest, Jo comes alive beneath me. Our hands grip hard enough to bruise as we both edge closer to the precipice of desire. And when I thrust fully into her, letting her have my length in its entirety, we tumble over that precipice together, free-falling into the depths, crying out for each other in the dark.

I love you, I think in the aftermath of our union, holding her tight. Pressing a kiss to the top of her head.

I'm not sure why I don't say it aloud. Why I don't tell her exactly how I'm feeling.

I should've.

I guess... I thought we'd have more time. I thought the happily-ever-after part would last more than just one night.

I was wrong.

WAKING up beside a stark-naked Josephine Valentine is as close to heaven as I've ever experienced. For a long while, I just stare at her — taking her in like a piece of artwork hanging on the wall of a museum.

Every freckle.

Every eyelash.

Every plane of her face.

Every curve of her body.

Until last night, I had no idea it was possible to lose yourself so completely in someone else. Physically, emotionally. Even spiritually. All I can think about is getting back inside her. Seeing that look in her eyes when she's about to explode into fragments under my hands.

A faint chirp makes me sit up. Moving quietly, so I don't disturb her, I fish my pants from the floor and pull my phone from the pocket. My eyes widen when I see the screen.

17 missed calls.

4 text messages.

I click open the first one. It's from my father.

COME HOME NOW. URGENT.

My heart begins to pound. When I click open the second message, it stops entirely. It's from Rico, with a timestamp about 25 minutes after the one from Pa.

I WARNED YOU AND YOUR BROTHER NOT TO FUCK WITH ME, KID.

The third message is a picture. In it, I see my parents duct taped to metal chairs. I have no idea where they are. All I know is, they look terrified as they stare into the camera.

The final message chills me to the bone.

1318 CABOT STREET

11 AM

COME ALONE

NO POLICE OR THEY DIE

Fear spikes through me as I check the time.

It's already 10:35.

I have 25 minutes to get there. And I don't even know where 'there' is, yet. I shoot one last look at Jo as I grab my clothes and start running.

CHAPTER TWENTY-FIVE

JOSEPHINE

WHEN I WAKE UP, Archer is gone.

I'm alone in the Hinckley cabin. The boat rocks lightly beneath me as the tide comes in. I sit up, throwing an arm across my chest to cover myself.

"Archer?"

Silence greets me.

I don't panic yet. Not until I slide off the bed, step into my dress, and walk toward the cockpit.

"Archer?" I call again, louder this time.

There's no reply.

Surely, he wouldn't just leave.

Not after last night.

But there's no sign of him anywhere. Not a note, not an article of clothing. No trace of him at all, except for the slight ache between my legs and the small bloodstain on the v-berth's white sheets.

My first reaction is worry that something terrible happened to him. I reach for my iPhone to call... before I remember I don't have one. In the chaos of finals week, prom, and graduation, I haven't gotten around to buying a replacement, yet.

Shit.

Graduation.

That's today.

I yelp as my sluggish brain registers the position of the sun. It's already high in the sky. I need to be at Exeter by noon, dressed in my cap and gown, prepared to give a speech in front of three hundred people.

I jolt into motion, stripping the sheets off the bed with a yank, balling them into my arms, and carrying them off the Hinckley. I feel like a criminal disposing of evidence as I shove them into the trash can, pushing them all the way down to the bottom.

Barefoot, I leave the boathouse behind and race up the path to the house. It takes all my self-control not to turn off onto the side route that leads to Gull Cottage.

Maybe he went home to get ready...

But why not wake me first?

It makes no sense at all. The way he made love to me last night... it was a revelation. It swept me away on a tide I didn't even know existed, carried me to places I'd only dreamed about. There's no way he didn't feel it, too.

He might've made love to you, an annoying voice whispers from the darkest corner of my mind. *But he never actually told you he loved you.*

Did he?

I push the voice aside, trying to hold onto the parts of last night that aren't in question. The look on his face when he pulled up in the Hinckley. The break in his voice when he called my name. The passion in his hands when he pulled me into his arms. The reverence in his eyes when he pushed inside me for the first time, so gently it made me cry.

Archer Reyes loves me, I assure myself. *I'm certain of it.*

And yet... as I step into Cormorant House's ever-constricting emptiness... as I shower away all traces of the boy who took my virginity... as I stare at my own reflection in the mirror while swiping on mascara.... as I pull on my cap and gown and collect my speech cards from my desk...

I don't feel certain of anything at all.

I MAKE it to Exeter with minutes to spare, the Porsche screeching to a stop in the first free spot I find. My hair is still slightly damp as I pull on my dark green graduation cap. The tassel tickles my cheek with each step.

I hustle toward the courtyard. Hundreds of white chairs are lined up along the grass, facing a narrow stage. A podium awaits at the center, with a green and black Exeter pennant hanging from the front.

Avoiding the dense crowd of parents and faculty, I wind around the perimeter of the courtyard toward the side hall, where my fellow graduates are gathered in an animated cluster — boys in black, girls in green. I scan every face, looking for one in particular.

He's not here.

Someone grabs my arm. Hope springs to life in my chest. I whirl around, expecting Archer, but it's only Headmaster Lawrence.

"There you are!" he says, relief saturating his words. "I was beginning to worry we'd have to start without our Valedictorian!"

"Sorry. I overslept."

"Not a problem, not a problem at all." He rubs his hands together. "I, for one, am so looking forward to your speech. I'm sure your parents are as well! I made sure they were seated in the front row."

"Joy."

"I knew you'd be pleased," he says, missing my sarcasm completely. "Josephine, in case I don't have another chance, I'd just like to tell you how wonderful it was to have a student like you at this academy. You were a credit to your peers and a delight to have in class. You will be missed around here. Brown is lucky to have you!"

I'm somewhat touched by his unexpected sentiments. I never thought he cared much for me. "Thank you, Headmaster. I appreciate it."

"I should go — we'll be getting started soon." He nods at me. "Best of luck! See you up there."

All around me, my fellow seniors snap selfies in their caps and gowns, commemorating the day in photographs. Not one person asks to take a picture with me. No one even looks my direction.

The closer the clock creeps to noon, the more unsettled I become about Archer's glaring absence. I can barely remember my speech. Only last night, I had it memorized word for word.

"Five minute warning!" a woman with a clipboard calls. "Please start to line up alphabetically by last name! Two lines. A-L on the right, M-Z on the left."

People begin to shuffle toward their places. I take a deep breath, leaning back against a column for support. Reaching into my billowy gown pocket, I pull out the index cards and study the lines scribbled there.

Winston Churchill once said, 'Success is not final, failure is not fatal: it is the courage to continue that counts.'

I flip to the next one.

As we stand here on our graduation stage, ready to collect our diplomas and move into the next chapter of our lives, I cannot promise you instant success... but I can guarantee, without a shadow of a doubt, at least some failure.

I flip again.

We all fail. That is an inevitable part of the human condition. It is how we recover from those failures that truly defines us...

"Josie!"

The twins' voices jolt me away from my cards. I look up just in time to be folded into a double hug. They squeeze me tight, talking over the top of one another.

"What happened last night?"

"I can't believe you ditched prom!"

"And with *Reyes!*"

"Did you two do it?"

"Um, hello? Did you see that kiss he gave her? They totally did it."

"You're probably right. It was an epic kiss."

"Totally epic."

"Spill, Josie!"

"We're dying for details, here!"

I pull back, trying to smile. "I promise I'll tell you guys everything later. Right now, I just need to get through this speech without falling apart in front of my parents and everyone I've ever met."

"No fun." Ophelia pouts. "I hate waiting."

Odette's brows waggle. "You mean it? *All* the gory details?"

"As many as you can handle."

"Deal."

"Wait, what are you doing over here all alone?" Ophelia grabs my hand. "Come stand with the rest of the alphabetical rejects, at the back."

"I can't." I wave my cards in the air. "Valedictorian has to sit up on the stage."

"Ugh, I forgot about that." Odette groans. "God, I'm hungover. You missed a hell of an after-party. My date passed out on the front lawn. Didn't even make it to the limo."

"Charlie was sad to see you go, Josie." Ophelia grins at me. "Thankfully, we found it in our hearts to comfort him. *Twice.*"

The twins high five.

I laugh. "I'm glad his night wasn't entirely ruined because of me. It wasn't exactly nice of me to bail on him. In the moment, I wasn't really thinking clearly..."

"Mmm. Lust will do that to you." Odette's head tilts. "Speaking of... where is the man of the hour? I thought you two would be stuck together like glue after last night."

I chew my bottom lip. "I'm actually not sure. I haven't seen him since..."

"This morning?"

I shake my head. "Last night, actually. We fell asleep together, but when I woke up... he was gone."

The twins trade a glance.

"What?" I ask nervously. "What was that look about?"

Ophelia reaches out and squeezes my arm. "It's probably nothing."

"Totally." Odette strokes the other arm. "I wouldn't worry about it."

"You guys are bad liars."

They trade another look.

"Tell me," I plead.

"It's... well..." Odette is avoiding my eyes. "It could be a bad sign that he left without a word. It could mean that, in his eyes, last night was nothing but a hookup. Just sex, no strings."

"No," I say instantly. "That's not possible."

Ophelia nods. "You'd know better than us, obviously. It's only... when it comes to guys, we've had a lot of experience with being ghosted after giving them what they want."

"A lot," Odette agrees. "Like... *a lot.* Teenage boys can be pigs. As soon as you let them under your panties, they treat you like conquered territory. You're picking out the names of your future children, meanwhile they're..."

"On to the next girl," Ophelia adds gently.

"No," I whisper. "This isn't like that. Archer isn't like that."

He loves me back.

I know he does.

"No matter how sweet he was to you last night... he's still a guy. His brain is wired to want exactly one thing." Ophelia grimaces. "Based on what you told us before... about how he's been so crappy toward you lately..."

"And how he screwed Sienna at that party..."

"And how he's never returned your feelings before..."

"*Stop.*" My voice breaks. "Please. Just... stop. I don't want to hear anymore."

Their eyes widen at my blatant pain.

"Sorry, Josie."

"I hope we didn't upset you..."

"You didn't. It's fine." I smile thinly, lying through my teeth. "I'll see you after the ceremony, okay?"

"Okay..."

A teacher claps her hands three times, calling for attention.

"Seniors! Two minute warning. If you aren't already in your spot, this is your last chance. I need the Student Council President and the Class Valedictorian up here, at the front." She glances at a clipboard. "That would be... Eva Ulrich and Josephine Valentine."

"Here!" Eva chirps brightly.

"Excellent. And Josephine? Where are you?"

Numb, I walk to the front of the crowd.

"Here," I say. "I'm here."

But my mind is somewhere else.

HEADMASTER LAWRENCE CLEARS HIS THROAT. He's been droning on for fifteen minutes already, his opening marks rivaling Lincoln's Gettysburg Address.

"And now... it is my distinct honor to introduce to you our Class Valedictorian, Miss Josephine Valentine."

Polite applause fills the courtyards as I walk to the podium. My parents are in the front row, preening like prized peacocks. This is just another feather in their caps.

Our daughter, Class Valedictorian.

With genes like ours, how could she not be?

Blair didn't have the time to celebrate my birthday or see me off to the prom or even drive me to my own graduation ceremony... but apparently she found a few free minutes to pop into the salon for fresh highlights and a mani-pedi. She looks like a Jackie O knockoff in her vintage Chanel suit.

When I meet her eyes, she mouths something at me.

Posture!

My shoulders pull back. My spine goes stiff. I look around the crowd, searching for a friendly face. Flora and Miguel must be in the very back; I don't see them anywhere. And there's an empty seat in the R section, where Archer Reyes should be seated in his black graduation gown.

My grip tightens on the index cards. I glance down at the words written there. They swim before my eyes like gibberish. Fragments of a speech I wrote not for myself, but for the benefit of the two people sitting in the front row, staring up at me with frigid smiles.

Vincent gives a low, circular gesture, his eyes blasting a clear message at me.

Get a move on.

I set down the cards.

"I had a speech written for you today," I say into the microphone, flinching at the sound of my own voice booming across the courtyard. "It was a good speech. It had all the appropriate pauses, a few key jokes, and even a line to make you cry. I practiced it in the mirror precisely sixteen times, until I was able to recite it without stumbling over the pronunciation of the word *hegemony* even once." I pause. "Shame, since you won't be getting to hear it."

The audience titters, unsure whether or not I'm being serious. Blair and Vincent appear less than amused.

"Because now that I'm up here on this stage, on the day of my graduation, looking out at all of you fine people in the crowd... I am not, in fact, overcome with an urge to wax poetic about the value of working hard in order to get ahead in the world, or the benefit of a solid education in furthering your future interests. I will not stand here quoting Winston Churchill and encouraging you to sieze the day."

The crowd is silent, rapt. For the first time in my life, my parents are staring at me with something close to undivided attention.

I soak it in like a drug.

"Who am I to spend my allocated five minutes preaching? I'm not any kind of authority. I'm just an eighteen-year-old overachiever with stronger test-taking skills than my peers. How that qualifies me to give a speech about *anything* is, frankly, laughable. Yet, I am expected to step into this charade, playing my part convincingly. And you — you, sitting there, acting like I'm not just as messed up as any kid in this graduating class, simply because I happen to have a marginally higher GPA — are just as culpable."

Behind me, Headmaster Lawrence clears his throat.

Loudly.

I ignore him.

"Exeter Academy of Excellence taught me many things over the years, from anatomy to astrophysics... but the one lesson that isn't taught in textbooks is the one I'll remember best. We're all just playing parts. Pretending to be something we're not, hoping no one else looks close enough to notice." My eyes drop to the front row. My parents are glaring at me, mortification plain as day on their faces. "Whether you're a selfish philanthropist saving the world to cover your own narcissism..." I glance at Ryan Snyder, glowering in the second row. "Or an imposter bound for the Ivy-League..." My eyes move to Sienna Sullivan, seated beside him. "Or a mean girl lashing out to cover her own insecurities..." I look back out over the crowd. "Or even a clueless valedictorian asked to speak with some semblance of conviction..." I shrug, lips twisting wryly. "Life makes liars of us all."

The silence of the crowd is absolute.

"I'm so tired of pretending. Aren't you? I'm sick to death of acting like someone I'm not. So here's the truth about your Class Valedictorian, Josephine Valentine." I smile. "The essay that got me into Brown? It was complete and utter bullshit. A painstakingly plotted story, designed with the help of three tutors."

My mother claps a hand over her mouth.

"The mansion I live in, the one in the magazine spreads and architectural blogs? It's a sprawling, soulless box, empty of everything that makes a house a home."

The crowd stirs, whispers spreading like wildfire through grass. "The parents who raised me, teaching me to ride a bike and braid my hair? They're a housekeeper and a handyman, not the people with whom I share strands of DNA."

Furious, my father starts up out of his seat. My mother grabs his arm before he can fully stand, her fingernails digging into the fabric of his shirt. Holding him at bay.

God forbid they make a scene.

He sits stiffly. His eyes hold a dark promise that I will soon pay for my behavior.

A radiant smile spreads across my face. With each lie I strip away, I feel buoyant. So light, I could float up straight up into the sky.

"I can't stand parties. I like being alone, at home with my sewing machine or out on my sailboat. I know that isn't trendy or cool to admit, but it's true." I glance briefly at Odette and Ophelia. "I hate being called *Valentine* and *Josie*, but I let it happen because I was too desperate for friends to make waves." I take a deep breath. "And this fall, I have no plans to pursue a degree in Public Health so that I can take over my parents' foundation. I'll be studying fashion design instead."

Two hundred sets of eyes watch as I take a deep breath. I notice, some people in the crowd are nodding. Whispering behind their programs.

"So. Why am I telling you all this unnecessary information?"

There's a low, collective chuckle.

I direct my final words at my classmates. "We are eighteen. We are on the cusp of becoming real people. The choices we make now will define who we are for the rest of our lives. Make sure you choose wisely. Stop hiding behind a socially acceptable facade. Stop worrying about what everyone else thinks. Be a freak. Be a weirdo. Be offbeat. Don't force your sailboat upwind, simply because that's where others expect you to go. Adjust your course to somewhere that matters. And while you're at it... enjoy the journey. It's always far shorter than you expect, and usually better than the final destination." I pause for a long beat. "Thank you."

The silence is deafening.

I count out three long seconds before, finally, from the back row, people begin to clap. Before long, the entire courtyard is swept up into thunderous applause, cheering for me as I turn from the podium.

With one notable exception.

In the front row, Blair and Vincent Valentine are stone statues, their faces both contorted in shock, their hands clasped tightly in their laps.

I take my seat beside Eva Ulrich. In six years, we've never really spoken outside of class necessities. She's always been annoyed that I beat her out for the top GPA slot. But now, she's looking at me with a sort of grudging respect shining in her eyes.

"Good luck at Brown, Val—" She breaks off. " I mean *Josephine*. I hear their fashion program is amazing."

"Good luck at Harvard, Eva. And... thanks."

Headmaster Lawrence is back at the microphone. "Without further ado... I will now hand out the diplomas."

The first row of students rises.

"Steve Abbott!"

"Abigail Barlow!"

"Arther Bennings!"

With each name he calls, one of my classmates walks across the stage to shake his hand, collect their diploma, and switch their tassel to the other side of their cap. It takes a surprising amount of time. As he moves slowly through the list, the tension inside me grows so strong, I can barely sit still.

"Amanda Quinn!"

"Edward Reardon!"

I suck in a breath.

"Archer Reyes!"

The seconds tick by.

He doesn't appear.

Headmaster Lawrence looks around in confusion.

"ARCHER REYES!" he calls again, louder. As if Archer is simply hard of hearing.

Whispers circulate through the crowd as the seconds pass by. The ceremony has ground to a halt, waiting for him to materialize. But he doesn't.

Where is he?

Something is wrong. I can sense it. My mind spins a million directions, playing out unlikely scenarios to explain his absence. I want to fly from my seat and search for him. The need to know he's okay is so strong, it squeezes the air from my lungs, until I'm struggling to breathe. I'm about two seconds away from a full panic attack.

"It seems Mr. Reyes was unavoidably delayed," Headmaster Lawrence announces. "So. Where were we... Ah, yes. *Rebecca Rowland!*"

"Sienna Sullivan!"

"Ryan Snyder!"

"Eva Ulrich!"

"Kenny Underwood!"

Finally, after a million years...

"*Josephine Valentine!*"

When he calls my name, I walk up to the podium and accept my diploma with numb hands.

"Congratulations, Miss Valentine." He leans in to whisper something, muffling the microphone with his hand. "An interesting speech, earlier. Unexpected but refreshing. I admire your candor. And I hope you know... striking out on your own, outside the expectations of a family legacy, is something to be proud of. Never be ashamed of making your own way. No matter what your parents think."

"Thank you." My throat is tight. "I appreciate it, Headmaster."

He nods, then glances down at his sheet to call the next names. Blessedly, we're almost to the end.

"Odette Wadell!"

"Ophelia Wadell!"

They both wink at me as they collect their diplomas.

After the final name is called, Eva walks to the podium, grinning.

"Hat's off to the graduates!"

Snatching the cap from her head, she tosses it straight up. A second later, a hundred more join it, filling the air with green and black squares.

The crowd cheers. Their whistles and wolf howls are ear-shattering. In spite of everything, I find myself smiling just as wide as my fellow classmates. Soaking in the moment, before it slips away.

High school is over.

Welcome to real life.

All around me, parents are hugging their children, wiping tears of pride and joy. I walk down the steps of the stage, searching the crowd for signs of Flora and Miguel. Hoping they, at the very least, can offer some sort of explanation for Archer's absence.

But they're nowhere to be seen.

The anxiety inside me, momentarily subdued by the hat toss, returns with a vengeance. It multiplies when Blair and Vincent step into my path.

"Come, Josephine," my mother says in a frigid voice. Her eyes are like knives. "We're leaving now, before you can publicly humiliate us any further."

"But—"

"*Now.* I'm not going to say it twice." My father's voice is shaking with anger. "And, for the record... you can consider yourself grounded."

CHAPTER TWENTY-SIX

ARCHER

MY RIGHT HAND grips the steering wheel so hard, my knuckles turn white. My left holds my iPhone in a vise grip. Every few seconds, the truck's GPA system drones orders at me, directing me toward the address Rico sent.

"At the lights, turn left at Lexington Avenue."

The stoplight goes from green to yellow as I race toward it. I blast through the red without a thought, wincing as other cars swerve to avoid me with a racket of angry beeps. I'm usually the farthest thing from reckless behind the wheel. Today, I drive like a Formula 1 racer.

There's no other choice.

I'm still wearing my prom clothes, the white button-down now a mess of wrinkles. There was no time to change before I hopped in my truck. No time to do anything except sprint to the cottage, calling out for my parents. Praying this was all some kind of sick joke.

"Ma! Pa! Where are you?"

My own voice echoed back at me, desperation in every syllable. Signs of struggle were apparent — a dining chair overturned, a floor rug askew, a water glass on its side. Cold fear gripped my heart as I raced to my bedroom and grabbed the aluminum bat from the floor.

I glance at it now, sitting on my passenger seat beside the graduation gown I'll probably never get a chance to wear.

A boy with a baseball bat, against two gun-toting gang members.

The odds are not in my favor.

They never were. That doesn't change a damn thing, though. My parents are held hostage in some dark basement. There's no way I'm going to sit idly by while they're in danger.

I eye the dashboard clock.

10:57

I have three minutes to make a ten minute trip. My foot presses harder against the pedal, accelerating to twice the legal limit on this quiet residential street. The truck engine roars in response.

50mph

60mph

70mph

"At the stop sign, continue straight."

I glance around for other cars, then proceed to blow through the intersection without braking.

10:58

"In a quarter mile, merge onto Abbey Street."

Driving with my knees, I jab a finger against my iPhone screen and dial Jaxon. It rings three times before kicking over to his voicemail — just as it has the past three times I tried to reach him.

The caller you are attempting to reach is not available. Please leave a message at the tone.

When it beeps, I lift the phone to my mouth.

"Jaxon, it's Archer. I don't know where you are or what the

hell you did to piss Rico off... but you need to fix it. Now." I swallow hard. "They have Ma and Pa. I'm going to try and negotiate, but I could really use some backup. So just—" I suck in a breath. "Just show up. For once in your fucking life, just be there when I need you."

I rattle off the address before I disconnect. My eyes snag on the clock.

11:00

I'm not going to make it in time.

"Turn onto Cabot Street," the GPS instructs. "Then, drive three-point-two miles."

I take the turn on two wheels, relieved I'm nearly there. Not that I have any actual plan of action beyond that. I'm running on pure nerve, my mind circling madly around itself, like a snake devouring its own tail.

"Your destination is on the right in three miles."

My finger hovers over the screen. It would be so simple to dial for help. Three little numbers.

9-1-1

Rico's text message said not to call the cops; that he'd kill my parents if I did. I have no reason to doubt him. Every experience I've had with the Latin Kings has proven them to be merciless. They will stop at nothing to get what they want.

Nothing.

Which is why I know that, even if I do as he says, Rico won't think twice about killing us all. His endgame is the only thing he cares about.

"After the next intersection, your destination is on the right," the GPS intones in a robotic voice.

11:02

Before I can second guess myself, I close my eyes and dial. It connects almost instantly.

"9-1-1, what is your emergency?"

"There's a hostage situation at 1318 Magnolia Street!" I yell into the speaker. "Please, send someone right away."

"Okay, sir, I need you to calm down and give me some details," a soothing voice instructs. "You said there are hostages, can you tell me how many? And how many suspects?"

"Two hostages. Two suspects."

"And are there any weapons involved?"

"I think they have guns. I don't know for sure. But they're dangerous." My grip tightens on the steering wheel. My eyes flicker back and forth between the road and the GPS. I don't see the lights change as I fly into the intersection. "Please, hurr—"

The word never makes it past my lips. A 16-wheeler slams into the passenger side of my truck, crunching it in like a fist around a soda can. The phone sails out of my hand as the world flips upside down. Time seems to slow, suspended endlessly in the moment before impact.

There's no way to brace against it.

Gravity forces the truck back to earth, landing on its roof. Glass explodes all around me, raining down in razor-sharp droplets. Airbags burst out with a hiss of compact air. Metal screeches, showering sparks across the pavement as the momentum carries the truck across the intersection. It rolls three times before it finally slams to a stop against a telephone pole — upside down, tires spinning in the air.

Hanging limply against my seatbelt, I gasp in excruciating pain. There's so much of it, I can't pinpoint where it's coming from.

Everywhere, all at once.

It's blinding.

The pain in my chest is hard to breathe around — radiating down my arms, throbbing like a heartbeat. I try to move my limbs, but they don't cooperate. I taste hot copper in my mouth and know it's not a good sign.

In the distance, sirens approach, growing louder and louder.

Are they for me or my parents?

I hope its the latter.

The world outside the crunched cab of my truck is fading a bit more out of focus with each passing second. It's all rather hazy; as though my head is stuck inside a ball of cotton. My thoughts are equally muddled.

Time is a funny thing. More fickle than funny, actually — making promises and breaking them. Handing you hope for a future and then snatching it away.

You always think you'll get more minutes on the clock than you do. More play time on the field than you're given. You see the stories of lives cut short on the nightly news... you read the sad headlines scrawled across the morning paper... and you think to yourself, *That will never be me.*

How vastly unfair to learn you are not the exception, but the rule.

Something warm and wet is dripping into my eyes, making it hard to see. It might be blood. I lack the energy to search for its source. I let my lids flutter closed, embracing the cold reality of my present.

Because the present is all I have left.

One hour in the past, I was holding the girl of my dreams in the circle of my arms.

One hour in the future, I was meant to walk across the graduation state to collect my diploma.

And now, instead...

I'm dead.

CHAPTER TWENTY-SEVEN

JOSEPHINE

WHERE ARE YOU?
Where are you?
Where are you?

CHAPTER TWENTY-EIGHT

ARCHER

OKAY, so I lied.

I'm not dead.

I just feel like it.

Blinking awake, I wince at the bright fluorescent light beaming directly into my retinas. Machines beep all around me as they monitor my vitals — a mechanical din that intensifies my headache tenfold. My right temple throbs, swollen to twice it's normal size. I must've cut my head open.

I try to lift my arm to feel the gash, but meet unexpected resistance. I glance down for the first time and feel my stomach turn to stone.

A metal handcuff is fastened neatly around my left wrist.

I'm manacled to my hospital bed.

I barely have time to process that when I catch sight of my other arm. My pitching arm. It's encased in a thick white cast.

Fuck.

The door swings open. A doctor steps into the room. She looks around nervously as two police officers follow her in, pushing her glasses farther up the bridge of her nose.

"Archer, I'm Dr. Taggerty. I was the resident on call this morning when they brought you in. It's a relief to see your eyes open."

"What's going on?" I rasp. My voice comes out like sandpaper. "What happened?"

"You were in an accident," she tells me kindly. "Do you remember? Your truck flipped over several times at an intersection in Beverly."

"I remember that. I meant..." I inhale sharply as pain shoots through my chest. "What happened to my parents?"

"I'm sorry, I don't know. They weren't brought in with you." She glances at the policemen, brows raised. "I'm sure the gentlemen behind me will be able to offer more insight on that front."

One of the officers steps forward. He's middle aged, with sandy brown hair and the beginnings of a beer belly. His light green eyes are cold as they glare into mine. "I'm Officer Belkin. That's Minkoff." He jerks his head toward his partner — a few years younger and a few pounds lighter, but wearing the same inhospitable expression. "Your parents are at the station for questioning. We were able to extract them from the house where they were being held without injury. They're cooperating fully."

Relief floods me.

They're alive.

"And my brother?"

"We haven't been able to track Jaxon down yet. But it's only a matter of time."

"What about the men who were holding my parents? They're members of the Latin Kings. They've been threatening us for months."

"Look, I'm afraid we can't talk to you about any pertinent

details of the case until we know the extent of your involvement, Reyes. Active investigation and all."

"*My* involvement?"

Belkin nods. "If you'd like to answer some of our
questions—"

"No," the doctor says flatly. "No questions until he's had a
full examination. I want to make sure we're completely out of
the woods. He has some internal bleeding we're watching
closely. And he's still dazed from the general anesthesia."

"Fine." Belkin sighs. "We'll come back tomorrow."

"Are the handcuffs really necessary?" Dr. Taggerty shoots
me a look of sympathy. "He's just a kid."

"He's eighteen," Minkoff says. "And he was caught in possession of enough fentanyl to OD every addict north of Boston."

"*What?*" The word explodes from my mouth. "That's
insane!"

"So you deny the drugs were yours."

"Hell yes I deny it," I growl.

"Then how do you explain how they got into your truck?"

My mind spins, seeking out any possible explanation. I can
only come up with one.

Jaxon.

He must've stashed his supply in my truck when he came
home the other day.

God.

Fucking.

Dammit.

My hand curls into a fist inside the handcuff. "Look. I don't
deal drugs. I've never even taken drugs. Whatever you found, it
wasn't mine."

"His bloodwork was clear," Dr. Taggerty murmurs. "For
what it's worth."

The officers barely acknowledge her. They're looking at me with that familiar expression. The one that says, *You're a Reyes. You're trouble.*

I try to keep calm, but the anger brimming inside me is difficult to swallow. "I have no idea how the drugs got into my truck. I swear it. I—" I break off with a wheeze of pain. My cracked ribs ache so badly, my eyes gloss.

Dr. Taggerty rushes to my side, putting her fingers to my jugular vein to check the pulse pounding there. "That's enough. No more questions today, officers. As I told you before, you'll have to come back if you want to question him." She pauses. "And, if he's really under arrest, I don't think I need to remind you he's entitled to a lawyer."

Belkin scowls. "Fine. We'll come back tomorrow. But we're reading him his rights before we go."

I close my eyes, trying to shut out the words.

You have the right to remain silent.

Anything you say can and will be used against you in a court of law.

You have the right to an attorney.

If you cannot afford an attorney, one will be provided for you...

I don't open my lids again until the officers are gone. When I do, I find Dr. Taggerty watching me. Her eyes are full of sympathy.

"You've had a rough go of it."

"I can't lie, it's not exactly how I pictured my graduation day going." I scowl down at the clunky plaster cast on my right arm. "How bad is it?"

"You have severe bruising over your entire body, three cracked ribs, plus some pretty persistent internal bleeding we need to keep an eye on for the next few days. If it doesn't resolve on its own, you'll need surgery." She pauses to shine a light into my pupils, checking for reactivity. "This gash on your temple is pretty nasty. You've got sixteen stitches."

"Like Frankenstein? Perfect."

"You'll have a scar, but it shouldn't be too bad. Your hair-line will hide most of it." She lightly probes the wound, checking the bandage with deft fingers.

"And my wrist?"

She sighs. "A compound fracture. When you came in, the bone was protruding through your skin in a not-so-pretty way. We rushed you into surgery and set it for you. It will require some extensive physical therapy if you expect to regain your mobility."

"I'm a pitcher," I say inaudibly.

"What was that?"

My eyes lift to hers. "I'm a pitcher. A baseball pitcher."

Her face pales. "Oh. I didn't know that."

"I have a scholarship. If I can't play... I can't go to college." I wish my voice wasn't shaking. "Please. Just tell me. Will I be able to pitch again?"

"I will send in the orthopedic surgeon to discuss your prog-nosis in depth tomorrow. But I won't lie — injuries like this don't always heal perfectly. There's are pins in your body, where before there was only bone. Even with physical therapy, you may never regain the exact level of control or throwing power you had before."

I turn my head away. I don't want her to see the tears filling my eyes.

"Archer." Her hand lands on mine, squeezing warmly below the cold metal cuff. "You are young and healthy. There's no reason to assume the worst. And even if your baseball career is over... your life isn't. After the accident you had, you're lucky to be breathing."

My head swivels toward her in slow degrees.

"Lucky?" I choke out, my voice broken. I rattle my left hand against the manacle. "*Lucky?*"

She flinches at the ear-splitting clang. "That was a poor choice of words. I only meant—"

"Get out." My eyes press closed. "I don't want to talk anymore."

"Archer, I think—"

"*Go away.*"

I hear the sound of retreating footsteps. The door clicks closed a second later, leaving me alone for the first time since I regained consciousness.

In solitude, I'm finally able to process the gravity of my situation.

Even with physical therapy, you may never regain the exact level of control or throwing power you had before.

I want to scream.

I want to rage.

I want to cry.

I want to curse.

I want to wrap my hands around my brother's neck and squeeze until he stops breathing.

I want to hug my parents for five minutes straight, like a little kid after a bad dream.

I want to crawl into Jo's warm embrace and reassure myself that there are still things in this world worth living for.

But I can only lie here — a prisoner of my own choices. A victim of circumstances beyond my control. Breathing through the pain that radiates from the top of my head to the tip of my toes.

I am broken.

In more ways than one.

WHEN MY DOOR swings open the next morning, I assume it's the police back for another round of questioning. I sit up straighter in bed as the last people I ever expected to see walk into my hospital room.

Blair and Vincent Valentine.

"Mr. and Mrs. Valentine, what are you doing here?" I crane my neck, trying to see around them. "Is Jo with you?"

"Josephine is at Cormorant House."

"Oh." My hope deflates. "Maybe next time."

There's a long silence. Neither of them seems to know where to start. They stare at me with eerie, emotionless gazes.

"I asked for my phone so I could call her and explain what happened... but they won't let me have it. They only let me speak to my parents for a few moments last night." I clear my throat. "I'm surprised they let you in, to be honest."

"The State Police Superintendent is an old friend," Vincent informs me.

"Right. Of course." I suck in a sharp breath. "Maybe you could pass along a message to Jo for me. Tell her that I'm sor—"

"Oh, no." Blair cuts me off. Her eyes are locked on my handcuffs. "I'm afraid that simply won't be possible, Archer. Josephine is not to be told about any of this... *mess*."

My brows lift. "What?"

"She is in a fragile state, right now." Blair shakes her head in a poor mimicry of sympathy. "Frankly, now that we've learned what's been going on around here with your family... it's understandable why she's spiraling. She's been surrounded by chaos for weeks."

"Is she all right?" I ask instantly. "What happened to her?"

"Physically, she's fine. But mentally..." Blair shakes her head, lips pursed. "I'm afraid she has some soul-searching to do. Yesterday at the Exeter graduation, she completely devolved on the stage in front of hundreds during her speech. It was humiliating."

My brows pull in. "For her or for you?"

"That is a very rude comment to make, young man. Especially given that we came here to help you."

"You want to help me," I say dubiously. "Why?"

They exchange a look.

Vincent steps forward. "We understand our daughter has a certain... fondness for you. But I think we all know that teenage romances rarely last. You two are simply on different life trajectories."

I snort. "You mean in two separate tax brackets."

"Josephine is destined for great things. She shouldn't be bogged down by..." Blair trials off, gesturing vaguely at me. "By the many issues you're currently facing. Your recovery, your family drama..."

"Not to mention the heap of trouble you're in with the law." Vincent's voice is blunt. "You'll need a good lawyer to make those drug possession charges go away. I happen to have one on speed dial. And that's not even taking into account my personal connections to local law enforcement. I could make things significantly easier for you." He pauses for a long beat. "Or significantly harder."

"Are you threatening me?"

"Quite the opposite," Blair soothes, oozing civility from her every pore. "We're making you an offer."

"Which is what, exactly?"

"We plan to take Josephine away for the summer — overseas, to Europe, so she can get some hands-on experience at VALENT before she starts classes at Brown in the fall. If she likes Geneva, she may even defer a year. Stay on at the company to really get the hang of things."

My heart has turned to stone inside my chest. "Geneva."

"Switzerland," Blair clarifies, as if I have no idea where Geneva is. "Leaving tonight. It's a done deal."

"If it's such a done deal, why the hell are you here talking to me?" I hiss. "Shouldn't you be packing?"

They're silent.

"Let me guess... Jo isn't so thrilled about this new summer vacation arrangement."

"You know our Josephine. She can be quite stubborn." Blair sighs. "Sometimes, she doesn't know what's best for her. She needs a little push in the right direction."

"Stop talking in circles," I growl. "Tell me what you want from me."

It's Vincent, who finally speaks plainly. "Cut off all ties with our daughter."

"*Excuse me?*"

"You heard me." Vincent levels me with his best hardball stare — one I'm sure he wields effectively in board rooms. "Give her some incentive to leave Manchester — and the mess you've made — behind. Break her heart, if you have to. Whatever it takes to get her out of this town, before the blowback from your family implosion is spattered all over her bright future."

"Screw you," I hiss. "Get out of my room."

"Don't make up your mind so fast, Archer." Blair takes a few steps closer to the side of my bed. Her eyes are the same shade as her daughter's, but they contain none of Jo's warmth. "It seems your brother is still missing. When they find him, he will undoubtedly be going back to prison. You along with him, if you're not smart. As for your parents... unfortunately, we can no longer offer them employment at Cormorant House in good conscience."

I jerk against my handcuffs. "My parents have nothing to do with this—"

"Oh, but they do. They failed to inform us that their ex-convict, drug-addicted son had been released on parole. They concealed the fact that our daughter was in the crosshairs of *gang violence*, of all things." She presses a hand to her heart. "Much as it pains me to let good help go, I don't have much choice in the matter."

Good help.

That's all Flora and Miguel have ever been to these people.

"My parents have worked for you for over twenty years," I hiss through clenched teeth, so furious I'm barely able to breathe. "Gull Cottage has been their home for as long as they've lived in this country. And you're just going to throw them out on the street like... like... rubbish on trash day?"

"Certainly not." Vincent huffs. "We are in a position to provide them with quite a generous severance package. Enough money to get them set up with a house of their own anywhere in the world."

Anywhere except Manchester-by-the-Sea, he means.

"However..." Blair's lips twist in a fake frown. "We are under no such obligation to do so. Technically, as they are in violation of their contract, we owe them nothing. Not a penny. Not even two weeks notice." She pauses. "I doubt they'd find other work in this area. It's a small community. People talk. You know how it is."

Translation: we will use our extensive network to blacklist your parents from any potential job opportunities in a hundred-mile radius.

I look back and forth between them. My heart is lodged inside my throat. "So that's my choice. Either I lose Jo... or lose everything else. My future. My family. My whole fucking life."

Blair sniffs. "I wouldn't phrase it so crudely, but... yes. In a sense, if you cut your ties with our daughter, we will ensure that you walk away from this rather unpleasant incident a free man. And we will take care of your parents in such a generous manner, they can retire tomorrow, if they so choose."

My eyelids press closed. Jo's face appears behind them. A million versions of it. A million memories, embedded deeply in my mind.

Jo at 4, wearing overalls and lopsided pigtails.
Jo at 8, teaching me to skip stones in the cove.
Jo at 10, digging up quahogs on the shore.
Jo at 12, teaching me the basics of sailing.
Jo at 15, scowling at me under the stars.
Jo at 17, telling me she loved me.
Jo at 18, exploding into passion beneath me.

"I can't." My eyes open. "I won't."

"Don't be so stubborn, Archer." Blair scoffs. "Think it through. We all know your baseball career is effectively over. Which means... no scholarship. No college. Even if you beat the criminal charges, you're looking at a far smaller future than the one you planned on."

I try to block her out, but her words hit me like bullets, tearing into the fabric of my heart.

"Without our help... you'll be an ex-con, like your brother. Is that really what you want?." She pauses artfully. "Tell me — can you really picture Josephine in that future with you? Do you really think she'd want you like *this*? No talent? No prospects? No ability to provide the kind of life to which she is accustomed?"

I clench my fists. Pain shoots through my broken bones — a pain so intense, my eyes fill with tears. I can't bring myself to speak.

"You have nothing to offer," Vincent says flatly. "You can't elevate her to the heights she deserves. You will only bring her down, into a life of misery and despair. And, eventually... she will hate you for it."

I stare at the wall. For a long time, the room is completely silent. The agony inside my heart is stronger, even, that the physical pain of my broken body. I find myself wishing, just for a moment, that I really had died when my truck flipped. A quick exit might've been more merciful than this slow atrophy occurring inside my soul.

I have lost everything.

My future.

My dream.

My love.

Looking back at Blair and Vincent, I swallow hard. The voice that comes out of my mouth sounds like it belongs to a stranger.

Cold.

Dead.

Empty.

"I'll need a piece of paper."

CHAPTER TWENTY-NINE

JOSEPHINE

I PACE the confines of my bedroom, just as I've done for the past twenty-four hours, slowly going crazy. Since the commencement ceremony yesterday, I've been confined to the house, completely cut off from the outside world. Vincent and Blair took away my electronics in retaliation for the so-called *spectacle* I made during my speech.

I don't regret a single word.

Nothing can hold my focus. Not sewing, not my kindle, not even *The Great British Bake Off*. I stare up at the ceiling, consumed with worry about Archer. The more hours slip by without being able to talk to him, the more convinced I become that something terrible has happened.

I try not to think too much about Ophelia or Odette's opinion on the matter.

Teenage boys can be pigs. As soon as you let them under your panties, they treat you like conquered territory.

A knock on my door has me flying upright. I pray it's Archer — or, at the very least, Flora or Miguel. But when the knob turns, it's my mother who steps through the door.

"I haven't changed my mind," I say flatly. "I'm still not going to Switzerland."

Her brows lift. "Really? Even if your attendance at Brown is contingent upon it?"

"What?"

"Your father and I have decided, if you don't come to Switzerland, we won't be paying your tuition for the fall semester." She pauses. "Or any other semester, in fact."

My mouth falls open. "That's outrageous! You can't do that—"

"We can. We did. The matter is settled."

"Nothing is settled," I retort hotly. "You don't get to make decisions for me anymore. I'm eighteen."

"Wasn't your whole graduation speech about how we didn't parent you enough? Here we are, trying to parent, and you punish us for it."

I stare at her, unconvinced. "I don't understand why you have to *parent* me in Geneva. Why can't we just stay here for the summer?"

"Because our distribution headquarters aren't here."

"But—"

"You'll adore Switzerland, Josephine. I promise." She sits on the end of my bed and reaches out softly — almost tentatively — to tuck a strand of hair behind my ear. "Don't argue anymore. Pack your things. We're leaving for the airport in an hour."

She pushes to her feet and walks toward the door. Pausing in the frame she says, almost as an afterthought, "The Reyes boy came by earlier."

I practically fly to her side, then grab her by the arm. "What? What did he say? Why didn't you let him in to see me?"

"Slow down, Josephine." Blair presses a hand to her chest. "Dear lord, you're overexcited."

I take a measured breath, trying to calm my nerves. "What did he say?"

"Not much. I did invite him in. He declined."

My heart lurches. "No... that's not... he wouldn't..."

"He seemed to be in quite a bit of a hurry. Something about an opportunity regarding baseball — a training summer camp perhaps? In Nebraska, of all places. Honestly, Josephine, you know how I am when it comes to sports. It all goes right out of my head."

I feel like I've been sucker-punched.

I know exactly what she's talking about. For years, Archer has prattled on and on and on about the elite training camp run by former MLB players. It's nearly impossible to get accepted into their program. But once you're in, you train with the best of the best. There's a good chance he could be recruited to the major leagues.

It's the opportunity of a lifetime.

Not in a million years would he turn it down.

"Did he say anything else?" I ask, feeling the earth tilt beneath me. "Did he say when he was leaving?"

"No, he didn't." Blair sighs, sounding bored by this entire conversation. "Oh — he did leave a letter, though. It's on the table in the atrium."

I nearly bowl her over as I run out the door, into the hall. I round the staircase at warp speed and almost trip down them face-first, only managing to catch myself on the bannister at the very bottom.

The envelope is waiting on the entryway table, just as she promised. My fingers tremble as I rip it open. My eyes scan the words, devouring Archer's familiar, blocky handwriting.

Dear Jo,

I'm sorry to be doing this in a letter. Honestly, after the other night, I didn't know how to face you. I thought it would be easier to put everything down on paper, so there's no confusion.

Prom night was a lot of fun. I had a great time. I hope you did, too. But, as wonderful as it was to spend that moment with you... I think that's all it was.

A moment.

And moments pass.

As soon as I woke up the next morning, I realized we'd made a terrible mistake. I'm sure you realized it, too.

I've been given the opportunity to attend the MLB Elite camp in Nebraska this summer. I think it'll be best for both of us if I go. I won't have access to my phone or internet, so don't bother reaching out.

A little space wouldn't be the worst thing, anyway.

I hope you know, I value our friendship so much. Too much to risk it with something as meaningless as a hook up.

Have a nice summer.

Best,

Archer

THE LETTER FLUTTERS from my fingertips. It hits the floor with a soft *whoosh*, sliding beneath the table.

I do not bend to retrieve it.

Numb, I walk upstairs to pack my suitcase.

UP NEXT...

"We were never just friends."

Don't miss the stunning conclusion to Archer & Jo's love story in *WE DON'T LIE ANYMORE*, part two of THE DON'T DUET, available everywhere December 2020.

PLAYLIST

1. **Wish You Were Gay** — Billie Eilish
2. **Water Fountain** — Alec Benjamin
3. **Cotton Candy** - spill tab
4. **Love You For A Long Time** — Maggie Rogers
5. **I Like Me Better** — Lauv
6. **Don't Wanna Think** — Julia Michaels
7. **My Boy** — Billie Eilish
8. **I Hate Everybody** - Halsey
9. **Cardigan** — Taylor Swift
10. **Falling Like The Stars** — James Arthur
11. **I Miss You, I'm Sorry** — Gracie Abrams
12. **Watch** - Billie Eilish
13. **Exile** — Taylor Swift
14. **Forever (is a long time)** — Halsey
15. **Getting Over You** — Lauv
16. **If the World Was Ending** — JP Saxe & Julia Michaels
17. **Dancing On My Own** — Calum Scott

18. **Hoax** — Taylor Swift
19. **Josephine** — The Wallflowers

ABOUT THE AUTHOR

JULIE JOHNSON is a twenty-something Boston native suffering from an extreme case of Peter Pan Syndrome. When she's not writing, Julie can most often be found adding stamps to her passport, drinking too much coffee, striving  to conquer her Netflix queue, and Instagramming pictures of her dog. (Follow her: @author_julie)

She published her debut novel LIKE GRAVITY in August 2013, just before her senior year of college, and she's never looked back. Since, she has published more than a dozen other novels, including the bestselling BOSTON LOVE STORY series, THE GIRL DUET, and THE FADED DUET. Her books have appeared on Kindle and iTunes Bestseller lists around the world, as well as in AdWeek, Publishers Weekly, and USA Today.

You can find Julie on Facebook or contact her on her website www.juliejohnsonbooks.com. Sometimes, when she can figure out how Twitter works, she tweets from @Author-Julie. For major book news and updates, subscribe to Julie's newsletter: http://eepurl.com/bnWtHH

Connect with Julie:
www.juliejohnsonbooks.com
juliejohnsonbooks@gmail.com

ALSO BY JULIE JOHNSON

STANDALONE NOVELS:

LIKE GRAVITY

SAY THE WORD

FAITHLESS

THE BOSTON LOVE STORIES:

NOT YOU IT'S ME

CROSS THE LINE

ONE GOOD REASON

TAKE YOUR TIME

SO WRONG IT'S RIGHT

THE GIRL DUET:

THE MONDAY GIRL

THE SOMEDAY GIRL

THE FADED DUET:

FADED: Part One

FADED: Part Two

THE UNCHARTED DUET:

UNCHARTED

UNFINISHED

THE FORBIDDEN ROYALS TRILOGY:

DIRTY HALO

TORRID THRONE

SORDID EMPIRE